The Pirate's Pursuit

A Sapphic Seas Romance

Wren Taylor

EPICEA PRESS
TACOMA, WA

More from Wren Taylor

SAPPHIC SEAS SERIES

The Captain's Choice

The Pirates Pursuit

For Emily

Chapter 1

JANUARY 1710

"YOU SHOULDN'T BE HERE, Lisbet," her mother scolded, crossing her thick arms across her chest. "Why have you come?"

After five years, the harsh words shouldn't have bothered her, but the rebuke still felt like a knife stabbing into her heart. Mothers weren't supposed to reject their daughters, even if those daughters sinned, and her banishment from the village stung like a wound that still hadn't healed.

"I just came to bring you some things from town, Mama," Lisbet said softly, looking away. "For the babies. I know you need them." Not that her sisters were babies anymore, but it had been so long since Lisbet had been allowed to see them, that was the age they stayed in her mind.

"We need nothing from you nor the buccaneers you associate with," her mother said coldly.

"I saw how the crops were wilted in the field on the walk up. I know it hasn't rained well in months. Look, I've brought food from other islands, smoked meats and molasses." She held out her basket, nearly overflowing with the goods she had purchased from the bustling market in Nassau that morning. "I only want to help."

"Help gained through sin is no help at all, but a curse you won't trick us into bearing. God will provide." Lisbet's mother crossed her arms resolutely.

Lisbet gripped her skirt tightly to hide the trembling of her sweaty palms. Showing her rage, her grief, her fear would only serve to see her dismissed faster. There was so much she wanted to scream, so much her mother didn't understand. She had given up trying. If she was living a life of sin, it was because it was the only choice thrust upon her when she was told to leave her family home. But there was no point in arguing, no words she could yell that hadn't already been spoken.

"May I at least see Charlotte and Adeline before I go?" She asked about her younger sisters, knowing what her mother's answer would be.

"Your influence isn't welcome here." Her mother looked her up and down as if really seeing her for the first time since Lisbet crossed the little clearing to the village hidden amongst the tropical trees of New Providence. Lisbet had worn her most modest dress, a somber gray affair with a high neckline and long sleeves, yet her mother sneered as though her full bosom was on display.

"Where is Father?" He could overrule her mother, and an appeal to him was Lisbet's last hope to hug her sisters before she was chased out of the village again.

"Yonder," her mother said, nodding towards the church tucked up against the treeline at the far side of the clearing.

Lisbet set her basket down on the step leading into her family's house. Pride might stop her mother from accepting it or voicing her thanks, but practicality would prevent her from wasting the gift. She walked along a tamped down path through overgrown grass that led to the little wooden church that she had helped erect just a few years prior after the village of settlers had moved after yet another raid on Nassau by the Spanish.

"He's around back."

Lisbet jumped, startled to realize her mother was following her. There was a coldness in her tone, a flatness that made Lisbet's heart race with fear. The beating against her chest was only amplified by the absence of noise coming from the cemetery behind the church. She picked up her pace, trying to convince herself it wasn't true. He was just working back there, she rationalized. He was digging a grave for someone else. She couldn't hear the sound of the spade cutting into the rocky soil because he was taking a break. Her mother couldn't have been so cruel. Someone would have told her. She rounded the corner of the church into the small yard of graves with simple headstones. It was empty.

"Where?" Lisbet choked out.

"There," her mother pointed to a wooden cross planted in the ground a few paces away.

The grave was new enough that plants were just starting to sprout from the dirt that covered it, tender shoots rising from the loamy, black soil. *William Clarke. 1663-1709*. It couldn't be. Lisbet knelt beside the cross and read it again, but the name etched upon it didn't change. Slowly, she pulled her eyes away from the grave to stare at her mother in shock.

"When? How?" She forced the questions out before the settling grief began to suffocate her.

"Four months back. He fell ill with a fever. It nearly took Lottie from me, too."

"You didn't send for me," Lisbet sobbed, disbelieving.

"How would I have known where to find you?"

"Nassau isn't that big. You didn't even try."

"No, I didn't. I'll not walk into that den of thieves and harlots, nor send anyone there on my behalf. You made your choice years ago. You, Lisbet. I'll not allow you to blame me for it now."

Lisbet wiped away her tears angrily, wishing she had never come back to the hidden village in the forest. She had everything she needed in Nassau, and the village only reminded her of the pain of losing her family. How was she supposed to grieve a father she had already lost years before? Or her sisters, alive and presumably well, but just out of reach? Or the mother who looked at her with such disdain? Lisbet had always clung to the hope that one day her parents' anger would pass, but she realized she needed to lay it to rest as well. They were all as good as dead to her, and pretending otherwise would only lead to more anguish in the future.

"I'll pray for you," she hissed, knowing her mother would be bothered by the offer of prayer from a harlot and a sinner.

"You should leave," her mother said, not meeting her eye.

She glared at her mother for what she vowed would be the last time. There was simply no point in trying any longer. Her father was dead. It was such a final thing, impossible to comprehend. Yet, his death was no different at all than all the years of absence that preceded it. Tears escaped from her eyes to run hot down her cheeks, and she swiped them angrily away. She didn't want to cry any more for him, the man who had never dared to stand up to her mother against her mistreatment. She didn't want to mourn a man who didn't deserve it.

"Goodbye, Mother," she said, then turned to walk numbly back to the pirate town. Back home.

"You seem troubled," Mona said to Lisbet as she scrubbed the inside of a cage. It was one of a half dozen that had been hand-crafted by Mona's wife Elinor and was just large enough to hold a cat and her kittens. "Is everything alright?"

Lisbet sighed. "Yes, I'm fine. It's just been a trying day."

"Care to talk about it?" Mona stacked the clean cage on top of the others then motioned for Lisbet to sit.

"I went to see my family this morning. Found out my father died, and no one even thought to tell me."

"I'm so sorry." Mona winced with pity.

"Thank you. It's strange to find out this way, with four months already passed. And I haven't even seen him in years."

"You're still allowed to grieve," Mona said.

"Do you have a good relationship with your family?" Lisbet asked, uncomfortable with the pity from her friend.

"I suppose I did," Mona said. "My mother died when I was young, and my father only wanted the best for me. But he and I had differing opinions on what that was. I left without saying goodbye to him. I've always regretted that, even if he would be scandalized to see me now. Maybe enough time has passed that I should write him."

Lisbet knew that Mona had been a woman of some stature back in Wales, and she could see why some might find the life Mona built for herself to be scandalous. It was a life Lisbet could only dream of, no matter how content she was with her own. Her friend was married to a woman who loved her more deeply than any love Lisbet had ever seen. They had demanded respect, and the pirates had given it. At times, Lisbet's admiration of the couple strayed into jealousy, followed by regret. She'd had her chance at love with a woman who completed her, and she had ruined it. All to appease her parents. All for nothing.

"I shouldn't care this much," Lisbet said, blinking back tears as she was slammed by another wave of uninvited grief.

"Caring is what makes you better than them," Mona replied as she arranged a bed of fabric scraps and old rags in the cage. "If you want to go home, I can handle all the chores today."

"No, I'd rather be here. Helps me not to think about it as much."

"I understand that," Mona said. "Sail on, we used to say on the ship. Stay busy and keep moving forward."

Lisbet bent to pick up one of the cats roaming around the yard. The mean looking orange tabby with a missing fang that Mona had named Pendragon rubbed his face against her shoulder. He ruled the cat yard, asserting order and keeping the other felines in their place, but he adored human company. Lisbet had a special place in her heart for him, and every time a captain or quartermaster came by to find a new mouser for their ships, she secretly hoped no one would choose him.

The cats were free to come and go as they pleased, and often left the confines of the yard to roam about Nassau and follow the call of their instinct to hunt. The only ones confined to cages were the injured or those who had just had kittens. But most of the cats chose to spend their time lounging on the warm rocks placed perfectly around the yard to warm in the afternoon sun. Mona and Lisbet fed and cared for them until they could find new homes on ships that needed them to keep their stores of food safe from the rats that always found their way aboard.

The pirates of Nassau found their endeavors ridiculous, and heartily supported them by offering unneeded scraps of fabric, fish heads, or even their coins on occasion. It wasn't enough for Lisbet to make her living, but it helped to pass the time before her evenings of entertaining the town's drunk and debaucherous. The cats offered affection without judgment, something Lisbet had known little of. Taking care of them with her best friend was a privilege that Lisbet would never let go for granted, especially since Mona was the closest thing to family she had left.

Lisbet smiled a little at her fortune in finding such dear friends. It had taken time for Mona to warm up to her, but Lisbet fully understood why. Mona's wife had been one of Lisbet's frequent clients long before Mona had captured her heart, and their first interactions were charged with jealousy and vitriol on both sides. All of that had changed when they found a kitten that had been abandoned by its mother, half-starved and with a broken leg. Their common purpose bonded them, and had grown over three years to help dozens of cats.

"Won't you join us for supper tonight?" Mona asked.

"I can't," Lisbet said. "I've got to go up to the tavern, my purse is getting light."

"I'm sure Elinor can find some work for you in her shop, if you'd rather."

"No, I'll be better off up there." The offer was sweet, and one both women had extended before. But Lisbet didn't mind the work of pleasing men, and the oh-so-rare woman who paid for her services. She would earn more in an hour hanging around in the tavern than she would in a day doing menial chores for Elinor.

"Suit yourself," Mona said with a smile. She didn't understand, but that was okay.

The work of a prostitute wasn't for everyone, but for the women who sought wealth by any means, it was a steady and abundant source of income. When Lisbet had first been exiled from the village, she had worked as a barmaid in the tavern, but soon found that the long hours on her feet for a meager share of coin was not to her liking. The real wealth of Nassau lay in the pockets of the pirates, and all it took was a little charm to relieve them of it.

"I should be on my way," Lisbet said. The work in the cat yard was nearly done, and she had to change her clothes and freshen up for the evening. She bent to stroke Pendragon one last time.

"Will you be around tomorrow?"

"Sometime in the afternoon," Lisbet said. She walked from the house by the beach up the road that led through the town. It had changed so much since she had first moved there, a scared seventeen year old with nowhere else to go. Burned and damaged beyond recognition after repeated raids by the French and Spanish, the pirates had moved in to claim it as their own. Four years after the last raid, the town of Nassau stood in opulent splendor, the buildings reconstructed and painted in sumptuous colors that put the wealth of the pirate haven on full display.

Lisbet turned down the path that led to her little home. It had cost her more from her stash of gold than she'd wanted to part with, but it was a place that was all hers, one which no one could ever take away from her. She never entertained her customers there, or even her friends. It was just big enough for her mattress and a wardrobe to store her dresses, with a small area to cook behind it outside.

She went to the well she shared with her only neighbors– a widow and three children that mostly kept to themselves– and drew up a bucket of cool water. It was hot enough outside that she didn't need to warm it for a bath, the temperature would be refreshing after sweating under the sun in the cat yard all afternoon. She splashed water on her face, jumping as she heard a meow behind her. Pendragon had followed her. He sat, tail swishing in displeasure as he stared at her.

"What? You didn't get enough attention earlier?" She cooed, picking him up again. "Well, come inside then, but I won't be here long. I'm going to the tavern, and they won't take kindly to you following me there." Lisbet laughed. She was talking to the cat like a mad woman. Not that it mattered if no one was around to see her. She opened the door and let Pendragon jump to the floor. He immediately darted under the bed and lay there staring at her with pensive, green eyes.

"You better not shit in my house, cat," she said, still laughing as she walked over to the one floorboard in the back corner that hadn't been nailed down.

She lifted it and reached down into the hole below. The sack was there, just as she had left it. Her future. Although she considered herself happy, she knew she couldn't sustain the life she lived in Nassau forever. The pirates would find a new haven with new women, or she would get too old to attract their attention anymore, or she would lose interest in the trade entirely. She wanted to be prepared for that day, and have a way out. As long as she spent her money wisely and saved the rest, she would be able to sail anywhere in the world and use her wealth to buy an easy life. When she was ready, which she wasn't yet. She nestled the floorboard back into place and moved to the wardrobe.

She had a dozen dresses, each custom sewn for her body and designed to attract as much attention to it as possible, without giving away the full show for free. Her simple gray skirt fell to the floor as she selected the gown she would wear for the evening. It was a crimson so deep it was nearly black, with sleeves that just covered her shoulders and a plunging neckline that stopped just short of baring her entire chest. She laid it on the bed and sponged herself off before slipping into it, spraying herself with rose scented perfume and running a comb through her long, auburn locks.

Pendragon was still rolling around under the bed, wrestling with the dust balls she had neglected for too long. Lisbet called for him, but he ignored the summons. She shrugged. He could stay there while she was gone, though she suspected she would find him yowling at the door for his freedom when she returned.

She locked the door. It was a real luxury to have a lock, but also a necessity on the island of thieves. Though there was a general consensus among the pirates not to steal from each other in Nassau, she didn't trust a single one of them. Especially not when there was drink involved. The sounds of the tavern up the path beckoned to her, filling the evening air with music, and she practiced smiling demurely and fluttering her eyelashes. Her silver and gold was waiting.

Chapter 2

KIT MURPHY LEANED AGAINST the wall of the tavern, observing the way the other pirates moved through the crowd. She pulled her hat a little lower over her short cropped hair to better hide her face, but no one was paying her any mind at all. Two women were on a raised stage in the center of Nassau's favored gathering spot, wrestling one another as the men placed bets on which would be victorious. Their shrieks filled the room as they grappled, pulling at hair and tearing at each other's clothing as they tried to pin the other to the floor. Fabric ripped and the men cheered as one of the whore's breasts spilled from her bodice, the cloth no longer able to do its job to keep them contained.

Kit's eyes locked on a target, observing from the back of the crowd, his arms crossed over his broad chest. He seemed fully distracted by the wrestling bout, which would make her job easy. She slid between two chairs that had been abandoned for the spectacle, then crept up behind the tall man with dark hair whose pocket she was about to pick. Thieving from other pirates wasn't her preferred way to make a coin, but it was one she was skilled at. And she was in need of coin, since her own had been taken by the very men she called crewmates.

The man shifted his weight to his other foot, and his pocket gaped open, inviting her hand in. He would never even know she had been there, and she could finally buy herself some supper. Her fingers struck gold. Or maybe silver, it was too soon to tell. The man whirled around, catching her wrist in his fist with a quickness she hadn't anticipated from his hulking size. The coin gleamed between her fingers.

"Do you know who you steal from, boy?" The man growled, pulling her arm so high in the air she had to stand on tiptoe to avoid having her shoulder ripped from its socket.

Kit shook her head. She had never seen the man in her life, and he was one she would have remembered. He had a wicked scar winding around his forearm and was slowly drawing a pistol from his waistband. She dropped the coin. Its clatter on the wooden floor was drowned out by more cheers from the crowd. The giant man stepped on it. No one else had noticed the scuffle behind them.

His eyes narrowed as he glared at her. "What's your name?"

"Kit," she said, forcing her voice to sound deeper that it was.

"Who's your captain?"

"No one. I'm without a ship at present."

"Not surprising. Did you steal from your last one, too?"

She shook her head again. Her wrist was beginning to hurt, but she wasn't going to show it. At least he hadn't seen through her ruse yet.

"Well, Kit, you've put me in quite the predicament. Theft can't go unpunished."

"I didn't actually steal anything, though," she said looking down at his boot covering the coin on the floor. "It's still in your possession."

To Kit's surprise, he laughed and lowered his arm, loosening his grip a bit without letting her go. "Attempted theft, then. Still have to figure out what to do with you. How old are you, anyways?"

"Fourteen," she said, the lie flowing easily. Old enough that the men on the ships would take her seriously, but young enough that no one would ask why she was so much shorter, and her voice that much higher than was expected of an adult man.

He raised an eyebrow but didn't question her further. "Be a shame to cut the hand off one so young."

"I would really rather you didn't."

He laughed again. "You're lucky I'm in a generous mood today. You can keep the hand, as long as you use it to do some work for me. You said you're without a ship?"

"I am," Kit said cautiously.

"It so happens I'm looking for extra hands on mine. *Nimue's Revenge.* But you steal from my crew and I'll take more than your hand."

As fearsome as the man was, he could be no worse than her old captain, and she needed the work. And her hand. "I'll do whatever job you need," she said. "As long as you pay me my fair share."

His dark eyebrow darted up again. "Of course. I treat my crew well. So, if I let your hand go to shake on it, you'll be at my camp tomorrow morning?"

"I will," she swore.

"Good," he said, finally releasing his grip on her wrist. "If you're not, this island isn't that big. I'll find you, and you'll pay for trying to pick the pocket of Tristan Buell."

She shook his hand. His grip was as crushing around her fingers as it had been around her wrist. "Where is your camp?"

"Down the main road, behind Davies' supply store on the beach. When you see a bunch of cats, keep walking, and you'll find us amid the trees."

"I'll be there. Tomorrow morning," Kit confirmed, eyeing the exit. She wanted to leave before the captain could change his mind.

He bent to retrieve the coin from beneath his shoe, and handed it to her. "You seem like you might need this more than me. Consider it an advance for the work you'll do."

Pride told Kit not to take it, even though getting enough coin for a meal and a new blanket was her original intent. She didn't like handouts. Need overwhelmed pride, and she pocketed the coin.

He nodded to the door. "Stay out of trouble, Kit. Enough of it will find you here without you seeking it out."

As she wove her way through the crowd, the hairs on the back of her neck rose and she had the distinct feeling of being watched. A quick scan of the room confirmed her suspicions. One of the town's whores was watching her from across the tavern from her seat in the lap of a pirate who had his face buried in the neckline of her blood red dress. She was too far away and the tavern too dark for Kit to read her expression, but there was something familiar about her posture and the set of her jaw.

Kit darted out the door, cursing herself. She had gotten too bold, and attracted the very attention she had been hoping to avoid. Such carelessness was unforgivable, and would lead to her being discovered. She didn't want to imagine what the pirates would do to her if they found out she was a woman disguised as one of them.

Outside of Nassau's center, the main road was rocky and rutted, with weeds growing between the tracks left by wagons in a distant past. Few people traveled along it, though Kit knew that there was still an enclave of the original settlers of New Providence hidden further up the hill. She had grown up among them, until she had been sent away from the island when she was sixteen. It was tempting to follow the road to see what had become of her old home, but it wouldn't be wise. Five years was a long time, and some things were better left unknown.

Kit stepped off the road and into the trees, the darkness of night in the forest even more blinding after the moonlit walk up the open road. Her little camp was well hidden, far enough out of town that no one would think to go looking for her there, especially not the men of her old crew. The voyage from Bermuda to Nassau hadn't been long, but the older men had managed to pack as much torment into the short time frame as they could. From denying her rations to stealing her wages, they had seized upon every opportunity to bully someone younger and smaller, just as their captain mistreated them.

She lay down in her hammock, the interaction in the tavern racing through her mind. The man– her new captain– hadn't seemed as cruel as the other pirates she had known, despite being one of the most intimidating figures she had ever seen. He had shown her mercy, and whether she wanted to join his crew or not, she was a woman of her word. It was better than losing her hand over a stupid mistake.

D AVIES' SHOP, THEN PAST the cats... Kit peered into the trees. There were hammocks strung between trees and branches that had been driven into the sandy soil to form the frames of tents. Thin blue wisps drifted upwards from the center of the circle where the embers of a bonfire still smoked. The camp was quiet but for a few men snoring. She knew it was early for pirates, but she preferred to be early than late.

She'd slept poorly, apprehensive of what the day held for her. The captain hadn't told her to bring any of her belongings, so she had left everything up at her camp in the woods. Her assumption that they weren't going to sail that day seemed to hold true, judging by the men's late hour of slumber.

"There you are," Captain Buell's voice startled her as he stepped out between two tents. "At least you take direction well."

"Aye," Kit said, looking between the trees and across the sandy beach to the shallow harbor glimmering blue and yellow in the morning light. "Which ship is yours?"

"That one," he said, pointing. "With the three masts. *Nimue's Revenge.*"

"She's enormous," Kit said, awed.

"One of the biggest in the Caribbean." He smiled, radiating pride. "Used to be a merchant ship."

"How did you come by her?" Kit asked, expecting one of the pirates' wondrous tales of battle, chaos, and fortune. The captain seemed like he could take on any foe, and Kit wasn't surprised he helmed a ship with as intimidating a stature as his own.

"That's a long story, and one you'll surely come to know," he said. "But first, firewood. The men'll be wanting their breakfast and we burned through all we had."

"Aye, Captain," Kit said as he waved her towards the wood.

Firewood was easy enough. She walked among the trees, scavenging the ground for any fallen branches and sticks shaken loose by the summer winds and rains. The captain had shown her no malice, and she found herself eager to please him and prove she was capable. Soon, her arms were laden with wood, and she turned back to the *Revenge's* camp. More of the sailors were awake by the time she returned to deposit her load by the fire pit dug out of the sand.

"We'll need more than that," Captain Buell said. "Go get another bundle. Be quicker this time."

Kit felt the men's curious stares on her as she jogged back into the woods, anxious to please the captain. She felt as though she was being tested, like he could change his mind at any time about letting her off easily for attempting to steal from him. Pieces of bark bit into her hands and knees as she crawled on the ground, scrambling to collect as much flammable wood as she could carry.

"Better," he said as she returned with the second armful. He turned to address his crew. "Listen up, you lot. This is Kit, he's joining our crew."

A few of the men greeted her with waves or nods of their heads, but most continued to ignore her, taking no great interest in the addition of another powder boy to their ranks.

"Old Scab, Scabbard, is the quartermaster." The captain pointed to another man who sat in his hammock holding his head in his hands. "He's a little rough around the edges, but you have any problems, you go to him. He'll see that it's taken care of." He smiled wryly. "Assuming he's not piss drunk, that is."

It was clear Captain Buell ran a tight ship, and his men moved in well-practiced unison as some brought the fire back to life and others began clearing the camp of empty bottles of rum that lay discarded at the bases of trees. Kit wondered where she was supposed to fit in, what role would fall to her. Everyone seemed to know what to do without being ordered, and she was an outsider who didn't know their ebb and flow of tasks well enough yet to participate.

"Come with me," the captain said, as if he could read her mind. "I need to go to the shop, could use the extra hands to carry supplies back."

Kit followed half a pace behind him as they walked back up the beach, hugging the treeline where the sand was easier to walk in. They passed the dusty yard where cats were meowing insistently at a woman carrying a bucket. She waved cheerfully at the captain.

"Good morning, Tristan," the woman called. "Going to see Elinor?"

"Morning, Mona," he replied casually. "Is she in the shop?"

"Always," Mona laughed as she walked over, and Kit saw her bucket was filled with fish heads and bones. "It's been busy lately, but she didn't forget about you." A cat pawed at Mona's trouser-clad leg and she shooed him off.

"I hope not," the captain said. "Better see to the cats, then. They seem impatient."

"They can wait," she said, reaching to hug him across the fence. "It's always good to see you Tristan. And who is this?" She looked at Kit.

"New powder boy we're trying out. Caught him trying to pick my pocket up at the tavern last night, and offered him a better life than the one he was walking into. Providing he can pull his weight."

"Hmm." Mona looked at Kit as if she was trying to figure her out, but if the friendly woman suspected anything was amiss, she didn't say anything. "Well, it's nice to meet you. The *Revenge* is a good ship. Spent some time aboard her myself. Tristan will take good care of you."

Kit had to clench her teeth together to keep her jaw from dropping. The beautiful woman who was friends with the captain had served on his ship? It didn't seem possible, yet neither of the two laughed at what had to be a joke.

"He doesn't talk much," the captain said when Kit didn't respond.

"No wonder," Mona laughed. "You talk too much for him to get a word in edgewise. Where are you from?"

"Bermuda," Kit said, a half truth. It was where she had spent the most time recently, and admitting she was from New Providence would only lead to more questions about her identity that she didn't care to answer.

"I've never been there," Mona said. "Is it as lovely as Nassau?"

Kit shrugged. She hadn't found it to her liking, but that she was no fair judge.

Another cat was winding itself between Mona's legs, meowing louder as his attempt at attention was ignored.

"Okay, okay," Mona laughed and reached into the bucket to drop a fish head on the ground. "I won't make you wait any longer."

As if on cue, the other cats in the yard swarmed around her, hissing as they each clawed for a piece of the fish. Mona waved goodbye to Tristan and Kit as she moved across the enclosure, scattering the cats' food as she went.

"She was on your ship?" Kit asked, forgetting to deepen her voice in her awe. Tristan didn't seem to notice, but men never did. They were the most unobservant creatures, only seeing what they wanted and expected to see.

"Aye, but that was before *Revenge* was mine. She's as sure of a shot as they come, too. Struck a man dead at a hundred paces, wouldn't have believed it if I hadn't seen it with my own eyes."

"I didn't know that women could do that."

"I reckon there's a lot of things about women you don't know. But if you think she's impressive, just wait until you meet Elinor." Tristan's eyes twinkled as he smiled. "She was the captain."

Chapter 3

PENDRAGON'S BODY RUMBLED AS he purred. He had wormed his
way into Lisbet's bed when she returned home the night before, and
she hadn't had the heart to evict him once he had made his way under
her blankets. His companionship was soothing as the memories of the day
before flooded back in. She had earned her coin easily enough, the work of
seducing men a good distraction from the news her mother had given. But
when she was alone in her cabin again the death weighed heavily around
her, a shroud she couldn't escape.

Lisbet stretched, startling the cat from his contented slumber. He darted
from his spot on the bed to retreat beneath it. She sighed. It was time to
get up. She crossed the room and opened the door. Pendragon dashed out,
presumably hungry and making his way back to the cat yard to scrounge
up any remainders of the morning meal Mona supplied.

She pulled on the trousers and ragged chemise she normally wore when
she wasn't trying to solicit the coin of the pirates in town before locking
her door and walking down to the beach. A swim would help her clear her

head, and then she needed to speak with Tristan. She had seen him in the tavern the night before speaking with a face that haunted her memories. As unlikely as it was to be her, Lisbet had to know for certain. The tavern was dim, and she had been sitting some distance away. The woman she thought she had recognized could have just as easily been a figment of her imagination, an unrealized longing surfacing from the depths of an alcoholic stupor.

The town was alive with activity; Lisbet had slept later than she meant to. Not that it mattered, she had no obligations and no one to report to. Her life was hers to live as she pleased. A man whistled at her, but she ignored him. He would have to find someone else to fulfill his morning desire, and there was no shortage of women in Nassau who were up to the task.

The water was cool and the sun obscured by clouds as she swam parallel to the beach, heading for a far rock at the edge of the harbor. There was almost no current running under the water, and she savored the feeling of tiny waves breaking over her back as she swam. When she reached the rock, she pulled herself out of the water to lay in the sun, whose rays were just peeking beyond the edge of the cloud.

The only part of her life she would trade was the loneliness. She had friends, of course, Mona and Elinor and some of the other women in town. And Pendragon. But she didn't have a partner, someone to spend the slow hours alongside, someone to revel in companionship with. The men offered her coin but no comfort, and she longed for the partnership and support that a committed relationship provided. There was no use moping, though. The only two women on the island who had any interest in another woman were already married to each other.

When her clothes were dry, Lisbet walked along the beach towards the cat yard. Mona wasn't outside, so she went around to the front to knock at the door of the house that was next door to Elinor Davies' ship supply shop. She stopped dead in her tracks as she saw the trio of people in front of the shop: Elinor, Tristan, and the stranger from the night before. Lisbet felt the blood drain from her face as the three turned to look at her. So she hadn't been a figment of her imagination.

"Kate," Lisbet whispered, feeling like she had seen a ghost. It was her, even if she was dressed as a boy with a hat covering half her face and hair hewn off in a way that was oddly becoming against Katherine's delicate features. Lisbet could never forget that face, the sharp arch of her brow or the big hazel eyes. For a moment, Lisbet forgot she was supposed to hate her. "Is it really you?"

Kate paled, and took a step towards her. "Lisbet. I didn't think I would ever see you again."

"I'm still here." Lisbet had so many questions she wanted to ask her old friend. Her first love. She reached out a hand to touch her and see if she was real, had really returned to New Providence after all those years, but she didn't dare. She let the hand fall back to her side, still in shock over the appearance of someone she had spent years hating.

Tristan cleared his throat, and Lisbet remembered she and Kate weren't alone. Elinor and Tristan were staring at them, wearing matching expressions of confusion. They glanced at each other, then Elinor spoke.

"You know each other?"

"Knew each other," Lisbet corrected. "She left years ago." And Lisbet was still bitter about it, even though she was just as much to blame.

"I didn't leave by choice," Kate said. The pain in her eyes made it clear she hadn't forgotten either, but there was something more in the look she gave Lisbet.

23

"I think we should all go inside and sit down," Elinor said. "Mona is already making tea, and I'm sure Captain Buell has questions for you both."

She opened the door and held it as the group filed inside. Lisbet's heart thumped wildly, as if it had been caught up in a storm swell and was being pummeled on the rocks and reef below. Kate was back on the island. Her first love, her only real love. Back.

"Sit," Elinor said, traces of her years as a captain showing in her confidence giving orders.

Mona poured cups of tea as everyone sat around a table covered in pilfered books, inkpots, and quills. Lisbet grasped her cups with both hands, desperate for the warmth to seep into her hands, which had gone clammy and cold.

"First things first, are you Kit or Kate?" Elinor asked.

"Both, I guess. Most know me as Kit now."

"How old are you really?" Tristan wanted to know.

"Twenty-one."

"What else did you lie about?" He pressed.

"I only lied because I had to. How else was I supposed to find work on a ship? None would have me as a woman." Kit stared into her cup of tea.

"The *Revenge* is different," Tristan said.

"How was she supposed to know that?" Mona asked, coming to Kit's defense. "Don't you remember how hard it was for Elinor, or what happened to me on the *Bonny Lass*?"

Lisbet had heard the story many times, usually passed through the chains of gossip in Nassau as some great love story for the ages. Mona had boarded a smuggler's ship under the guise of working among the crew until Elinor hunted the ship down and won her heart back. What the stories often forgot to mention was how harrowing the ordeal had been for both women. Lisbet fully understood why Kit wouldn't have taken the same risk.

"You're right, you're right," Tristan yielded as all four women glared at him. "I'm sorry."

"So, can I stay on your crew?" Kit asked. Her hand reached to play with a lock of hair that wasn't there, a nervous habit Lisbet still remembered well.

"Of course," Tristan said. "As Kit or Kate or whoever you want to be."

Lisbet saw Kit exhale a sigh of relief. It was strange to see her again after so long. She looked older, which was to be expected considering the time that had passed, but was nonetheless jarring. Lisbet wondered if Kit felt as off-balance as she did.

"Why did you come back?" Lisbet asked, unable to keep the bitterness from her voice.

"I only went where the ship I worked on sailed," Kit said. "It wasn't my choice to come here. Just as it wasn't my choice to leave."

"I didn't realize you knew each other," Mona interrupted, smiling as she poured cups of tea for everyone seas at the table. She had missed the conversation outside.

"Unfortunately," Lisbet said, pursing her lips. She saw the flash of sadness in Kit's eyes before she looked down into her tea again. Everyone at the table shifted awkwardly, and Lisbet realized the assumptions they were making due to her profession. "We grew up together," she clarified.

"My parents sent me to live with my aunt and uncle in Bermuda seven years ago," Kit added.

"It must be nice to be back," Mona said.

"I never expected to be." Kit's tone was pleasant enough, but her expression said she would rather be anywhere else and she still refused to meet Lisbet's eyes.

25

"Well, Liss, we should be seeing to the cats now, shouldn't we? I'm sure these three have to get back to their negotiations." Mona winked at her wife.

Lisbet was grateful for a reason to leave, and pushed back her chair to rise hastily to her feet. "Tristan, Elinor, wonderful to see you as always." She paused, trying to think of something smart to say to Kit, but settled on silence.

As soon as they were outside and well out of earshot of the house, Mona turned to Lisbet. "I've never seen you act so bitterly towards someone."

"She ruined my life out of spite. So I ruined hers." Lisbet sighed. "We were young and dumb and in love and had a fight. I'm sure she feels the same way towards me now."

"That must have been some fight," Mona said.

"It was. She was the reason my parents sent me out of the village to fend for myself in Nassau. She wanted to run away together, but I wanted to stay. I was afraid. Nassau wasn't safe because of the raids, and neither of us really knew what lay beyond." Lisbet swallowed. The fight and the fallout wasn't anything she'd thought about in years, and speaking it aloud made her more emotional than she liked. "The village would have never accepted us, so I told her it was over, that I would find one of the boys in the village to settle down with, and we ended everything. I thought it was done then, but she was jealous. A few weeks later she saw me sneaking off into the storehouse with a boy, and she told my parents. They caught us right in the act."

"That's difficult," Mona said.

"It was," Lisbet agreed, wincing as she remembered the blows her father had dealt upon finding her with her skirts hitched up around her waist and bent over a grain barrel. He had been furious that she was tarnished. "They were going to force him to marry me, and he would have happily obliged."

"But that was what you wanted."

"Not him, not that way. Not to have my dignity taken from me, to have my future decided because of my lack of virginity. I didn't know what I wanted. So what I did was even worse."

"Oh?" Mona asked, curiosity mixing with pity in her green eyes.

"I don't want you to think less of me for it," Lisbet said cautiously, knowing she had already said too much about the past she had always hidden from her closest friend.

"I'm hurt you think I would. I could never think less of you for something done years ago, when you were what? Seventeen? I know who you are now, Liss, I won't judge you for what you did then."

"I confessed to her parents and mine in church that I was no virgin, but not of Andrew's doing. I blamed Kate for all of it, said that she had bewitched and seduced me and I had fallen into her carnal trap. They believed me, because I had professed it before God, and sent her away."

Mona looked horrified and Lisbet couldn't blame her. It was an awful thing she had done, and it had put both her and Kate's– Kit's lives at risk. Andrew's parents had immediately withdrawn from the marriage arrangement, embarrassing Lisbet's family and earning her more lashes with her father's belt before she was told to leave and never return.

"Liss–" Mona said, putting a hand on her shoulder.

"I'm over it now. I don't need that part of my life dredged up again, so the less I see of her, the better."

"Might be hard to avoid her if she's sailing on the *Revenge*." Mona looked towards the ship's encampment, just visible through the trees.

"Maybe you could talk to Tristan? I know he has a soft spot for you."

"And tell him not to take her on? I'm sorry, Liss, I can't. I don't involve myself with the business of the ship, it's not my place. Besides, what other

27

crew is she going to join? I wouldn't feel right exposing her to that risk. The *Revenge* will treat her well."

"I know," Lisbet said. "I just wish she would disappear again."

"Don't let it bother you too much," Mona advised. "It's long in the past and nothing you can change. Just carry on as though she's not here, and the *Revenge* will sail again soon enough."

"You're right. It just took me by surprise. I saw her last night at the tavern with Tristan and thought it was her, but I was too far away to tell. Seeing her again today was quite the shock."

"I can imagine."

"But enough talking about the past, we have chores to do." Lisbet grabbed a rake and began amassing the droppings the cats had left since the afternoon prior.

Kit and Tristan appeared on the other side of the fence, walking to the *Revenge's* camp together. Lisbet turned her back to them, feeling Kit's stare behind her. Once the shock had faded, the old hatred had set back in, and she seethed at the audacity of Kit to come back at all. Just when Lisbet had finally found her path to happiness, fate decided to push out new and gnarled roots for her to stumble over. Twice in two days. She was almost afraid what the next held.

Pendragon emerged from the bushes and began weaving through her legs, pressing his head to her calf as he purred in happiness. He, at least, was someone she never minded seeing.

"Had a quartermaster down here looking at him earlier this morning," Mona said.

"He can't take him," Lisbet said immediately. She and Mona had promised each other they wouldn't grow attached to the cats they looked after. Their lives would be better off the island on the ships where they could gorge themselves on the pests that traveled with the stores of food. They wouldn't be able to breed as quickly when they were isolated. But Pendragon was different.

"Why not?" Mona asked. "You know they care well for the cats on the ships. He'll have a good life."

"I need him," Lisbet explained. "I don't have a good reason why, other than I feel like he was meant to be mine."

Pendragon meowed, as if in agreement. Lisbet picked him up, his whiskers tickling her face as he nuzzled her cheek.

"Oh, if you say so," Mona cooed, speaking to the cat. "Looks like he chose you, too."

Chapter 4

"WHEN IS THE *REVENGE* due to sail again?" Kit asked. It was a struggle to keep her tone nonchalant, but she didn't want the captain to see her malaise.

"A few weeks, maybe," Tristan said. "We're in no rush."

That could be either good or bad, Kit still hadn't quite sorted out how she felt yet. There was shock, of course, at seeing her first, her only love. Guilt and sadness lingered as well. She had never even gotten the chance to properly apologize to Lisbet all those years ago, and it was clear the other woman still carried a grudge. Buried beneath it all was longing, shadowed by doubt, but burning so intensely she couldn't ignore it.

Lisbet had grown into a woman even more beautiful than Kit had ever thought possible. The scar above her eyebrow that had dominated her features for a good year when she was fifteen had faded completely, only visible to those who knew to look for it. Her face had thinned, matured into the cutting cheekbones and sharp jaw of a woman. Kit wished she had run into her alone, so they could have had time to talk away from the curious ears of the captain and his friends. There were so many questions she wanted to ask, so many things she still needed to say.

"Kit?" Tristan said, jarring her from her thoughts.

"Yes?"

"I asked if you'd like to stay down here at our camp. Where are you staying now anyways?"

She nodded towards the hill but didn't give anymore detail than that.

"You'll be safe here," he continued. "But if you don't trust us yet, I understand. If you don't want to stay, be back at the same time tomorrow morning, to gather the firewood. I'll give you a piece of eight every day til we sail, then you'll get a normal crewman's share."

"That's very generous," Kit said. Retrieving the firewood was a fairly light task, and the compensation he offered handsome.

He handed her a coin. "For today's work."

"Are you going to tell your crew who I really am?"

"Only if that's what you want."

"Not yet." She shook her head. Even if he seemed to think she would be safe, it wasn't his life or well-being at stake, and Kit refused to take the risk. He may have been the captain and his orders ruled the ship, but how could he know what was truly happening in the crew's quarters? Her last captain had turned a blind eye to the bullying his crew had wrought upon the perceived young powder boy in his crew, and she didn't want to imagine how much worse it would have been for her if they knew her true identity.

"Then you'll find your secret is safe with me," he said with a wink, before turning to go speak with his quartermaster Scabbard.

Kit took this to mean she was done for the day, though she was loath to walk past the cat yard and risk seeing Lisbet again. All things considered, it could have gone a lot worse. She brushed the sweat from her palms on her breeches, thankful to still have both hands to do so. The new captain had shown himself to be merciful, but if he showed the same mercy to his crew when they transgressed, it could still bode poorly for her.

Her stomach growled, determining her next priority. She headed to the tavern, hoping to claim a seat at one of the long tables before it became almost too crowded to move. A bowl of stew and a few pints of ale would help her clear her head. The chance of seeing Lisbet again– for she was sure it had been Lisbet staring at her from across the room the night before– was an irresistible lure, no matter how much Kit tried to pretend she didn't want to see her.

The curiosity burned stronger than anything else. What had happened in Lisbet's life since Kit had left the island? Did she ever regret it? Had she been able to mend the relationship with her parents, as Kit one day hoped to do? Did the tip of her nose still wiggle when she was trying to stifle a laugh?

Lisbet wasn't anywhere to be seen in the tavern when Kit sat down at an empty table in the back corner near a large window that let in the sea breeze. A barmaid brought her a bowl of stew and she tucked in ravenously as she watched the patrons of the night trickle in. The pirates were a lawless bunch, rowdy men who wore the scars and grizzled faces of those who had seen, and done, horrible things. They walked and talked as if they were gods deigning to court the earthen realm, reveling in the bacchanal splendor as they vied to make their names immortal. They dressed as if their garb was a competition to see who could display their wealth the most ostentatiously, and Kit knew many of them had riches more more fabulous than that they wore on their coats.

But they didn't intimidate her. Beneath all their facades, she knew they were still men. They still bled, and cried, and one day they would all die.

33

Their names would be as lost as the treasures that were rumored to be buried around the isles.

A few of the men in her former crew walked in, and Kit ducked her head to avoid their notice. The noise in the tavern grew as the crowd did, and tankards of ale and grog were poured liberally by the barmaids flitting between benches. Kit's table filled with pirates, and the man across from her challenged her to a game of cards. She declined, having no silver to waste on losing bets to a man who looked like he was adept at cheating. When night fell and the crewmen were well sotted, the women of Nassau arrived to seduce the men into parting with their coin.

Kit's heart began to hammer in her chest when she saw Lisbet finally step into the room. She ducked her head and watched from beneath the brim of her hat. Lisbet was even more stunning than she had looked that morning, having shed the utilitarian braids and breeches for cascading waves of dark brown hair and a dress as blue as the waters of the Caribbean. She moved so gracefully she seemed to be dancing as she made her way to a table in the center of the room. Leaning forward so the pirate she'd selected had a full view of her cleavage, Lisbet bent to whisper in the man's ear. He grinned and wrapped an arm around her waist, pulling Lisbet into his lap as the both laughed at whatever she had said.

Kit felt a pang of jealousy, mixed with disgust. Flirtation had always come easily to Lisbet. She knew she turned the heads of men and she'd never minded their attention. It wasn't fair, but it never had been. It was different for Kit. She had tried her whole life to find men attractive, had searched for the desire everyone else seemed to have and always come up empty. She only wanted Lisbet, had only ever wanted Lisbet.

"Another ale," she said when the barmaid passed by her table again.

Even after five years, the rejection still hurt. What she had thought was true, deep, lasting love had been nothing more than a teenage dalliance for Lisbet. Lisbet, who was all too happy to have the man's face buried in her neck as she stroked down his shoulder. Kit sipped her ale as the jealousy simmered persistently. Emboldened by too many drinks, she stood and pushed past the other men at her table to stumble across the room and confront the couple.

They rose before she could get to them, so she intercepted them at the door, barring their path out.

"Move aside, powder boy," the pirate scoffed as a cloud of anger darkened Lisbet's face.

Kit ignored him and spoke directly to her. "I want to talk to you. Alone."

"Too late for that, she's already comin' with me. Try your chances with one of the other ones." The man stepped forward threateningly.

"You couldn't afford me, anyways," Lisbet said coldly. "Move aside."

The harsh rebuke stung, and Kit stepped out of the way without trying to stop Lisbet. Trying to speak to her there had been a bad idea, one she would have recognized sooner if she wasn't blinded by ale.

"Who was that?" The man say as he walked away with Lisbet, his hand groping her ass as they disappeared into the night.

"Someone I would have never waste my time on," came Lisbet's husky reply. "Not with strong, handsome men like you around."

Kit felt her heart break all over again. It was clear Lisbet had finally figured out what she wanted after claiming uncertainty for so long. Tears welled in Kit's eyes, then spilled over to run down her cheeks. She wiped them away as she stared at the figures in the distance, wondering vaguely where they were even going. There was no one to blame but herself, she knew. She had come to the tavern with the hope of seeing Lisbet, knowing what she did to earn her coin, so she didn't know why it was such a blow to see her doing just that.

She went back into the tavern to order more ale. There were other whores milling about, and Kit briefly entertained the thought of trying to recruit one for her services. She'd never been with anyone except Lisbet, and it was beyond time she moved on from the memories that still pushed her to climax when she was alone and the desire burned too hot to ignore. Patting her pocket she smiled nervously at a red haired woman standing a few paces away. The woman didn't even notice, but that was for the better. Kit didn't have the coin to spare, and she had to begrudgingly admit that Lisbet was right about one thing. She couldn't afford it.

"Hey. Powder boy," a man called. The hair on the back of Kit's neck rose. She recognized the voice as one of her tormentors from the ship that had stolen her wages and put her in such a predicament to begin with. "Come sit with us." His words may have been friendly, but his tone was not.

She whirled around to find him within arm's reach, a malicious glint in his eye. She backed up, but the tavern was crowded and there was little room for her to move. Her hand drifted to the knife she carried at her waist, and she drew it from its sheath. No longer on the ship, she wasn't afraid to defend herself from the attack she was sure would come.

"Leave me alone, Edward," she said, keeping the knife at her hip and out of his line of sight. He was so drunk she didn't know how he was still standing, a state she had seen him in many times before.

"It wasn't a request, powder boy," he said, and lunged towards her.

Kit thrust the knife up as he plowed forward, feeling the brief resistance as the sharpened point met his leather vest before piercing through to his soft flesh beneath it. Edward howled in pain as she jerked the knife out, brandishing it again defensively. Stirred by Edward's yowls, three more of his crew stood up to join him, spreading out in a semi-circle around Kit. All eyes in the tavern were had turned to them, interested in the fight that had broken out. Kit slashed the air in front of her, a warning to them to keep back, but she was penned by men on all sides with nowhere to retreat.

Edward lay on the floor at her feet, groaning as he clutched his stomach with both hands. Blood seeped between his fingers, dark and slick against the pale timbers of the floor. If nothing was done to help him, he would likely be dead within minutes. His camarades were drawing their own weapons, steel glinting in the lanternlight and anger burning in their eyes. Everyone in the tavern seemed to be holding their breath in anticipation of the slaughter that would happen next, for Kit stood no chance against three men that seemed twice her size.

"Move aside, move," Kit heard a man yelling in the crowd, and saw the pirates and prostitutes parting to avoid the man's swinging elbows as he charged towards her. His face looked vaguely familiar, and she realized it was one of the men she had seen that morning at the encampment of sailors who crewed the *Revenge*. He was flanked by two other men from the ship.

"What's happening here?" The man demanded of Kit's old crewmates.

"Stabbed our mate, didn't he?" The other pirate said furiously. "Like that, over nothing. It's none of your concern, though. We'll handle this with the powder boy."

Edward was still on the floor between them, though he had stopped moaning and his face had turned sickeningly pale.

"Your mate attacked him first. We all saw it." Tristan's men stepped in front of Kit. "You have an issue with one of our crew, then you have an issue with all of us."

"One of your crew?"

"Yes." Another man pushed forward through the crowd, and Kit knew him as the one the captain had called Scabbard. Her new quartermaster. "One of ours." A fifth man pressed through, and a sixth, until Kit's attackers were the ones surrounded. The tension in the air changed as the support of the crowd shifted to the men of the *Revenge.*

"Go get Tristan. Captain Buell," the first man said over his shoulder to Kit. "He might be down at the Davies' house. We'll hold them here. If you can't find him, go to camp and stay there."

Kit nodded, and turned to flee. The crowd parted to let her through, and she ran down the main road towards the candlelit house closest to the beach. She hesitated at the door. The hour was late and she didn't want to disturb the shopkeeper and her wife. She heard laughter inside, including a deep baritone that had to be the captain. Knowing he was there gave Kit the courage to raise her fist to the door and rap upon it.

Elinor answered, one eyebrow jutting up sharply in surprise when she saw who her visitor was. "Kit," she said, smiling graciously, "We weren't expecting you. Come in."

Kit stepped into the little house for the second time that day. "I'm sorry, I didn't mean to interrupt your evening. There's just been... a situation at the tavern. The crew sent me to fetch Captain Buell."

"What happened?" The captain was on his feet before he could even finish the question.

"Some of the men I knew before were none to pleased to see me," Kit said warily, worried the Captain would find her to be at fault. "I defended myself, and your men defended me."

"Any injured?"

"Only the one I stabbed," Kit said. "Unless something has changed since I left."

38

Elinor tossed the captain his jacket from the coat rack by the door, then donner her own on before placing a three cornered hat with a long, black feather on her head. She belted a cutlass around her waist as Tristan did the same.

"Well, let's go see what we're dealing with," Tristan said with a grin.

"I'm sorry to have interrupted your evening," Kit said again, surprised at their apparent delight. She had expected he would be angry with her for causing trouble on her very first day, and decide she wasn't worth having on her crew. Instead, he seemed as ready to defend her as the crewmen in the tavern were.

"Interrupted?" Elinor laughed. "This could be the most excitement I've seen in weeks. I'll never turn down an excuse to keep my skills sharp."

Kit trotted behind as Tristan and Elinor raced up the road to the tavern. She wasn't nearly as eager to face the men again, even with an entire ship at her side. The sounds of yelling and scuffles drifted down to meet them; the standoff had erupted into a brawl while Kit was fetching the captain. Elinor grinned at Tristan, then drew her cutlass and charged in. Kit watched in awe as she slashed at a man who was sneaking up to smash a bottle over the head of Kit's first defender. Elinor's blade swiped the man's forearm and a sliver of blood appeared as he dropped the bottle. It shattered on the floor, breaking Kit from her reverie. She had caused all this, and she needed to help end it before anyone got hurt on her behalf.

All around her was mayhem, but she quickly found another man from her old ship in the fray. Her fist flew towards the hiss face before she even realized she had thrown the punch, and it connected with the satisfying crunch tof a broken nose. Good. He deserved it. He was one of the group that had cornered her in an alley as soon as she stepped off the ship and robbed her of the purse she had earned alongside them. He snarled in pain before lunging at her, and she spun out of the way before he could knock her to the ground.

"Enough!" Tristan yelled. He raised his pistol, but no one in the tavern heeded his order to stop. Kit saw the spark of powder igniting before the booming shot ripped through the air. A hush fell over the tavern as men's blades dropped back to their sides and a whores poked their heads out from the corners where they cowered.

"Enough," he repeated. "*Revenge* crew, get back to our camp. Everyone else, get back to your own. Enough blood has been spilled tonight."

The pirates groaned and protested as the heat of the moment faded.

"You've done enough damage here," Elinor shouted, her cutlass glistening with crimson blood in the lamplight. "Don't you want a tavern to come back to tomorrow? Then go home tonight."

Men glanced around the tavern, taking in the overturned tables and broken bottles littering the floor, then began shuffling to the door. Their bloodlust had been sated for the evening, and they were exhausted from the drunken burst of exertion. The prostitutes trickled out after them, chasing down those without wounds to nurse to try to salvage their nights. Within a few moments, the tavern was cleared of everyone but Elinor, Tristan, Kit, the barmaids, and Edward's dead body laying still in the center of it all.

Elinor began righting overturned benches, and Kit followed her lead. The thrill of the fight had faded, and the rush of panic and fear and fury had drained from her body to leave her exhausted and trembling. She pushed a bench under one of the long tables, then leaned on it to catch her breath. It had been a close call. Too close. If the men of the *Revenge* hadn't been there, the barmaids would have had two bodies to clean up that night. Kit couldn't stand to look over at him again, but Edward's presence still hung over the room, taunting her. She stared at her hands instead. To kill was sickening, and her stomach turned. Even if he had deserved it.

"You're making quite the impression on this town." Elinor stopped cleaning to stand beside her.

"It's made quite an impression on me," Kit said. "I've never been somewhere this... lawless before." Nassau had barely existed when she'd been forced away from the island, and Bermuda was too tightly controlled by the crown to have descended into such pits of debauchery. Even on the ship, the pirates had deferred to their captain and followed a system of rules and order. But in Nassau they were beasts unbridled.

"We've never had a place like this before, where we aren't ruled by the restrictions of men in distant towers who look at us as scum," Elinor explained. "And we're more civilized than you might think. But it's impossible to take crews that fight at sea and expect them to have peace on land. We maintain it as best we can, but there will always be scuffles of this nature. Just be glad you were on the better side of it this time."

"I am," Kit said, "and I'm not afraid if it happens again. I can defend myself. It's just so different from how Nassau used to be."

"For all its ugliness, there is beauty here, too. Opportunity, free for anyone to take. Mona and I can live the life we want without the judgment we would face elsewhere. If you look past the danger, you'll see paradise."

Kit reached for one of the abandoned tankards on the table and drank deeply, gripping the handle until her knuckles were white to quell the shaking of her hands. The warm ale slid down her throat, soothing her frayed nerves.

"Walk with me," Elinor said with an air of authority that Kit didn't dare defy, even though it was late and her hammock was waiting in the dense copse of trees just up the hill.

The men and women of Nassau who weren't exhausted by the fight were continuing their merriment in the streets, passing bottles between them as they laughed and danced under a sky filled with stars. Kit noticed one pirate and prostitute openly fucking against a building for anyone to see. She felt guilty for noticing, but curiosity lured her eyes back for a second glance, just to make sure. It wasn't Lisbet. Kit breathed a sigh of relief, unwarranted. If not that man, then surely Lisbet was off spreading her legs for another.

She followed Elinor down a narrow alley, passing between rows of houses with brightly painted wooden siding as they walked parallel to the harbor. A full moon hung over the waters of the Caribbean, reflecting white in the gentle waves that broke against the shore.

"Where are we going?" Kit asked, wary about following the dangerous woman into the dark. She was one of the pirates, and though she had been pleasant enough to Kit, she still wasn't to be trusted. Even in their short interactions, Kit had learned enough about her to know her loyalties lay with her wife, *Nimue's Revenge,* and Tristan Buell. If Elinor Davies decided Kit was a problem that threatened any of those, Kit knew she wouldn't hesitate to handle it herself.

"Just up here," Elinor said, pointing to the ruins of the old fort that rose from the shadows to stand watch over the bay.

Kit remembered when it had been built thirteen years earlier. The settlers on the island of New Providence demanded a new way to protect their home, and the fort had been erected. It had failed in its duty, and fallen quickly in the repeated attacks on the island. The ruins were a reminder of what had been, and what had become. She followed Elinor up a path hacked through the plants that had grown in after the fort fell into disuse.

"Sit," Elinor ordered as she took a seat on the old wall that overlooked the water. "I wanted a chance to talk to you alone, without pretense or curious listeners."

"About what?" Kit asked, still wary.

"How did you fall in with the pirates?"

Kit shrugged. "Same as anyone, I guess."

Elinor crossed her arms and stared at Kit, waiting for a better response.

"My aunt and uncle no longer had a use for me in Bermuda." Kit gave in to the battle of wills quickly. She just wanted to go to bed. "They were going to send me to the Colonies to work as a servant and pay some of their debts. I had other ideas."

"I see," Elinor said. "How long ago was that?"

"Six months, no more. Why does it matter?"

"I just want to know who you are. Besides Mona, Tristan is the closest thing I have to a family. I have to look out for him when he won't do it himself."

"Look out for him? You think I'm some sort of risk?"

Elinor smiled grimly. "You did just kill a man from your old ship, did you not?"

"He attacked me," Kit argued. "I only defended myself."

"Will your aunt and uncle be looking for you?"

"I doubt it. They're probably pleased I'm gone. They only ever said what a burden I was to them, even though..." Kit trailed off. She didn't want to reveal too much of herself.

"Even though?" Nothing slipped by the shrewd, retired captain.

"I did everything for them, everything I was told. All the housekeeping, the laundry and the dusting, everything." Penitence, her mother had called it when she pushed her onto the ship bound for Bermuda. Atonement for her transgressions against her family and God. Yet, no matter how hard Kit had worked, forgiveness had never been granted.

"Who taught you how to fight?" Elinor asked, though her face had softened.

"The men on my ship," Kit said bitterly. "I had to learn, or I would have been an even easier target."

"Do you regret it? Wish you had gone to the Colonies instead?"

"No."

"Not at all?"

"The time of my life for regrets has passed. I only wish to live on my own terms, as I'm sure you and Mona understand."

"Mona spoke with Lisbet. I know you used to be affectionate with her."

"At one time. It's been years though, any desire has faded." Kit hoped Elinor couldn't see through her lie.

"I hope you won't betray your new captain as quickly as you betrayed her, should the situation ever arise."

"I was a hot-headed girl then. I know the meaning of loyalty now. I could never turn on Tristan, not after the kindness he's shown me," Kit insisted, wondering if anything she said would be enough to appease the suspicious shopkeeper.

"Good," Elinor said. "Because I will kill you if you ever do."

Chapter 5

LISBET FOUND IT SURPRISINGLY easy to forget about Kit's presence on the island. She avoided crossing paths when she saw Kit's familiar hat bobbing through the market, and peddled her wares outside of the tavern where Kit had taken to spending her evenings. The only times she really had to think about her past lover at all was when Kit walked to and from the *Revenge's* camp on the other side of the cat yard while Lisbet was out working. Otherwise, it was as though she had never returned. At least, that was what Lisbet told herself.

She definitely wasn't thinking about Kit as she shopped for a new dress in the market, running a finger over the slippery blue fabric that would drape seductively around her curves. She certainly wasn't wondering what Kit would have thought about the low neckline or the delicate lace accents that would kiss her collarbones and draw attention to her slender neck. She wasn't thinking about how Kit's eyes would widen and her pupils would darken with desire if she saw the way the bodice clung to Lisbet's waist . No, she wasn't thinking about Kit. She refused to.

"Lisbet? A word?" Kit appeared behind her, as if she had been summoned by Lisbet's thoughts.

"No," Lisbet said coldly, without turning around. She wasn't ready to face Kit and own up to her mistakes. She wasn't ready to admit she had been wrong about so many things.

"If you won't give me an hour of your time, then let me buy it." Metal clinked on metal as Kit dug the coins from her pocket.

"I already told you, you can't afford me." And even if she could, Lisbet had no intention of bedding her again. No matter how tempting the offer was or how much she missed the touch of another woman, sleeping with Kit was a bad idea. There was too much history and too many feelings. It would only end in heartbreak for both of them again.

"It's been five years. Don't you think it's time we talk?"

"I could have gone a lifetime without seeing you again and it would have been too soon." Lisbet spat out words that were crueller than intended. She never expected Kit would be open to a reconciliation, and the thought scared her more than she cared to admit. "There's nothing to talk about." She turned to stalk away. The dress would wait. If it was meant to be, it would still be there when she returned.

Kit's hand darted out to grab Lisbet's shoulder as she brushed by. Her grip was stronger than Lisbet remembered. Short hair poked out from under Kit's hat like straw from a scarecrow, but Lisbet liked it. Kit's high cheekbones were flushed with island heat, and her nose crinkled between sparkling eyes as she squinted up into the sun. "How much for an hour?"

"Look, just because you're waving a purse of coins in my face, it doesn't mean you have any right to my time. Let me go." Lisbet needed to get away before she was pulled into Kit's trap. A deep sense of longing clenched deep in her loins, her shoulder on fire where Kit's hand lay. She brushed the feeling away. Any woman's touch would have set her aflame. Kit was trouble.

Kit's face crumpled and hurt flashed in her eyes. "The *Revenge* is leaving in a few days. I wanted to apologize before I go, in case I never sail back here again, or if something happens. I don't want to part on ill terms again."

"And you think you can do that by buying my time? Like I'm some kind of..." Lisbet trailed off, insulted. Even if she was a whore, that wasn't how she wanted Kit to see her.

"How else was I supposed to talk to you? You've been avoiding me."

"I can't do this right now." Lisbet didn't deserve an apology without giving one, and she was not prepared to do that. It was better to leave the past behind. "I have other things to see to."

"A man," Kit said flatly.

Lisbet shrugged. It wasn't any concern of Kit's what, or who, she had to do.

"Go on, then." Kit let go of Lisbet's shoulder and her voice rose in frustration. "That's all you ever wanted, right? To spread your legs for men? I was just practice?"

Lisbet glanced around the market to see if the argument was drawing stares. It didn't seem like anyone was paying them any mind. She wanted to walk away, but she couldn't. "You weren't practice," she hissed, trying to bring the volume of the conversation back down. "I cared for you."

"I don't believe you. If you cared for me, you wouldn't be so keen to fuck men all the time. Look at you, Lisbet, you've built your whole life around it."

Lisbet sighed. Kit had never understood how she could desire the company of both men and women. "Only because there's a lot more men around her who want to fuck me than women, and they pay handsomely for the privilege. You were gone. I moved on." She pursed her lips in annoyance. Though she would never call their lives easy, at least Kit and Mona and Elinor had always known with certainty what they wanted. She had been made to feel broken, always pulled in two directions by people who could never understand.

"I shouldn't have told your parents about you and Andrew," Kit said. "I was angry, and jealous, but I never wanted you to get hurt."

"No, you shouldn't have. Though maybe I should thank you for it. Had you not told them, I would still be in that village, constrained by their religion and their silly notions of sin. At least I have my own life now."

"I've missed you," Kit said, her voice raspy. "Every single day since I left."

She couldn't admit how much she had missed Kit, too. There was no point. Kit would be sailing away again soon, and Lisbet would stay behind to nurse the reopened wound alone. Just when she thought she had finally figured everything out. "Better to let the past rest."

Kit looked disappointed in that response, but it was the best Lisbet could give her. She had wasted too many hours on daydreams and what-ifs.

"I do have to go now," Lisbet said. She ignored the unspoken question in Kit's eyes. It would only hurt her to know the truth. "I wish you calm seas and good fortune."

"Goodbye, Liss," Kit whispered.

Walking away from her was as hard as it had been five years earlier, but it had to be done. Even if fate had decided to thrust Kit back into her life, there was no way in which the relationship could be salvaged. Kit would always be jealous of the men from whom Lisbet earned her coin, and the freedom of wealth wasn't something Lisbet would ever give up.

The pirate was waiting for her. He leaned lazily against a tree in front of the tavern, idly chewing one frayed end of a stick as he glanced around the square. The scent of rum clouded around him, and Lisbet had to fight to keep herself from rolling her eyes. By the smell of him, he wouldn't be able to get it up. She would take his money anyways for wasting her time. She let him lead her to his ship's camp, mind still lingering on the conversation with Kit. She hadn't thought to ask if Kit had loved anyone since her. She didn't want to know. The pirate pulled her into a tent made of canvas sails precariously propped up by driftwood. The whole thing threatened to collapse with one wrong move, so she lay as still as possible and let her mind drift. When she emerged from it a quarter of an hour later, her purse was heavy with silver coins, the pirate was snoring inside, and Kit's disappointed parting stare still occupied her thoughts.

Lisbet skirted the main road as she returned home, avoiding the bustle of the town. Pendragon was sitting on her doorstep, flicking his tail as the breeze ruffled his orange fur. She pulled her key from its chain around her neck, and pushed the door open for him to dart in. He retreated to his typical spot underneath her bed while she deposited the coins in her secret stash and sponged herself off with tepid water from her washing bowl.

She had mending to do. The drunken pirate had ripped her underskirt as he pawed at her in his heat of desire. A small, wooden box with her needles and thread was on top of the wardrobe, and she brought it over to the bed to begin the task. But when she sat on the edge of the mattress, she was overcome by a wave of emotion, and buried her face in her hands, sobbing. She cried until she had no more tears left to release. It was over, it had to be over. She wouldn't cry over Kit again. Something rough was scraping across her hand, and she opened swollen eyes to see Pendragon licking it, as if to remind her she wasn't completely alone. Lisbet's damp cheeks lifted in a smile. She would be fine. She had everything she needed.

***

The canoe bobbed in the waves as Mona dropped a fishing line into the crystal clear waters beneath them. Lisbet wrinkled her nose as the scent of rotting fish guts was blown her way by the breeze. The putrid bucket sat between them, alongside a pot large enough to hold twenty crabs or more. She watched as the line drifted down to the sandy bottom, weighted by a musket ball tied partway up the line.

"Come on, bite," Mona said, leaning over the edge of the canoe to watch.

A large crab sidled sideways beneath the boat, approaching the bait. Both women held their breath waiting to see if he would take it. The line jerked, and Mona pulled it in as Lisbet whisked the lid from the pot. The crab fell in, and she slammed the cover back on quickly, before the crabs could clamber over one another and up the walls of the pot in a desperate bid to escape back to the tranquil blue depths.

"How many do we need for supper?" Lisbet asked.

"Five or six more should be enough," Mona replied. "Let's paddle closer to the rocks."

"Six more? Are you having a party?"

Mona laughed. "Better to have too much than too little, and if any's left over we'll give it to the crew. Besides, Tristan is coming, and you know how he eats."

It was true, Lisbet had once seen the man put away a whole roasted chicken after a long journey at sea. "We might need ten more, in that case."

In the end, they settled for another eight, the crabs making the work easy as they teemed from the dark rocks at the end of the beach, lured forth from their lairs by the fish entrails. Lisbet's stomach growled as they paddled their way back to the little pier on the beach closest to Mona and Elinor's house.

Tristan saw them rowing in, and met the canoe at the beach to carry the heavy pot into the yard. Lisbet and Mona followed him past the shop where Elinor was finishing a sale with a customer, and into the back kitchen area that boasted a well shared with the *Revenge's* crew, and a large, dugout firepit in in the sandy soil.

Lisbet froze when she saw her, recognizing the slender, spry figure even from a distance. Kit sauntered into the yard, dropped a load of firewood, met Lisbet's eyes, and froze as well. Lisbet spun on her heel and walked back around to the front of the house, Mona right behind her.

"You didn't tell me she would be here," Lisbet said, angry at her friend's deception.

"I didn't know, Liss, I swear. Elinor must have invited her, or Tristan. I would have told you if I'd known."

"I'm going home."

"Please don't. Can't you just make peace for one night? This is the last night the *Revenge* will be here for God knows how long, and we want to see her off right."

Lisbet crossed her arms, unswayed by her friend's plea.

"Please, just stay. Otherwise I'll be bored to tears when they start talking about ship things."

"Fine. But I don't want to sit near her."

"You won't. It will be fun, I swear. You won't even know she's there."

Lisbet laughed bitterly. Kit's presence was impossible to ignore. But she would try, for Mona's sake. After all, they had already put in so much effort to procure the meal, and she may as well try to enjoy it. She followed Mona back into the rear yard and drew up a bucket of water for the pot of crabs. Mona chopped some onions and potatoes on a slab of wood and added them to the pot, along with a palmful of salt. Together, the women hoisted the pot over the fire, attaching it to a metal chain with a hook that hung suspended between three iron legs that straddled the blaze.

The crabs' claws and legs scratched at the sides of the pot in awful screeches that raised the hairs on Lisbet's forearms. The noises ceased quickly as the water began to bubble and steam lifted the lid ever so slightly to escape into the evening air. Tristan appeared from inside the house, bearing a large platter in his arms.

"It smells delicious," he said as Mona loaded it with seafood and potatoes. "The table's set, we're just waiting for you two."

They led the way inside the house, Lisbet holding the door for Tristan. The table was cleared of all Mona's writings and Elinor's maps, and a rich purple table cloth draped over it and hung nearly to the floor. Candles were lit along the table's length, bathing the simple room in a warm, flickering glow. Steam wafted up from a basket of hot rolls, and the colorful fruits of the Caribbean adorned another platter. Lisbet's mouth watered at the sight of the feast.

Tristan set the crabs down in the center of the table and took his seat to the left of Elinor, who was at the head. Mona sat to her right, across from a man Lisbet recognized as Reddy, another member of the *Revenge's* crew. Two more of the crewmen separated her from Kit, at the other end of the table. Lisbet glanced away before Kit could notice her staring, and turned her attention to Elinor, who had risen to address the party.

"Tomorrow, *Nimue's Revenge* sails on, to continue her legacy under the greatest captain she's ever know," Elinor said. She smiled at Tristan, who shook his head in disagreement. "Tonight we gather to celebrate these months we've had together, and to toast the ones we'll have again when you return." She raised her glass, filled with deep red wine. "To Tristan, Reddy, Scab, Jack, and the newest crewman, Kit!"

"To the *Revenge!*" Lisbet said in chorus with the rest of the group. She sneaked a look at Kit, who was blushing furiously at the mention of her name. Lisbet drank thirstily from her glass, hoping the wine would calm her nerves. It was half empty when she set it back down as Mona prodded her in the side.

"It will be fine," Mona leaned over and whispered.

Tristan passed Lisbet a plate, and she realized he had begun serving food. Good. The tedious work of pulling apart the crab and drawing the meat out of the shell would provide an easy distraction. She tucked into her plate, the soft meat practically melting on her tongue as she glanced down the table at Kit again.

"So where are you sailing for?" Elinor asked Tristan.

"Hispaniola," he said. "The bloody Spaniards'll be sailing for Spain this time of year, and their ships are full, or so I've heard."

"A safe wager," Elinor said. "But I've also heard talk of greater treasure coming from further out, ships laden to the brim with gold."

"Talking to Avery again? You know he likes to spin tales."

"Aye, but his purse was heavy when he came by the shop."

"Could be, but we'll stick to safer waters this time. Hoping to be back before Christmas."

"Suit yourself," Elinor said with a grin.

"Sounds like you want to come along."

"Don't you dare," Mona glared at Tristan.

Elinor laughed. "Don't worry darling, those days are long behind me. I have the greatest treasure I could ever dream of right here."

Lisbet looked down at her plate so no one could see her scowl. She loved Mona and Elinor, but sometimes they were so affectionate towards one another that it was irritating. Especially when Lisbet was so alone. She couldn't help herself as she stole another glance down the table at Kit. She was laughing with the men, her perfect pink lips parting to eat another bite of crab in between jokes. Lisbet almost choked on her own bite of meat as the memories of kissing Kit rushed back all at once.

She struggled to breathe as tears welled in her eyes, and she realized she hadn't almost choked. She was choking. She tried to cough, to force her airways to release the morsel of food lodged there, but her attempts were futile. Her eyes widened in panic as people laughed around her, oblivious to her distress. If she didn't get air soon, she would die. The realization washed over her, flooding her body with an eerie calm.

Lisbet pushed her chair back as black spots began to dance in the corners of her eyes. If she was going to die, she refused to do it at the dinner table and ruin the party. The conversation at the table lulled as she stumbled to the door and pushed out into the dark night. Her chest fought to expand, burning as her lungs were denied the air she so desperately needed. She knelt on the wooden porch, the motion jarring loose an acrid memory of all the times she had been forced to her knees in prayer between the pews of the tiny church up the hill. She clutched her throat, feeling the same ache as when she'd pled with God to make her stop loving Kit.

Lisbet closed her eyes, willing forth the images of Kit she had pushed away for so long. If she was on her way to eternal damnation, she wanted her last moments on Earth to be reliving the closest she'd come to heaven. All of a sudden, she was a rebellious teen again with Kit by her side. Running through the field together, feeling the tug of Kit's hand as she urged Lisbet to keep up with her longer strides. Inventing excuses to steal away to the storehouse and discovering each other there. The secret, soft kisses, and the harder, more urgent ones. The certainty that Kit was the one she was fated to love, and the fear of what that meant.

"Lisbet?"

She could almost hear Kit's voice calling her name, like a nearly forgotten dream. *I'm here*, she wanted to call back, but there was something caught in her throat and she couldn't get the words around it.

"Oh God, Liss. Help! She needs help."

Something hit her in the back and she fell forward onto her palms. Another blow struck between her shoulder blades, and the bite of food dislodged itself, falling unceremoniously to the porch as she coughed and gasped for air.

"Breathe, just breathe," Tristan said, his quiet authority soothing as he knelt beside her. "We've got you."

Lisbet felt her lungs fill. The cool evening air was sharp in her chest, but it cleared the black spots from her vision. She slowly realized everyone from the party had abandoned the table to circle around her on the porch, the looks in their eyes ranging from concern to relief. Her face went hot as she flushed from embarrassment. The last thing she wanted was to attract so much attention.

"I'm sorry for disrupting your meal." She smiled wanly at the others.

"Don't be ridiculous," Mona said, kneeling at her other side. "You didn't disrupt anything. We're just all grateful Kit realized something was wrong, and Tristan knew what to do."

"Thank you," Lisbet whispered to Tristan, ignoring Kit. How could she look her in the eyes, knowing they would betray her inner feelings to the other woman who knew her all too well?

"Come, come." Elinor ushered the watching crowd back into the house. "Give her some room to breathe."

Mona and Tristan hauled Lisbet to her feet again, her knees shaky from nerves as she realized just how close she had come to death. She sucked in another long breath of fresh air, appreciating it like she never had before.

"Are you alright?" Mona asked.

"Just shaken," Lisbet said with a sigh.

"Understandably so, but nothing a hot tea and a nip of rum won't fix. Come in, I'll fix you a cup."

Lisbet shook her head. "I'd rather go home to rest." She couldn't go back to their sympathy and stares.

Mona raised a copper eyebrow. "I'm not sure that's a good idea, considering the fright you just had."

"I'm fine, truly. Please extend my goodbyes to everyone else." Lisbet looked up at Tristan as she dropped into a shallow curtsy. "Thank you again, for coming to my rescue. I wish you smooth seas and good fortune on your next voyage."

Tristan nodded deeply. The sound of laughter floated out from the open door; the party had already resumed inside.

"Be safe, Liss," Mona called as Lisbet walked away, still trying to digest what she had just been through and discern its meaning.

Kit had been the last thing her mind had shown her in the moments before death, and that had to mean something, no matter how hard Lisbet wished it didn't. Guilt washed over her. She shouldn't have been so cold, but she was out of time to mend things. Kit was sailing the next morning on the *Revenge,* and Lisbet was staying behind. Just like she had done before.

Chapter 6

I F *NIMUE'S REVENGE* WAS an impressive beast from shore, then she was truly terrifying up close and in person. Long rows of black cannons on each side of the deck gleamed in the breaking sunlight, reflecting the soft pinks and purples of the dawn on their polished barrels. Three heavy masts towered overhead, bedecked in a veritable maze of complex rigging and billowing canvas sails. The sheer size of the ship was enough to awe Kit. It dwarfed any other vessel she had sailed on, including that of her former captain, and was clearly designed to wreak maximum destruction upon its foes.

"Raise the anchors," Tristan called to the men.

Metal creaked and clanked and the crew winched the heavy anchors up, freeing the ship from its tether to the sea floor. Kit stood at the rail, awaiting her first orders on the *Revenge* as she looked at Nassau in the distance. She couldn't help but wonder what Lisbet was doing in the early morning hours, then decided she didn't want to imagine the possibilities. They would only anger her.

Kit's hand slipped into her pocket out of habit, fingers wrapping around a small rock, worn smooth from years of her rubbing it as a nervous habit. Lisbet had given it to her because it looked like a heart, and she had carried it every day for almost ten years. Her fingers curled into a fist that she extended out over the water.

Lisbet had done nothing but push her away. Even the night prior when Kit had saved her life, Tristan had gotten all her thanks. She hadn't even come back in to say farewell. It was time to leave Lisbet, and New Providence well and truly behind, yet her fist refused to unclench no matter how much she willed it to. She wasn't ready to let go. She slipped the stone back into her pocket.

Something brushed against her leg, making her jump. She looked down to see a gray cat staring back up at her.

"Why, hello there," she said, stooping to give the cat a scratch on the head.

"Has Igraine escaped from the hold already?" Tristan asked, strolling up as the ship lurched into motion.

"Igraine?" Kit asked, the name unfamiliar.

"It's Welsh," he explained. "She was the mother of King Arthur. Mona gives all the cats she finds Welsh names, says it's so the Crown can't erase our history." He picked up the little gray cat. "She should be below deck filling her belly with stowaway rats, not prowling up here. Take her down to the hold, then find Scab for your station."

Kit took the cat that was passed to her. A wave rocked the boat and the cat dug into her shoulder with her claws, piercing through Kit's clothing and dotting her shirt with red. She wrapped one arm around Igraine, keeping a firm grasp on the nape of her neck as she stumbled over to the hatch that led to the great underbelly of the ship. Her sea legs had escaped her in the few weeks she had spent on land, and she had to take care not to trip as the ship pitched side to side in the deeper waves as they left the harbor.

She climbed down the ladder, no easy feat with an angry cat attached to her, the crossed through the crew's sleeping quarters to another hatch that led down to the hold. She made her way quickly across the dark room, the path already committed to her memory from the multiple trips carrying crates of food and drink to the *Revenge's* storeroom. Igraine seemed to recognize where she was supposed to be and wriggled free from Kit's grasp with a hiss, darting towards the hatch and leaping down into the hold below.

Kit heard a noise behind her and stiffened against the assault she was sure was coming. The hazing on her old ship had begun within hours of her boarding, as soon as a few members of the crew had managed to corner her beyond the sight of the captain who turned a blind eye to their intimidation practices. The two men of the *Revenge* just nodded in greeting though, and maneuvered around her, holding a large crate between them. She breathed a silent sigh of relief as they passed without incident, then scampered back up to the top deck to find the quartermaster.

Gruff and grizzled, Scab looked every inch a pirate, with a perpetual scowl that showed he was missing two of his top teeth. The crew had explained to Kit that his name was short for Scabbard, because he'd once been run clean through by a cutlass— turned into a scabbard, as it were— and lived to tell the tale. He commanded the crew through their daily activities brusquely, but she had come to learn he had a sly sense of humor and a quicker wit than he showed.

"Can you read and write, boy?" Scab asked.

"A bit," Kit said. "Not well." Her parents hadn't thought it suitable for a girl to learn anything but a few Psalms and prayers and how to scrawl her name.

"A shame," Scab said. "But there's plenty of other work for you to do. I suppose you can swab a deck?"

Kit nodded.

"Ever fired a gun?" He motioned to the large cannons lined up across the deck.

"I've seen it done enough times, I'm sure I'd manage. I ran powder on my last ship, I know how it's done," Kit said with more confidence than she felt.

"Good enough for me," Scab said. "Join up with Reddy and Diego, they'll show you the ropes." He peered at her, narrowing his eyes quizzically. "Speaking of ropes, you any good on 'em? You've got the stature for climbing."

"I'm alright at it," Kit said, swallowing nervously. Truth be told, heights made her knees tremble a bit more than she preferred, but she was eager to please her new quartermaster.

"Good, good. Might make use of that. Run on, then, the work doesn't wait."

"Aye, aye," Kit said, jogging across the deck to join Reddy, the russet-haired crewman who had come to her defense in the tavern. She recognized Diego from the pirate encampment as well. He was a lanky teenager who spoke with a slight Spanish accent and towered over her, nearly as tall as the ship's intimidating captain. Kit had given him a wide berth around camp, having found before that the younger the crewman, the more likely he was to try to assert dominance over what he perceived as a weaker boy in the ranks. But Diego greeted her with a toothy smile, and she wondered again if she had misjudged the crew of the *Revenge*. They had been nothing but pleasant with her, following the example set by their captain.

"Want to race?" Diego asked, handing her a bucket.

"Race for what?" She asked.

"First to clean two cannons, and the deck around them, wins."

"Wins what?"

Diego shrugged. "Nothing, I guess. Gambling's not allowed on the ship. Just for the competition. It makes the time pass faster."

"I'll take these two," Kit said, nodding to the two cannons nearest to her. She'd never been one to shy away from a challenge. She reached into the bucket to retrieve a brush and dropped to the deck, scrubbing vigorously at the base of the heavy cannon.

"Cheating already," Diego scolded, but he was laughing as he hurried across the deck. "I guess you're a real pirate after all."

The race did help pass the time faster, and Kit rushed through the task. She was eager to prove herself, but she had scarcely started on the second gun when Diego strolled back over.

"Taking a break because you know you'll lose?" She teased.

"Already finished." He grinned smugly. "Maybe you'll get me tomorrow."

"Help Kit finish off the last gun," Reddy told Diego after looking over his station and deeming it sufficient.

"How long have you been on the *Revenge?*" Kit asked as Diego joined her alongside the weapon.

"Three years."

"I've never met a Spanish pirate," Kit said. All the crewmen of her old ship had been British sailors, defected from the navy or merchant ships for the chance to make more money on their own terms. She was used to fighting against the Spanish, not working alongside them.

"I assure you, we exist," Diego said proudly.

"Clearly. But how did you come to be on a Welsh ship?"

"The old captain, Captain Davies, saved me. I was pressed into service on a Spanish ship by no choice of my own and she offered me work here. It was an offer I couldn't refuse." Diego's tone was light, but he smiled wryly, and Kit wondered what threat the pirates had used to get him to agree to join their crew.

"How do you find this ship?"

"Better than the one I left. The captain treats us well, makes sure we're not wanting for gold." Diego patted his pocket, which sounded empty. He laughed.

"Makes sure we have plenty of opportunity to spend it all, too," Reddy said, polishing the cannon with a dry rag. "She's a good ship, helmed by a good man."

That was reassuring. Kit felt her guard slipping down a little more. The men were dangerous, and she wouldn't want to face them in battle. But among themselves, they acted almost as a family, and she sensed no threat against her from the crew. Across the deck, other men had already broken out a bottle of rum and were lounging on crates pulling long swigs as they passed it around. Judging by the sun's position overhead it was scarcely midday, far too early for Kit to be interested in drinking, but her feet seemed to follow Reddy and Diego of their own accord as she strolled to join them.

By the third day, Kit was fully settled into the routine of life aboard *Nimue's Revenge*. She no longer flinched when she felt the footsteps of someone behind her, and found herself opening up little by little as the sailors swapped stories of adventure over tankards of grog into the late evening hour. The camaraderie was unfamiliar, a sensation she hadn't experienced since she had been exiled from the village, but Kit embraced it. It felt good to belong somewhere again. She was finally part of a community, even if it was built upon a lie. Guilt tugged at her conscience, a reminder of the secret she still withheld from all of them but the captain.

She wanted to tell them, knew it would be better to get it out in the open than have them discover it later and label her deception as malicious. It would be a relief for her, too. She was tired of being looked at like the child she pretended she was, and even more exhausted by having to keep up the pretense of being a boy. Her throat hurt from deepening her voice all the time, and her shoulders ached from keeping them hunched to hide her figure. Yet, each time she opened her mouth to admit the truth, the words caught in her throat. It wasn't time.

Chapter 7

"*A BOTTLE OF RUM, and then one more*
Far we'll sail to distant shores,
And fill our ship from deck to hold
With rum, and whores and chests of gold!"

The pirates cheered on the last note of the popular shanty, their roar seeming to shake the layers of palmetto leaves that made up the roof of the tavern. A buccaneer handed Lisbet a bottle of wine, and she set it on the table without drinking from it. She was bored.

"Drink." He handed her the wine again, dark brows knitting together in a scowl.

"Don't want to," she replied, but she held onto the bottle, if only to prevent him from passing it to her a third time.

"I don't care if ye want to, wench, I'm givin' ye an order. Do ye no' know who I be?"

Lisbet sighed, not in the mood to play games of stroking men's egos. He would tell her soon enough. They always did. "No, and nor do I care."

"I'm Captain John Wood." He rose and withdrew his cutlass from its leather scabbard at his waist. "Greatest captain in all the Caribbean. And if I say drink, ye'll drink."

"I could think of a dozen better, easily. Put that away," Lisbet said, looking from the blade to its sheath as she feigned boredom. The pirates feasted upon fear, and respected the bold. "You're making a fool of yourself."

He glared at her, but she held his gaze while tightening her grip on the wine bottle. If he lunged at her, she would smash it over his head. The pirates usually fought with each other and left the women of Nassau alone, but as more and more flooded to the island, their behavior became more erratic. To her relief, the captain laughed and returned his weapon to his waist.

"I do hope ye're as feisty in bed as ye are now," Wood said, leering at Lisbet's chest.

"You'll not be finding out," Lisbet said lightly, as she sidestepped around him. He was too unpredictable. There was no way she would be following him anywhere, not for all the coin in Nassau. She wasn't looking to get stabbed by some captain drunk on power, riches, and rum.

Well out of reach of the menacing pirate, she drank from the bottle she still clutched. The red wine was as sour as the feeling he had given her, like it had turned to vinegar. She glanced around the tavern, but the worn black hat covering tousled hair was nowhere to be seen. Not that she was expecting to spot it, it had only been a week since the *Revenge* left the harbor, and it would be at least a few weeks more before she saw Kit in Nassau again. If she even came back.

Lisbet recognized a pirate who had paid for her services a few nights before, and slid onto the bench next to him to watch the game of cards in progress. She stroked his thigh under the table, wishing it was the thigh of a woman she was running her fingers over. They were at least interesting to lie with. The last woman whose touch she had known had been Elinor, before she had ever met Mona. It had been too long since Lisbet had been with someone who understood her, who saw her as more than an object to be used and endeavored to give as much pleasure as they took.

The pirate laid his cards face down on the table and slid a coin to his opponent. He turned to Lisbet, a gold tooth gleaming from his mouth as he reached for her. If it was pleasure, not coin, that she sought, she was unlikely to find it with him. But coin was a better consolation than nothing, so she let him take her by the elbow and escort her into the night. When he was done, she returned to the tavern to find another drunken fool to prey on.

That night her dreams were filled with visions of Kit. Lisbet awoke before the sun, burning with an aching need. Pulses of desire throbbed between her legs, sending ripples of lust up through her core to her breasts. She trailed a hand over her stomach, imagining it was someone else's. Goosebumps raised across her skin and made her shiver. She rolled a nipple between her thumb and index finger, feeling it harden with another jolt between her legs.

It wasn't the same. Her mind was too connected to her hands as she fondled herself, unable to maintain the illusion that it was Kit cupping her breast or dipping a finger between her moist folds. Lisbet wiped her hand on the blanket, unsatisfied. She needed the togetherness to truly feel satisfaction and dissolve into a million pieces. Groaning, she rolled back onto her side to try to fall asleep again.

She couldn't stop thinking about Kit's damned lips, how they were so perfectly pouty and the way they parted just before she leaned in for a kiss. Or her eyes, how they burned with an intensity and seductiveness that left her body tingling wherever they rested. Lisbet had heard that the pirates liked to torture people, but she didn't know Kit's return would torment her like this, driving her mad with forgotten desire and pushing her to the brink of explosion. She touched herself again in frustration, pressing into her sensitive nub and grinding her hips into the mattress. The pressure within her mounted but never released, leaving her panting and unsatisfied.

When the unbearable tension receded, she got up, even though there was nowhere she wanted to go and nothing she wanted to do. Nassau was growing, but the island felt too small for Lisbet to find what she was really looking for. For years, she had contented herself with the freedom her work allowed her, and the riches that accompanied it. But all the gold coins in the world couldn't ease her loneliness in the quiet cabin.

She treasured her friendships forged with Mona and Elinor, though it was becoming harder and harder not to resent their happiness. Each time they gathered together was a painful reminder that they had what she couldn't. And the hardest part of all was knowing it was of her own doing. Even if she had given in and talked to Kit, nothing would have changed from it. Kit was disgusted by her, by the life she had chosen. Lisbet wondered if she would ever be able to feel real pleasure, or love, again.

Her stomach wouldn't allow her to stay in any longer, and so Lisbet wandered into town to do some shopping before the stalls got too crowded with rowdy pirates. Freshly baked bread was being pulled from wood fired ovens, luring her to the vendor's tent by the aroma wafting between the stands. She couldn't resist ripping the heel from the hot loaf to devour it in the middle of the road. Steam curled up from the bread to dance in the morning rays of sun. No matter her woes, bread always seemed to make them a little better.

"Lisbet," a woman called.

She recognized the voice of her friend Emily, another of Nassau's women who made her living from the men occupying it.

"How are you?" Emily asked, approaching to air kiss Lisbet on the cheek.

"Ah, busy as always," Lisbet replied, skirting around the question. "And you?"

"If the town is thriving, so am I." Emily shifted her basket to one arm and raised her other hand to her brow to block the sun. "But anyways, there was a man asking around for you earlier. You just missed him."

"A man?" Lisbet asked. It wasn't unusual for the men who favored her to seek her out, but it was out of the ordinary for one of the other women to let her know and not try to part the poor soul with his gold themselves.

"Didn't look like any pirate I've seen," Emily continued, "and far too proper. Reckon he musta been one of the villagers."

"Did he say what he wanted with me?" Lisbet asked. There was only one villager she could think that might seek her out, and that was Andrew.

"No," Emily said, cocking her head to one side. "But I assume it's what they all want. He said you would know where to find him."

"I see," Lisbet said, mind racing. She knew the most logical reason Andrew was looking for her, but she feared the worst– that something had happened to one of her sisters.

Emily giggled, oblivious to Lisbet's internal panic, and dropped her tone to a conspiratorial whisper. "Is he... a suitor? Someone you care for, perhaps?"

"No, it's not like that at all. He's just a man, like any other." Adulterous, manipulating, and her only link to the village and the two people she still loved there.

It was probably nothing, but the doubt gnawed at her. Lisbet excused herself quickly as another woman came over to join them and spread the morning gossip of the town. There was only one place Andrew could have meant, the place of all their youthful trysts. The old storehouse at the end of the field below the village in the woods. Worry for her siblings grew as she jogged up the path and cut through the rows of withered stalks. The drought hadn't abated, and it seemed the village would have nothing to harvest. The field was empty of people working, a further testament to the struggle the last holdouts faced.

She arrived at the storehouse and ducked through the door that hung partially open. It had been burned during one of the Spanish raids on the island ten years prior, and still stood as an unintentional monument to the life of terror the settlers had known before the pirates' arrival. Most of the ceiling had collapsed into a pile at the back of the chamber, but the charred walls had held fast, and still offered some semblance of privacy.

Andrew wasn't there yet, and she considered leaving, but her desperation to know that her sisters were alright won out. It wasn't the first time he had summoned her to the storehouse, and she hated the way he baited her into coming by the information he held. She scoffed. And to think she had thought she could love him, once.

He made her sit with her memories for what must have been close to an hour, but finally the storehouse door creaked as its rusty hinges were called into service and his imposing silhouette filled the frame. Broad shoulders and tight muscles acquired from years of chopping wood for fires would have qualified him as handsome, if not for his cold, gray eyes that stared at her with calculating desire.

"Andrew," she greeted him tersely, rising. "Are my sisters well?"

"I didn't know if you would come," he said. "I'm glad you did."

"Where's your wife?"

"At home, with the wee ones. We're expecting another in a month or so."

Lisbet rolled her eyes. So that was why he had come, same as the last time. He was bored. "You should be with her, not here."

"She doesn't give me what I need. Refuses to let me even touch her. What else is a man supposed to do?"

"Are my sisters well?" She repeated, ignoring his question.

"There will be plenty of time to discuss that later." Andrew stepped towards her, reaching out to wrap his fingers in her hair as he rested his palm at the nape of her neck. "I missed you."

"Fifty gold pieces." Lisbet crossed her arms and named a sum she was sure he didn't have.

"I can offer you something better." He leaned down and pressed his lips to her forehead. "I'll bring your sisters to see you." It was an offer that was more valuable to her than gold.

"God damn you," she cursed, and he flinched. Her hands drifted to his belt buckle. She felt a tiny bit of sorrow for his poor wife, and wondered if she had any inkling what her husband was up to. The pity was overwhelmed by relief at having avoided the woman's fate.

"I thought you might be interested in that," he said as his trousers fell to the dusty floor.

"You're going to Hell."

"Then I'll certainly meet you there." His grip tightened in her hair as he spun her around and bent her over.

He never lasted long and that day was no exception. Lisbet's skirt fell to her ankles once more as Andrew removed his hands from her waist where he'd been holding it up. He stepped back and wiped sweat from his brow with the hem of his shirt, then pulled his pants up and rebuckled his belt. She turned around to lean against the grain barrel, crossing thighs that were slick with his spilled seed.

"Sounded like you missed me just as much." His smile was too smug. "I knew you did."

"You flatter yourself," Lisbet spat back. "It's playacting, a performance."

"You're lying," he said, but the smile was gone. "You wouldn't be here if you didn't want it just as much. You can't get enough of it."

"Take me to see my sisters."

"Oh, you didn't think I meant today, did you?"

"Andrew…" She warned, crossing her arms.

"After you just insulted me?"

She wanted to smack him right across his smug mouth. He was toying with her, like one of the cats with a mouse it was torturing. "A deal is a deal. Honor your side of it, or pay the fifty gold."

"Don't think I want to anymore. What are you going to do about it?"

"Andrew, be reasonable. Does your word, your honor, mean nothing?" She knew it didn't, or he wouldn't be there. Lisbet's jaw twitched as she clenched it in frustration.

"I want to know. What will you do if I don't?"

"Kill you."

He laughed sharply in disbelief, then fell silent as he noticed the look in her eyes. "Now who's being unreasonable, Lisbet?"

"If you refuse to honor your side of the deal, then you've stolen from me. I don't take kindly to it."

"So you threaten to kill me?"

"It would be doing the world a favor."

"And how would you manage that? If you had any weapons on you, I'm quite confident I'd've found them just now." He smirked, ever arrogant.

"By coin and connections. It wouldn't be hard." Lisbet could easily think of three men from the *Revenge* alone who would be happy to take on the task for the right price.

"You've spent too much time with the pirates. It's changed you." He tsked as he looked her up and down. "All this talk of murder is quite unbecoming."

"Of course I've changed. Now take me to my sisters."

"You should have married me and let all the nonsense with Kate die quietly."

"Why? So you could run off to fuck whores the moment I was with child, like you've done to your wife?"

"My wife has everything she wants. A home to fill with children and a husband to provide. She's happy. Something tells me you aren't, debasing yourself for every cock that wags at you. It took a long time spent in prayer to find the strength to forgive you, but now I've come to see I'm better off without you as a wife. I can still have you whenever I want, after all."

Lisbet couldn't restrain herself any longer, and slapped him firmly across the face. Her palm stung as she pulled it away from his reddening cheek. He stared at her in shock while raising a hand to rub the welt, then anger flashed in his steel eyes and he stepped towards her.

"You'll pay for that," he threatened.

"I already have," she spat, "and I never will again." She pushed past him, furious at being used and duped and mad at herself for falling for it.

"Come back here Thursday at dawn," Andrew said to her back. "I'll take you to see your sisters then."

She paused. "I don't believe you."

"Then don't come. It's all the same to me."

"I'll be here. But if you're lying to me again, Andrew, I swear it will be the last thing you do."

She stormed off, the encounter still lingering in her thoughts. She never thought much about the work she did, removing herself from her actions as her mind distanced itself from her body. Andrew got under her skin, though, and his touch made it crawl with his casual familiarity. Even worse, she knew that was why he did it. It was the one power he still had over her, and he took pleasure in wielding it.

Lisbet had no one to blame but herself, for she was the one who had given in so quickly the first time he appeared in Nassau. She'd been too eager for news from the village, of her family, and he had seen that weakness and exploited it. Sometimes she hoped the news would be bad, so that she would never have to see him again. It would be easier to know they were all dead and buried than cling to the hope of being accepted into their fold again.

He had never offered to take her to see them before, and she still didn't believe it was true. She had tried, and each time had been pushed away by her mother. But she had to trust Andrew and follow the flame of hope he had reignited within her, even as it led her into the dark.

Chapter 8

K IT LAY BACK AND propped her feet up on a wine cask that was turned on its side and lashed to the timbers of the deck. The best part of nights on the water was the hour when the sky faded to a deep, dusky blue and all the stars twinkled to life over the Caribbean. It was a time she looked forward to every day, a moment of calm between the bustle of work and the revelry of night. Diego sat beside her on a crate, bent forward with his elbows rested on his knees and his chin on his fists, and Reddy sat across from them, leaning against one of the *Revenge's* three, tall masts.

They'd been at sea nearly a fortnight and had yet to encounter another ship worth engaging. The only other vessel they'd seen was a large frigate flying the flag of the British navy, and the captain had ordered them off course to evade crossing its path. No prey, no pay. It was clear the other pirates were becoming bored, and they spent long hours lounging on the deck talking about everything and nothing as they wished the time away.

"When we get back to Nassau, I'm taking the first whore I find and having her right there in the road if I have to," Diego groaned.

Reddy laughed. "Seems it'll be some time yet afore that day arrives."

"And when it does, we'll get Kit his first taste of a woman, too," Diego chuckled.

"I've known a woman already," Kit said, propping herself up on an elbow to drink the grog that was making her forget she was supposed to be fourteen.

"Oho, have you now?" Reddy said. "Good lad. Which of Nassau's ladies had the honor?"

"Lisbet," she said wistfully. She probably shouldn't have told them that, but her tongue was too loose. It felt good not to lie to the men who had become her friends.

Reddy's head whipped around to stare at her. "Captain Davies' friend? The brown haired one with the big tits at supper the other night?" He snickered. "You are bold. Mind you don't cross her."

"Why's that?" Kit asked, curious what Reddy might know about Lisbet's life after the village.

"No man on the *Revenge* would lay a finger on her. Our old captain had a claim on her, and seein' as her and Miss Mona have become close, well it just don't strike any of us as somethin' wise to get entangled in."

"What do you mean the captain had a claim on her? Elinor?" Kit's stomach clenched. "But what about Mona?"

"It was before she met Mona, though for all I know they've carried on as three. They're together often enough." Reddy shrugged. "Not my business, but not something I care to be caught up in, neither."

"I'd pay to be caught up in that." Diego smirked. "The three of them and me? Take every coin from my pocket."

"Lisbet... and Elinor?" Kit repeated, struggling to comprehend what seemed impossible. "But that doesn't make sense."

"Why not?" Reddy frowned. "You do know the whores fuck other people."

Diego elbowed Reddy. "Look at him, he's jealous." He turned to Kit. "I fell in love with my first one, too. It'll fade fast, right about the time you fall in love with your second."

The men laughed and raised their tankards to each other. Kit rose. Even though it was lighthearted in nature, their teasing made her uneasy. It was too comfortable. She was too close to revealing everything to them. Reeling from Reddy's revelation, she staggered to the rail and stared into the night. Lisbet and Elinor. The knowledge of that hurt worse than seeing Lisbet selling herself to men. As terrible as it seemed, that at least made sense. There were few other opportunities for women to earn their living. But Elinor, and maybe Mona, too? Kit had always found consolation that Lisbet had rejected her for a man. There was nothing she could do about that. But if Lisbet still desired women, then that meant her rejection had been of Kit. It stung.

"Kit," Scabbard called across the deck, startling her as she gazed out to sea. "Going to need you up the ropes. This lout won't wake up for his watch."

He nudged one of the pirates sleeping on the deck with his boot toe. The man let out a great, rasping snore and rolled over.

"Aye, Quartermaster," Kit said. She felt a little wobbly herself, and hoped she still had enough of her wits about her to scale the rigging to the lookout perch high among the web of ropes.

He handed her a spyglass and shooed her off towards the main mast with a wave of his hand. It was a dark night, but the sky was clear. A half moon shone off the water and illuminated everything in its path. Kit grasped a rope so thick her hand barely fit around it. Fibers pricked uncomfortably into her palms, but she didn't dare loosen her grip. The rope swayed as the ship did, and Kit paused to get a feel for the movement before hoisting herself up. She could feel Scabbard's eyes on her from below, judging her performance to see if she was fit for the task he had assigned.

Finally, she made it to the perch. Her stomach turned as she looked down. A rogue wave would be enough to knock her down, and a fall to the deck from that height was almost certain death. She inched towards the mast, sighing with relief as she felt its sturdy girth behind her back. Once she was settled, she decided it was kind of nice on the perch. Elevated above the world, Kit could be alone with her thoughts. The stars looked close enough to touch, and she nearly reached out a hand to try, then remembered she had a task to do.

She pulled the spyglass from her pocket and extended it. Holding to one eye, she squinted off into the distance. The dark shadow of an island rose against the horizon to her left, a mound of black silhouetted against the dark blue sky. Kit yawned. On a normal night, she would have already been in her hammock below the deck. It couldn't hurt to close her eyes for just a few moments.

The ship rocked and Kit's eyes flew open. She had no idea how long she had been asleep but for the location of the stars above. They had shifted ever so slightly. She'd only been dozing a few minutes at most. Raising the spyglass to her eye again, she surveyed the horizon. There was a black speck on the lens of the instrument, and she rubbed it with her shirt, cursing in frustration that the speck hadn't gone. In fact, it almost looked to be moving.

"Ship!" Kit yelled down as she realized what she was looking at. The attempt was futile. Tristan and Scabbard had both retired to their cabins, leaving only the navigator at the helm. A few pirates still milled about near the stern of the ship, but they were much too far away to hear her over the sails flapping in the wind.

"Ship," she yelled again, forgetting to lower her voice in her urgency. She waved her arms, trying to attract the attention of the navigator, but his gaze was fixed ahead and he didn't notice her.

Kit threw one leg over the edge of the perch, searching for a foothold on the net of rope. Her toe caught in the rigging and she swung the rest of her body over the ledge. Palms slippery with anticipation, she almost lost her handhold. *Careful,* she reminded herself. There would be no share of the spoils for her if she was dead from a fall. She raced down the ropes, jumping the last few feet to land with a thud on the deck. The pirate nearest to her stirred.

"Ship," she yelled, and this time they could hear her.

The men leapt to their feet, revived from their drunken slumbers by their lust for gold. Kit raced across the deck to pound on the door to Scabbard's cabin.

"What is it?" His grizzled face scowled down at her as he came to the door.

Kit quickly told him what she had seen.

"Coming towards us?"

"Aye, sir, it seemed that way."

"Go wake the captain, I'll rouse the crew. You been in a fight before, boy?"

Kit nodded. "Aye, sir, a time or two." The brutality of it had stunned her. And thrilled her. She'd never realized what a bore her life had been until she was swinging a knife as she leapt through the air at a man who was just as intent on killing her. She'd never felt so alive as she had in the first moments after, when she knew she had survived.

"Go on then, we've much to prepare."

Kit ran to wake the captain, but he was already stepping out of his cabin, awoken by the noise on the deck.

"A ship?" He asked, rubbing sleep from his eyes.

"Aye, captain."

"Merchant or navy?"

"It was too far and too dark to tell," Kit said.

"Little matter," Tristan said with a smile that lacked his usual humor and warmth. This smile was cold, arrogant, and sent a chill racing down Kit's spine. "We'll take them either way. Get to your station and await my orders."

Kit felt the familiar chill rush over her body. Battle at sea wasn't an endeavor for the faint of heart and each one she survived was another step closer to the one she wouldn't. Her right hand went to her hip, grazing across the leather-wrapped hilt of her knife. It was like greeting an old friend, reliable and reassuring. She never looked forward to using it, but she'd never regretted it either.

Tristan cleared his throat, and Kit hurried to obey his order. Reddy and Diego were already waiting by the cannon. She squinted past the rail, but the ship wasn't visible from the lower vantage point yet. The darkest hour of the night was behind them, and they were sailing into the dawn.

"Was it you that spotted it, Kit?" Reddy asked.

"Aye," she said, "from the perch."

"How big?"

"It was hard to tell. It was just a shadow in the moonlight." In truth, Kit was starting to doubt what she had seen. Maybe it had all been a dream, wishful thinking of the riches a conquest meant.

An uneasy tension had blown in and settled across the deck, carried by the morning mist rising from the sea. Some of the men inspected their weapons, making sure knives and cutlasses were well sharpened and pistols and muskets clean. Others leaned against rails and masts with their eyes closed as they tried to regain whatever few minutes of lost sleep they could before an exhausting fight.

"That's all you have?" Diego asked as Kit pulled her own knife from its sheath.

"It is," she said, brandishing it defensively. "Claimed three men already, she has."

"We'll have to find you something better than that today, if the damned ship ever appears." He showed her his pistol, the wooden grip smooth and gleaming in the first rays of dawn.

His curse was apparently the incantation the other ship needed to come into view. The pirates ran to the rail to catch a glimpse as it slid across the calm water, its two sails full of wind that pushed it on a path directly towards the *Revenge*.

"Hoist the flag!" Tristan yelled, and the men scattered.

Kit ran to the powder keg to collect enough for Reddy and Diego to fire the cannon. The black powder was coarse and gritty like sand, with an acrid smell that she could never get acclimated to. She wrinkled her nose. Taking care not to spill any as she raced across the deck, she heard the creak of a pulley and rope as the pirates' black flag was raised.

Each buccaneer's ship had their own flag they used to signal their intent of piracy, and the *Revenge's* was no exception. It was blacker than the gunpowder she carried, and was adorned with a white skull in the upper left corner. The bottom right held a large, red dragon– the proud symbol of Wales. Kit had never seen it stitched to a pirate flag before and wondered if that, too, was Mona's doing. Either way, it made for a fearsome sight, proclaiming the threat of the ship before the crews were within shouting distance of one another.

Just as the first streaks of dawn broke through the night, a powerful boom ripped through the air, followed by the sharp crack of wood. *Nimue's Revenge* shuddered as the cannonball ripped into her just above the waterline.

"Fire," yelled Tristan. "All guns."

Kit took off running for more powder. The flashes of the guns on the ship blinded her, and her ears rang with the sound of the powder igniting to thrust the eight pound balls down their barrels and arcing across the water to meet the other ship. Smoke filled the air, choking her as she stumbled back to her station.

"Fire," Tristan roared again, raising his pistol into the air.

The other ship was still careening towards them, as though they planned to ram into the *Revenge* and sink her to the ocean floor once and for all. The men at the cannons loosed their next shots. Through the haze, Kit could just make out a man on the deck of the other ship, wearing the fine dress of a captain and waving his arms frantically.

"Hold your fire," Tristan commanded. "They're surrendering."

Silence fell on the water as both ships ceased their onslaughts.

"I recognize that vessel," Reddy muttered.

"So do I," Diego said. "The *Bonny Lass*."

"One you've come across before?" Kit asked.

"Aye, a few years back. We've a history with this ship, and her captain, if he be the same."

"What ha–" Kit's question was cut off by a bellow from the *Bonny Lass*.

"Davies! Show yerself!"

"Seems he hasn't forgotten, either," Reddy said.

The pirates looked to Tristan, who shrugged.

"Davies! Bring me the salty bitch or I'll sink yer ship."

"She's not here, Payne," Tristan yelled back. "I'm the captain of the *Revenge* now."

"I don't believe ye. Let my men aboard to search for themselves."

"You think me so gullible?" Tristan scoffed. "Captain Davies has moved on from this life, into her next."

"Who's takin' who for gullible? I'll not believe ye til I see for meself."

Tristan scowled in exasperation. "Try it and we'll shoot you down before you can get your ropes over our rails."

"Have it your way," the captain said, matching Tristan's scowl with one of his own. He raised his arm, and Kit could see the gleam of gold thread embroidering his rich, red coat. She couldn't hear the words— he was no longer yelling as he instructed his crew— but she could read them on his lips. *Sink them.*

The cannons roared once more and Kit dove for cover as bits of the deck exploded around her. She felt a fleeting sense of anger. All her hard work scrubbing day in and day out, ruined in the blink of an eye. It was enraging. A man yelled as he was struck by debris before toppling over the rail and into the sea with a splash.

"Fine," Tristan yelled. He was waving a white flag. "Board us. You won't find what you're looking for."

The *Revenge* was in poor shape, and Kit recognized that surrender was their only option if they were to keep the ship afloat. Her eyes burned from the spent gunpowder in the air, but through she was able to see the destruction around her as the acrid smoke blew away. Holes were punched through the timbers of the deck, and shards of wood blanketed what remained.

"Diego? Reddy?" She whispered, hoping against hope she would hear their reply.

"We're here," Diego said behind her. He sounded shaken.

"How could we lose?" Kit had begun to think the *Revenge* was infallible and the surrender shook her to her core.

"Lose what?" Reddy asked. "We're still here. Alive. They'll board the ship but there's nothing to take. We haven't lost yet."

"But the ship—"

"Will be repaired. Luckily we know a good outfitter in Nassau." Reddy cracked a grim smile, and Kit knew he was putting on a brave show.

"Why does their captain want Elinor so badly?"

"There's bad blood there, from three years back. I guess he doesn't know how to let bygones be bygones," Reddy said.

"We only sold him some cargo, then stole a bit of it back. See, he had the Captain's wife on the *Lass*, well, she wasn't her wife yet then, but Captain Davies wanted her to be," Diego explained, glancing uneasily toward the other ship.

Their sailors were rowing over to the *Revenge* in a skiff lowered from the *Bonny Lass,* the splash of their oars breaking the stillness of morning. Tristan threw down a rope ladder, and the men began to climb aboard. The ease of her captain's surrender chafed at Kit, but no one else seemed bothered.

"Are we going to attack them?" Kit asked, barely louder than a breath. She unsheathed her knife. "We could still fight them off while we have the high ground, before they get over the rail."

Reddy silenced her with a sharp glare. "The captain knows what he's doing."

Payne, the smuggler, climbed up last, after his men had safely arrived on the deck without interference from the *Revenge's* crew. He eyed the groups of men clustered around their cannons, gripping weapons with expressions that ranged from anger to resignation. Reddy stepped in front of Kit, blocking her view.

"Where is Davies?" Payne demanded again.

"I told you, she's gone to her next life. You're wasting your time."

"Tormenting Satan himself now, I'm sure." Payne spat on the deck.

Kit peered around Reddy just in time to see Tristan shrug.

"See, I still don't believe ye," Payne said. "If Davies had died, I'm sure the news would have made its way to me." He turned to his men. "Search the ship and bring her to me. Search the men too, she may be disguising herself among them."

Kit's blood ran cold at the order. Even if they were seeking Elinor, she didn't want to risk her identity being discovered either. Payne and his sailors did not seem like polite gentlemen, and there was no telling what they would do if they discovered her deception. She was gripping her knife so tightly her fingers were going numb, and she forced her hand to relax, though she didn't resheath her blade.

The smuggler's sailors fanned out across the deck, with some descending into the belly of the ship to search there. Payne walked slowly around the *Revenge's* crew, pausing as he inspected each group. When he got to Kit, his eyes narrowed. Her breath caught in her throat, and she fought to keep her face neutral as she stared him down. His beady eyes bored into her, the lines in his furrowed brow giving him a menacing air. He had a grizzled beard and one gold tooth that caught the sunlight and sparkled when he spoke. The hairs on the back of Kit's neck raised as his glare turned from curious to something else. Desire, almost, but with shades of malice that made her finally break his stare.

"Put that away," Payne said. He pointed to her knife.

Kit slipped it into its sheath at her hip.

"How old are ye?"

"Fourteen," she said quickly.

"Come with me." Payne raised his pistol and aimed it directly at her. He glanced over Reddy, then looked at Diego. "And you?"

"Sixteen."

"You come, too."

He led them across the deck towards Tristan's cabin, keeping his gun trained on them. Halfway there, they were intercepted by one of his crewmen.

"Searched the whole ship, top to bottom. Didn't find no one hiding," the man said.

"What is there to take as payment for our time wasted?" Payne asked.

"Nothing. A few barrels of food and water, a few bottles of rum."

"There must be something!" Payne's face reddened with anger as his voice rose. "These are pirates. There must be something of value on board this ship." He turned to Kit. "Where is it?"

"We only just set out," she explained.

"Where is your real captain?"

"Right there." She nodded to Tristan.

"I suggest ye tell me. I'll get the information I'm seeking either way." He waved his men forward and nodded to Diego. "That one first. I'd rather have this one unharmed."

The men surged forward, surrounding Diego before Kit even realized what was happening. His wrists were wrenched together behind his back, and then the men shoved him to his knees on the timbers.

"Hand over your knife," Payne ordered Kit.

She shook her head. Whatever they were going to do, she wanted no part of it. His men had knives aplenty, they had no need for hers.

"I'll ask ye once more, and then ye'll be joinin' him." Payne threatened.

Kit's hand trembled as she reached to her hip, bile biting at the back of her throat. She was a terrible pirate and a worse person for giving in so quickly, but it was the only way to save herself from whatever torture awaited. Diego wouldn't look at her, didn't see her mouthed apology, but Tristan noticed. He didn't try to hide his look of disappointment.

"Good lad," Payne said. "At least there's one of ye with some sense." He took the knife from her and handed it to one of his men.

The man held the point of the knife to the nape of Diego's neck while Payne moved away from Kit to face him.

"Last chance," Payne said. "Where's Davies?"

Diego spat on the deck, and remained silent. The man with Kit's knife jerked his arm downward, rending Diego's shirt in two and baring his back. Blood trickled down from a shallow cut Another sailor emerged from Tristan's cabin to hand Payne a whip with a thick handle and a long, snaking tail.

"Ten lashes to start, then. We'll see if ye've reconsidered talking after."

Kit's heart raced. She didn't want to see her friend tortured, but at the same time, she was relieved Payne hadn't chosen her to go first. Her secret was still safe. But it wouldn't be for long, not if Diego kept his composure and refused to speak. When they were done with him, they would turn to her. Kit realized Payne was attempting to manipulate Tristan by picking out the youngest of his crew, assuming he might have more pity for them and crack sooner. She glanced at her captain. His face was stoic as he watched the scene unfold, and she knew he would never break. Even after only a few interactions, it was clear there wasn't person on Earth he would do more to protect than Elinor. No, Kit was on her own. And she needed to think of something fast. Payne cracked the whip next to Diego, testing it.

"Stop!" She yelled.

Everyone on the deck turned to look at her.

"I'll tell you what you want to know. I'll tell you where to find Elinor Davies." She kept her eyes trained on Payne, but she could feel the disappointment and betrayal from the glares of the *Revenge's* crew.

"We'll see about that," Payne said. "Take him into my cabin."

The two sailors grabbed Kit by the elbows and led her into Tristan's cabin. It was the first time Kit had been inside the room, and she bristled at Payne calling it his. The men shoved her down into a chair at a table in the center of the room with her back to the door. Sunlight streamed through large windows at the rear of the cabin, and Kit focused on the horizon as she heard the crack of the whip from the deck. Diego cried out in pain. She felt another pang of guilt, but the longing for self preservation was stronger. The door slammed open behind her and Payne's heavy bootsteps crossed the room. He sat across from her and crossed his arms on the table.

"Why did you whip him?" Kit asked angrily. "I said I'll tell you everything you want to know."

"I promised him ten lashes and I'm a man of my word." Payne chuckled. "But you're not. Why did ye betray yer ship?" He asked.

"I don't want to die," Kit said.

"And ye think that's what I'm going to do to yer maties?"

"I'll not take my chances."

"Smart lad." Payne flashed crooked teeth in a grin full of malice. "That's precisely what I mean to do. And if you join them or not depends on if ye tell me what I'm seeking to know."

"And what is that?"

"What's become of the great Captain Davies."

"What do you want with her?" Kit asked, feeling unwell. She couldn't believe she was about to betray the only people who had shown her kindness. But it had to be done.

"She owes me a large debt. Cost me thousands of pieces of eight, or more. Slandered my good name among the buccaneers so now I can't get goods to sell. The bitch nearly ruined me." Payne frowned. "And it's past time she pays me back for it."

"I'll tell you where she is if you let the crew go."

Payne laughed. "Ye think ye're in some kind of position to be negotiating? Ye'll take me to her, and if she's not where ye say she is, ye'll be meetin' yer end, too."

"Nassau," Kit said bitterly. "She's running a shop in Nassau."

"See? That didn't have to be so hard. Pity you didn't speak up sooner, could have helped yer friend out there. Little matter, he won't be feeling much of anything soon enough..." Payne's smile relaxed into one more genuine, as though the thought of the murders he was about to commit pleased him. "Get the lad on the *Lass,*" he commanded his men, who dragged Kit back to standing.

Exiting the cabin, she saw the men of the *Revenge* clustered around the main mast in the center of the deck. They were bound hand to foot, and again with a rope around their waists that encircled the main mast. Kit swung her elbows, shaking the men loose.

"I can walk fine alone," she said. Sensing no threat from her, the men left her free to march behind them.

A gleam of silver caught her eye. Her knife, hastily shoved in her captor's pocket, hilt half-hanging from it. It was the one small thing she could do. He would never notice. Her hand darted out and she pulled it back quickly, treasure in hand. She glanced over at the *Revenge's* crew again, ignoring the daggers Tristan's eyes were stabbing into her. To get to the ladder off the ship, Kit would have to walk right past them. The two sailors were grumbling about the lack of gold or valuables on the ship, and how much effort the meager pay had cost them. She would never have a better opportunity. Captors fully distracted, she crouched next to Reddy and pressed the knife into his hand.

"Sorry," she mouthed before standing and quickening her stride so the men wouldn't notice she had fallen back. It was the best chance she could give them, a last glimmer of hope to ease her conscience as she swung a leg over the ship's rail to descend the ladder.

Chapter 9

L ISBET CROSSED HER ARMS, then uncrossed them again. She was in a foul mood, awake before her usual hour and upset that Andrew was keeping her waiting. Dawn, he had said. She had arrived at the burned out building before the first light had broken the horizon, and had waited until the colorful streaks had faded from the sky. The sun was well and truly up, and it was impossible that she had missed him. She rolled her eyes. Another one of his mind games.

It was going to be a hot day, and Lisbet wished she had brought something to quench her thirst. She could feel her hair escaping its pins to curl at the nape of her neck in the humidity. The tickle of the wisps in the breeze gave her the eerie feeling of being watched, raising the hair on her arms in response. She whirled around, but no one was there. Just the burned out husk of the storeroom.

Andrew wasn't coming. He had lied. Again. And she was the dimwit who had trusted him far too many times. Lisbet turned to leave, vowing it would be the last time she would let him manipulate her, when she heard a giggle up the road. She froze. There was another giggle, and then they came into view. Lisbet would have recognized them anywhere, even after all the time. Her heart jumped into her throat. Charlotte and Adeline.

They were looking at her with suspicion, and Lisbet suddenly felt self-conscious. Unsure what she was supposed to do, she waited for them to approach her. They both took after their father, tall and lanky, their limbs in that awkward childhood phase where they appeared too long for the girls' bodies. Adeline smiled shyly at Lisbet, revealing deep dimples and three missing teeth. Charlotte, two years Addie's elder, was more reserved, but she always had been.

"Hello," Lisbet said softly, using the same tone she did with the scared cats she brought to the yard.

Adeline's eyes widened when Lisbet spoke, and Charlotte darted behind Andrew.

"Run along and play a moment, girls." Andrew shooed them away. When they were well out of earshot, he spoke to Lisbet. "I didn't tell them who you are, and you'd be wise not to, either. I know you'd like to see them again, but if your mother catches winds of this..."

So they didn't remember her. She'd prepared herself for that, but the realization was still crushing. Her parents had effectively killed her, erased her very existence from the memories of those she loved most.

"What did you tell them, then?"

"Just that you're an old friend."

"Is that what we are, Andrew? Friends?"

He shrugged. "We're far more than acquaintences, wouldn't you agree?"

Adeline had settled onto a rock with Charlotte behind her, braiding her hair. Lisbet longed to join them in the simple act of sisterhood. It was supposed to be her, combing their hair and weaving pretty ribbons or flowers into the strands. Gone were the days when they would cling to her skirts, and beg her to tell them just one more story. They had grown up so much. In that moment, she would have given anything to go back to those days, even if it meant being back in the village under the oppressive rule of her parents and the church.

"How did you manage to bring them?" She asked.

"I told your mother I needed help fetching boards for the new babe's cradle. She was eager enough to have them out of the house for a while." He gestured to the storehouse. "We'll salvage something here."

Lisbet cast another quick glance towards her sisters. They were fully occupied and not paying the adults a bit of attention, so she leaned up on tiptoe to kiss Andrew on the cheek, all annoyance with him gone. "Thank you. I didn't think you were coming."

"I keep my promises." *Unlike you,* his frown seemed to say. "You should go."

"Go? I haven't even gotten to talk to them yet."

"I said you could see them, not talk to them. The less they can tell your mother, the better."

"But Andrew–"

"Go, Lisbet."

"I'll do anything you want. Anything," she begged. Surely he wasn't going to rip them away from her again so quickly.

"Anything? I'll keep it in mind for next time."

"When?"

"I'll find you."

There was nothing she could say to change his mind, and deep down, Lisbet knew he was right. Her mother would be apoplectic if she knew. She looked over at her sisters one last time, staring long and hard as she tried to commit every detail of their faces to memory. There was no telling when, or if, she would be able to see them again, but at least they were healthy, and seemed happy. That was all Lisbet could ask for.

She felt lighter as she made her way back through the streets and alleys of Nassasu, unburdened by having seen her sisters outside of her dreams. Andrew had shown he was a man of his word. It was nothing short of a miracle, and she had to remind herself she had paid for the privilege before she fell back into the trap of believing he was benevolent or kind. She only wished there had been another way.

Her stomach growled, angry at having been ignored for an entire morning and stirred to protest by the scent of roasting pig wafting through the alleyway. She followed the smoke to the back of the tavern, where a large fire had burned out into embers that glowed beneath a whole hog. Maggie and Ann, two of the tavern maids, tended to the spit, turning it slowly to allow all sides of the beast to cook evenly. Lisbet's stomach grumbled again, loudly, attracting their attention before she could greet them.

"Liss!" Maggie said with a broad smile as she wiped her hands on her apron. "It'll be a while before she's ready."

"Just a little nibble?" She wheedled, "I'm so hungry."

"There's bread and cheese in the kitchen, you remember where."

Lisbet nodded and slipped in the back door, remembering well from her time working as a bar wench. Wooden bowls and tankards were piled high in the small room, but she quickly found a basket filled with loaves of bread and the linen-wrapped chunk of hard, white cheese. She sawed off a thick slice of bread, then, catching a whiff of the cheese's pungent odor, decided she was better off without it. The bread was good though, chewy and dense with a thick crust that crackled when she bit into it. And it took the edge off her hunger. She stepped back outside.

"Been a while since we've seen you around here," Maggie said casually, but her expression showed she was slightly hurt.

"I was here last night," Lisbet replied.

"You've been around the tavern, but only at night when you've coin to earn. But I suppose you've gotten too busy to drop by and see your friends during the slower hours?"

"I'm sorry," Lisbet said. "There has been a lot going on recently."

"We forgive you, of course." Ann put her arm around Lisbet's shoulder and pulled her in for a hug. "But we have so much to tell you."

Lisbet took the handle of the spit from her. "Well, I'm here now. What have I missed?"

"Did you hear about Jane?" Maggie asked, naming one of Nassau's whores.

"I heard she was getting married," Lisbet said.

"Well she did. To a pirate. And not just any pirate, he's a captain."

"Yes, and she's already pregnant. Rumor has it, it's not his."

"No way to know for certain. She certainly was no virgin before," Lisbet said. Most of the whores of Nassau tried to avoid pregnancy by various means, some more effective than others, but it was still a risk that never abated completely.

"And of course he's already run back to sea," Ann said, reaching a ladle into a pot of fat and juices. She poured it evenly over the pig, making the crisp skin spit and whistle.

"Well, that is what pirates do," Lisbet said. That was why she would never get mixed up with one. They were nice to have around when they had coins to spend, but as soon as it was gone, they would be too, sailing on the first amenable tide. And they were never guaranteed to come back.

"Wish I could do that," Maggie said. "Must be better than washing dishes and carrying tankards all day."

"Why don't you?" Lisbet asked.

Ann laughed. "Can you even imagine our Mags on a pirate ship?"

"Why not? Elinor captained one, for a spell."

"I'm no Elinor Davies," Maggie said, chuckling. "But I do wonder what it would be like."

"I think you'd be brilliant," Lisbet said. "You're strong from carrying all those tankards, and tough from dealing with the louts that stumble in and out of here. I've seen you carve a whole hog down in less than five minutes, surely you could butcher a man as easily."

"Lisbet!" Ann faked offense. "How could you say such unladylike things?"

"Oh, as if you don't see worse in the tavern on a bad night," Lisbet laughed. "But anyways, what else have you heard?"

"Oh, I heard a good one last night," Maggie said. "They found a body out at the old fort."

"A body? You didn't even tell me that," Ann said with a raised eyebrow.

"Just heard last night. Well, overheard. A group of men talking about it inside. Didn't hear who, though."

"A man or a woman?" Libet asked.

Maggie shrugged. "They didn't say, I didn't ask. You haven't heard of anyone missing, have you?"

"No," Lisbet said, as Ann shook her head. "But it's worrying."

"It's Nassau. Weren't you just the one talking about butchering men?" Maggie asked.

"When there's good reason to," Lisbet said.

"And there may have been good reason for this one, too. We just don't know it."

Lisbet's arm was beginning to tire from keeping the spit rotating, so she stepped aside for Maggie to take over the turning. "Are you sure I can't have just a bite?"

"Go on then," Maggie said. "Shave some off the leg there, it should be well enough done it won't kill you."

Ann handed Lisbet a heavy knife, and she hacked off a piece of meat. It was steaming, and she tossed it from one hand to the other until it was cool enough to eat. When she finally bit it, fat exploded in her mouth in a wash of flavor. The meat was tasty but tough, and she chewed vigorously to get it down. "Needs to cook longer," she said with a sly grin.

Maggie shoved her with her free hand. "Didn't I tell you?"

"It was still good, though."

"So are you going to join the other girls starting a brothel?"

"I hadn't really considered it yet." Lisbet knew there was talk among some of the whores of opening a brothel. The pirate population had grown enough to support it, and so had the number of ladies in Nassau. A brothel would allow them to entertain the pirates on the premises and a safer place for their women to transact their business. "But I'm not keen to lose a portion of my profit to support it."

"I hope you don't join," Ann said. "Then we really won't see you anymore."

"Plus, it hurts our business. You're half the reason the pirates come to the tavern in the first place. If you all go, what will happen to us?" Maggie asked.

"Maybe you can become a pirate yourself," Lisbet said. "I haven't decided yet, but I don't think I will. I spent too much of my life answering to others, and I've come to appreciate my freedom too much to give it away now."

Ann hugged her. "Even if you do decide to join them, we'll still be your friends, right?"

"Of course," Lisbet said. "I would never give that up, even if I should come by to see you more often."

The sun was high in the sky, and as much as Lisbet wished she could stay to make up for lost time, it was beyond time for her to be getting down to the yard to tend to the cats. She made her goodbyes, then headed towards the beach. It was a good day, a remarkable day that stood out among all the other days of drudgery.

Lisbet stared out over the water, catching herself looking to see if the *Revenge* had returned to the harbor yet. She had seen her sisters, and her friends. The only thing missing was someone to love, someone to melt into at the end of a long day and share her deepest secrets. Had she made a mistake pushing Kit away again? Surely not. Kit was a pirate, and even if she returned she would only leave again. And again. Lisbet needed to learn to be happy with everything she had, and let such foolish daydreams go.

Chapter 10

K IT CLUNG TO THE rope. The guilt of her actions weighed on her so heavily it threatened drag her down to the depths below. Every step she took caused the ladder to writhe and sway in the air, and for a brief moment, she contemplated letting go. She hadn't meant to become friends with them. The affection she felt for Diego, Reddy, and the rest of the crew had snuck up on her, and the feeling that she had betrayed them stung more than she had imagined.

"Torch the ship!" Payne shouted from the deck of the *Revenge.* The crew howled cries of protest, but Payne only laughed. "Thought I would give ye a chance to escape, did ye? I've been waiting too many years for this. *Nimue's Revenge* has sailed her last, and all the songs will sing that it was at Payne's hand."

Kit's heart raced, and she felt as if she might throw up, but she couldn't go back. She settled into the skiff, and was soon joined by the last men of the *Bonny Lass.* Black smoke trailed into the sky, marring the otherwise clear morning with its haze. She climbed aboard the waiting ship in a stupor. No stranger to cruel captains, she wasn't surprised by Payne's decision. That was the way of the lawless Caribbean. Flames rose from the deck of the *Revenge*, and she could see her former crewmates writhing against their bonds. One of the sails caught, burning quickly in a blaze of yellow and orange and sending glowing canvas embers down in an infernal rain. Kit felt numb as the yells carried across the water, and she clamped her hands over her ears so as not to hear her friend's screams.

A hand squeezed down on Kit's shoulder and jerked her around. Payne. "You. Into my cabin."

She didn't dare protest, and let him push her across the deck as she struggled to take in her surroundings. The ship was smaller than the *Revenge*, though armed just as heavily with eight pound cannons lining the deck. The crew rushed to sail away before the burning *Revenge* could strike her last blow in the form of fiery sparks blowing towards them in the wind. Kit was marched into the captain's cabin as the *Bonny Lass* lurched forward. The room was much more richly furnished than Tristan's had been, with an ornately carved wooden desk at one side of the room and a large bed built into the other.

"So Elinor Davies is in Nassau?" Payne asked.

Kit nodded.

"Tell me everything ye know of her."

"I'm afraid it isn't much."

Payne crossed his arms and looked at Kit expectantly.

"She owns a shop, I told you that. Right on the beach." Kit shrugged, unsure what more he wanted her to say. "She lives in a house next door, and her wife looks after the cats of Nassau."

"Wife?" Payne raised an eyebrow but didn't comment further. Kit wondered what he was thinking. "Have you been in the house? What arms do they keep?"

"A pistol and a cutlass are all I've seen."

"Surely the great Captain Davies stays more prepared than that?"

"Perhaps, but I can only tell you what I've seen."

"If you've told me anything untrue, now is your chance to correct it. If I find any of this to be false, you'll pay with your life."

"I haven't lied to you," Kit insisted.

"How old did you say you are?"

"Fourteen."

"Old enough. Ye're awful pretty for a boy. Something about your face."

Kit flushed and Payne reached forward to stroke her cheek. He gripped her jaw tightly and he turned her face up to look at him. Every muscle in her body tensed, wanting to run but having nowhere to go.

"Unhand me," she said calmly.

"Do you know how long its been since I had a warm body beneath me?"

"Plenty of whores in Nassau to choose from when we get there," Kit said, horrified by what he was implying.

"Oh, I'll take my due from Davies and her wife before I kill them, too." He sneered. "Don't know that I care to wait that long, though, when you're right here."

Kit was in the worst possible situation she could have found herself in, and the regret that had calmed to a simmer erupted into a violent boil again. Had she not sold out her crew, she would be among them. Perhaps on her way to a watery grave, but with her dignity intact. If Payne were to discover her, she knew she would be wishing for death anyways.

He grabbed her hand, moving it to his crotch so she could feel the lump of flesh bulging beneath his trousers. Kit tried to pull away, but he held her there to feel his twitching member that had seemed to take on a life of its own. She couldn't bite back her laugh at the absurdity of it, and her mind flashed to Lisbet as she wondered how she put up with such awful men so frequently.

"Something funny about that, boy?" Payne snarled, and she realized she had offended him. "Let's see yours, then."

He let go of her wrist to reach for her waistband. She pulled away as he fumbled at her belt, when a knock at the door interrupted him.

"Not now," Payne yelled. "I'm busy."

"It's a matter that requires your urgent attention, Captain."

Payne swore, then strode over to the door. The man standing there whispered something to him and he nodded before turning back to Kit. "Go make yourself useful somewhere," he ordered, pointing to the crewmen who were teeming about the deck.

She didn't need to be invited twice, and hurried out of the cabin. Hopefully whatever matter the captain needed to see to was distressing enough that he would forget about her. She would keep her head down and fade into the background. Out of sight, out of mind. Nassau wasn't too far away, if they were sailing straight there, and she would find a way to escape once they arrived.

"You're the new one," a man said to her. "Can you stitch? I've a task for you."

"Well enough," Kit said cautiously, hoping she wouldn't be asked to stitch up men. Her stomach was far too squeamish for that. "What am I stitching?"

"Sails," the man said. "One of your balls put a hole clean through. Need to get it up again if we're to catch the winds."

"I can manage that," she agreed. Anything that would put her out of sight from the captain, who had disappeared into the belly of the ship.

She took the thick needle and thread the man handed her, and numbly sat on a crate with the torn sail draped across her lap. The work was welcome, requiring enough focus that she couldn't dwell on the fate of the *Revenge*. Black smoke still rose in the distance where the ship burned, and Kit forced herself to look down at the sail instead of squinting into the horizon for a sign that the crew had made it off. She didn't want to know.

The needle punched through the thick canvas and into Kit's thumb. She cursed as a pinpoint of blood appeared, staining the fabric where she had gripped it. A small penance for what she had done. She pulled the needle the rest of the way through, then stabbed it into the fabric again, taking more care to avoid herself. Stitch by stitch, the sail knitted together again, the scar of its destruction almost invisible.

Kit flagged down the man who had assigned her the task. He inspected the sail, then gave her an approving look.

"Better than me own mum coulda done," he said.

Kit cursed herself. In her determination not to focus on the *Revenge,* she had forgotten to focus on being a fourteen year old boy. She would have to remember to make her stitches sloppier, more unevenly spaced and less like a woman who had spent her entire life mending. She would have to be more careful.

F ORTUNATELY FOR KIT, PAYNE'S interest in her waned with the moon as the week went on, and she never found herself alone with him again. His crew didn't seem to share his same propensity for wanton violence, at least not that she had seen in the day to day operations of the ship. She was accepted as one of their own, for she had given them no reason not to. It wasn't uncommon for pirates to change their allegiances at the drop of a hat, and she had proven herself to be a hard worker. For the most part, her presence on the *Bonny Lass* went unnoticed and unremarked upon.

Maybe too unnoticed. Kit cleared her throat elbowed past one of the hulking men that blocked the stew pot to ladle out a plate for herself. It was the same stew they had eaten the night before, and the night before that. Food aboard the *Bonny Lass* was an abysmal affair that consisted primarily of salt pork boiled with beans in musty water until they were tender, but she was grateful to be allotted a ration at all. She took her plate and sat on a crate lashed near the ship's stern to look out over the wake the ship cut through the water..

She had come to learn that the ship was sailing directly for Nassau, and she wondered what Elinor had done to Payne to make him so hellbent on revenge. Surely it couldn't just be the double crossing or stolen loot. Those things were just one of the many risks a captain undertook when they decided to helm a ship to seek their fortune. There had to be something deeper, but the captain had given no indication what. Her crewmates on the *Bonny Lass* had been mum on the subject, and she didn't dare risk undue attention by asking.

The shapes of the islands rising up from the sea were familiar, and Kit knew they were getting close to the island of New Providence. Guilt still nagged at her, no matter how much she reasoned with herself. Any one of them would have done it, in the interest of self-preservation. Except none of them had. But that didn't make them better than her. She wasn't wrong to look out for herself. It was all she knew how to do, all life had taught her to do.

And Kit wasn't a completely horrible person; she had given Reddy the knife. There was still a glimmer of hope, that maybe they had freed themselves in time. That maybe their blood wasn't on her hands. She'd given them a chance to escape, one they wouldn't have had if she'd stayed with them to be tied to the mast and burned like a witch.

The knowledge that a second betrayal loomed near weighed even more heavily than the first. Not only had Elinor and Mona shown her exceptional kindness, she felt a deeper kinship with them. They proved it was possible to love on their own terms in the haven they had helped create. They were everything Kit hoped she could be one day. The thought of either of them falling into Payne's hands plagued her nights as she tried to sleep, as if their ghosts were haunting her before the act was even done. Kit knew she needed to find some way to warn them of the coming storm, to give them a chance, or she would never forgive herself.

The next day, Kit was on the deck, swabbing as unobtrusively as she possibly could. A few higher ranking crewmen were speaking furtively nearby, and she listened closely in the hopes they would mention Payne's plan upon the *Bonny Lass's* arrival in Nassau. Kit knelt behind a cannon, scrubbing as she listened intently to the quartermaster and master gunner.

"What is it, three years now since we left Nassau?"

"At least."

"I don't think they're ready for our return." The quartermaster chuckled. "How many small arms do we have?"

"Enough to take down a couple of women without much worry, I'd imagine."

"Well, one of them *is* Davies."

"Still no match for twenty of our best men."

Twenty men? Kit stifled her gasp of surprise. That seemed excessive, even for a fighter as renowned as Elinor. It would be a slaughter. The men were moving away from her as they spoke, and she crawled closer to stay within earshot, still scrubbing away at the deck.

"So is it to be tonight?"

"Dawn tomorrow, more like. We're still a few hours out."

"I'll see that the best men are well armed."

"And keep them off the drink tonight. We need them sober enough to swing a sword."

The master gunner was looking at Kit, and she realized was engrossed in the conversation and had stopped scrubbing. She looked away and quickly picked up the brush again, but the master gunner was whispering something to the quartermaster. He nodded, and both men walked away towards the captain's cabin.

Kit didn't know what sense compelled her, but suddenly every one she had was screaming at her to flee. She had lived long enough to listen to that instinct, and she abandoned her scrub brush where it lay to make herself scarce. She slipped through the hatch that led below deck and climbed down the rickety ladder, cursing that the ship wasn't larger. The men had said they were only a few hours away from Nassau, and she just needed to go undiscovered until then.

It was eerily quiet in the belly of the ship, below the waterline and away from the hubbub of daily life on deck. A few men lay sleeping in their hammocks, light snores breaking through the silence as she tiptoed past them. A large storeroom lay just beyond a door with hinges that creaked loudly anytime they were called into service. Kit pulled the door slowly, trying to keep that wretched screech from breaking the stillness and alerting others to her presence there.

The room was packed with goods the smugglers had purchased from buccaneers to be resold in the ports the pirates couldn't reach, and Kit crawled over crates and large sacks as she retreated to the furthest corner of the room. If they were looking for her, it would take the men a few hours to even disinter her from beneath all the piles of fabrics and sacks of sugar. She wedged herself between the rough timbers of the ship's hull and a stack of casks of cognac. Only a few moments had passed when she heard the first footsteps, along with Payne's angry voice just outside the door.

"Have any of you seen him come through here?" He roared.

"Who's that?" One of the men asked. He sounded half-awake.

"The little bastard that we picked up off the *Revenge*."

"We was all sleepin', Captain. Didn't see nothin'."

"Well get up and help me look."

Kit heard the men scrambling to obey their captain's orders, and then the door creaked open. She held her breath.

"We'll find ye if ye're in there, lad," Payne called. His shadow loomed, dancing menacingly as the flame of his light flickered through the darkness. "It'll be better for ye to come out now. My mood will be much more charitable."

Kit squeezed her eyes shut to block out the shadowy figure and ignored him, hoping his bravado was a ruse. Surely she wasn't so important to him that he would upend his ship to find her. The sound of crates scraping against the floor made her shrink back closer to the wall.

"This is yer last warnin', boy," Payne growled.

"Don't think he's in there, Captain."

"Search the rest of the ship then. If we don't find him elsewhere, we'll come back here."

"Can't've gone far," Kit heard as the door closed once more.

She breathed a sigh of relief, and then another, before standing and stretching. Her legs tingled as feeling rushed back into them. Whatever Payne wanted her for, she was sure it was nothing good.

A few hours til Nassau, and then she had to find a way off the boat and to Elinor. She knew where the skiffs were lashed to the deck, but there was no way she could manage one alone, and certainly not without anyone noticing her escape. She was going to have to swim. The thought filled her with dread, but her fear of the monsters that lurked in the depths of the ocean was quickly replaced with an image of Payne's leering face and the echo of his threat against Elinor and Mona.

And Lisbet. The very notion made Kit's blood run cold. Lisbet was at their house often, and if she was there when Payne and his men arrived... Kit couldn't even allow herself to think of it. She would get there first, or she would drown trying. But she was tired of good people being tortured and killed by cruel men, and she couldn't let the cycle continue. Even if it cost her everything. The footsteps returned, and Kit crouched down just in time to avoid being seen as the door to the storeroom swung open.

"We've looked over every damn inch of this boat." The man who spoke first sounded annoyed.

"Well, we didn't really look here before."

"He's not here, Sam. Bastard probably fell overboard, little as he is."

"Payne won't like that."

"Fuck Payne. I'm sick of his orders and his stupid vendettas. We've money to make and he's wasting our time on this fool's errand."

The man's companion shushed him. "Never know who's listening. Don't want whispers to start that you're speaking of mutiny."

"I'm not, but I'm thinking long and hard if I really care to return to the *Lass* when she sails again. I quite fancy the idea of getting my own ship."

"You, a captain? You haven't the guts for it."

"I might, if I weren't in the employ of the worst smuggler in the Caribbean. The buccaneers might have the right idea of things." The men laughed as they backed out of the room and Kit's relief deepened that they didn't share Payne's vigor in finding her.

She tried to nap to pass the time, but nerves gnawed at her so incessantly that sleep eluded her. Instead she stood stiff and still as the scarecrows she and Lisbet had constructed to guard the fields in their youth. As much as Kit tried to focus on her immediate goal returning to Nassau, it was impossible not to think about Lisbet, so inextricably tied to the island was she. But one thing Kit wouldn't do was seek Lisbet out again. She wasn't so desperate to mend things that she would go against her wishes. But if Lisbet sought her out, or if their paths crossed by chance, Kit was ready to let go of the heartbreak and lingering animosity to start anew.

A flurry of activity on the deck above her was followed by a splash, and then the *Bonny Lass* jolted as her anchors caught on the rocky reef below. They had arrived. The ship drifted on its tether, and Kit wished she had a way to see how far out they were in the harbor, or if darkness had fallen yet. Her stomach growled, but fortunately no one was near enough to hear it. All of the men were up on the deck seeing to their tasks of coming to harbor, furling the sails and securing the hatches for the ship to prepare to rest.

Another hour passed, or maybe a bit more, and the noises from above grew more distant as the men moved to the stern for their nightly libations.

She climbed back across the crates and pressed her ear to the door. There was no movement she could from the sailor's sleeping quarters, so she opened the door just wide enough to slip through and crept back across the ship. Yells drifted down from near the hatch and Kit froze in place. Her heart raced as quickly as her mind as she struggled to find an explanation that would convince them she was hiding for innocent reasons. No one descended the ladder, and after a few minutes the voices moved on. Kit tiptoed over to the ladder and climbed up a few rungs to peek across the deck.

Two men were standing at the rail with their cocks out, pissing windward as they argued about who was achieving the greater distance. They were paying no attention to what was happening behind them, so Kit held her breath and climbed the last rungs. She was so focused on them that she forgot to look where she was going and she stumbled over a coil of rope. Her foot thudded heavily on the timbers as she caught herself, loudly enough to catch the attention of one of the sailors. He glanced over his shoulder just as she ducked into the shadows behind a crate of cannonballs. She waited, unmoving, until the man shook his head as if to clear it and turned back around.

Since the ship was anchored, there was no one at the helm, and Kit rushed past it without worrying about being seen. To her surprise, the crewmen had already lowered the skiffs into the water and set the rope ladders in place. Kit had no idea how she was going to manage one alone, as they were designed to be rowed by up to ten men, but it was far preferable to taking her chances swimming in the choppy black water. Night was when the monsters were said to attack, rising from the depths under the cover of dark to take ships back to their lairs, never to be seen again. Kit had never seen one herself, but she had heard enough tales of long, scaly serpents and fish with mouths large enough to swallow a skiff.

Kit looked over the railing, second guessing her plan. Maybe it was too risky for her to go alone. Maybe Elinor had recognized the *Bonny Lass* as she sailed into harbor and was mounting an army of her own. Another shout behind her pushed her past the hesitation, and she climbed down the ladder and into the boat. She listened intently, but all the voices floating in the air came from further down the ship. The skiff bobbed in the water, occasionally drifting into the wooden hull of the *Bonny Lass*. The second boat was tied to the first, and Kit cut it loose with a knife she had stolen from the kitchen before giving it a shove into the waves that rolled towards the distant beach. Anything to make their raid more difficult. Losing both their skiffs would set them back a few hours, at least.

She struggled against oars that would have been unwieldy even if she was rowing with a full crew of men, but slowly she got the skiff turned to the land. Anyone who glanced off the deck towards the island would be certain to notice her, but by then it would be too late for them to do anything about it. Each wave pulled her a little closer to the shore, and she silently thanked the gods of the sea for their help on her mission.

Finally the little boat bumped against the sandy shore. Kit jumped out into knee-deep water and ran up the beach, not even bothering to drag the skiff onto the sand or secure it in any way. She didn't care if the tide took it away, she just needed to get to Elinor and Mona. The night was still young in Nassau, and the air was filled with music and revelry from the pirates' camps along the beach and further into the town. Smoke rose from the firepit behind the Davies' house, and Kit ran faster, weaving around men who turned to stare at her urgency.

She pounded at the door. Candlelight flickered behind the curtains that covered the windows, but no one came to answer. She pounded again, until she finally heard movement and Mona opened the door. She held a quill in one hand and looked quite annoyed to be disturbed at such a late hour. Her expression softened as she recognized Kit, then turned to confusion.

"Come in," she said with a hesitant smile. "We didn't expect the *Revenge* back for many weeks more. Will Tristan be along soon?"

Kit's heart felt like it shattered the instant Mona said the name of the ship. How was she supposed to tell her about the *Revenge?* How was she supposed to tell Elinor?

Mona reached for her hand and squeezed it. "Kit, you're trembling."

Was she? She hadn't even noticed.

"What happened? Sit. I'll make you a cup of tea." Mona pulled Kit to the table. She was too kind, too pure.

"I need to talk to Elinor," she said, pulling her hand away. She wasn't worth the misplaced sympathy. "Urgently."

"She's up at the tavern negotiating a deal, but I expect she'll be back soon."

"This can't wait." Kit turned back to the door. "The crew is in trouble." Or dead, but Kit couldn't bring herself to say that.

She ran up the road, Mona's longer strides easily keeping pace with her. The tavern was packed but Elinor Davies was easy enough to find among the crowd. She seemed to command the attention of every room she stepped into, her very aura drawing the respect and admiration of those around her.

"Darling," Elinor rose to greet Mona with a smile before noticing her expression. "What's wrong? Kit?"

"I need to talk to you," Kit said, staring down at the table covered in tankards. "Away from here."

Elinor was already striding to the door before Kit finished her sentence. Kit and Mona followed her down the alley beside the tavern until they got to a quiet spot between two half-constructed buildings.

"What is the meaning of all this?" Elinor demanded.

"The *Revenge* is gone," Kit said, and the tears she'd held back for days began to stream down her face. "And you're both in danger."

"Gone? Gone where?" A storm began to gather in Elinor's eyes as her brows came together in a deep frown.

"To the deep," Kit sobbed. "And now Payne is coming here. He is here. In the harbor. For you."

Elinor's hand went to her hip to rest on her cutlass as her tone turned icy cold. "Pull yourself together and tell me exactly what happened. Payne did this?"

Kit nodded.

"And the crew?"

"I did everything I could to help them. I can only pray they made it off the ship."

"Help them?" Elinor's fingers wrapped around the hilt of the weapon, as if she was seconds away from drawing it. The warning she had given before the *Revenge* set sail echoed in Kit's mind. "Were you not with them?"

"Elinor, I'm sorry. I had to. It was the only way. I tried to help them. They might have been able to escape."

"You betrayed them." Elinor's eyes narrowed.

"I had to," Kit stammered again. She had been so focused on reaching Elinor and Mona that she hadn't prepared a defense of her actions. It had been foolish to think they would be grateful to Kit for warning them, that it would exonerate her deeds at all. But Elinor was a reasonable woman, and surely Kit could get her to understand why she had to do it. "He was torturing Diego. He was going to torture me. They would have found me out."

"You. Betrayed. Him." Elinor growled, drawing her cutlass and pressing forward.

"Ellie, stop." Mona stepped between them, her face pale with shock.

"Go back to the house, Mona."

"Hear her out," Mona insisted.

"She's said all I need to hear already."

"She said they might have survived." Mona looked to Kit for verification, and Kit nodded.

Elinor returned the cutlass to its place at her hip. "Give me your belt," she demanded, holding out her hand to Kit.

Kit complied, untying the leather at her waist and handing the strip over to Elinor. If she was going to be beaten, she'd rather it be over quickly. Instead, Elinor bound her wrists in front of her. Kit didn't even try to resist. Being cooperative would make her seem more trustworthy, and she still needed to warn them that Payne was coming.

"What did Payne do to my ship?" Elinor asked through clenched teeth.

"He attacked, and his cannonfire was truer than ours. He was looking for you. Tristan allowed him to search the ship to prove you weren't there, and he burned it."

"And you...?"

"I told him you were here, in Nassau. But that's why I came to warn you. They're coming for you, and Mona, too. At dawn. You have to hide."

Elinor and Mona exchanged a long glance that Kit couldn't decipher. Mona shook her head slightly, and Elinor raised an eyebrow. Mona cocked her head to one side, as though she were listening to Elinor's unspoken argument, then nodded.

"I'll go see if Lisbet is inside," Mona said.

Lisbet? Kit's blinked in confusion. What did she have to do with anything? As soon as Mona's back was turned, Kit sensed motion in the corner of her eye. Elinor's fist connected with her cheek before Kit could move out of the way. Her knees buckled, and she tumbled face first onto the ground, unable to catch herself with her bound hands. Kit couldn't hold back her howl of pain as Elinor's booted foot struck her in the back. The attack ended as quickly as it had begun, and Elinor hauled Kit back to her feet.

"I'm not done with you, yet," she said, rubbing her knuckles. "You said Payne is coming for me?"

Kit nodded. "At dawn," she repeated, tasting blood in her mou

"Good. I have a gift for him." She shoved Kit forward, dragging her back to the little cottage by the sea.

Kit looked around, but Captain Davies was well respected enough in the town that no one milling about was willing to interfere. At least she had told them. If she was to die at Elinor's hand, it would be with one part of her conscience clean.

"If Payne is looking for a woman pirate, we'll give him one to find," Elinor said, shoving Kit into a chair at the table and tying her to it. "He'll know you double-crossed him just as you did us, and I'm sure he won't take kindly to it." Elinor stuffed a rag into Kit's mouth, then tied that off with more rope. "You sold out my wife, my best friend, and me, and for what? A few extra days of life? I hope Payne takes his time with you. I hope he makes you suffer as much as they did. And then I hope you burn in Hell for all eternity."

Kit's eyes widened as she tried to speak through the gag, but her muffled pleas went ignored by Elinor. She could see in Elinor's eyes that the former captain knew exactly what fate awaited Kit if she was left to Payne. She could also see that the former captain didn't care. Elinor moved about the house gathering things into a large sack. Kit struggled against her bonds as soon as Elinor moved into the other room, but the ties were secure, and there was no one coming to slip her a knife. Elinor walked back into the room, blew out the last candle, then hurried away into night, leaving Kit to wait for Payne alone.

Chapter 11

"SHOW YOUR CARDS," THE pirate across the table said.

Lisbet revealed her hand, groaning as she did. The man had called her bluff, and taken another shining piece of eight from her. It was of little concern, though. She reached under the table to stroke the man's thigh and saw his eyes darken with lust. He was handsomer than most, with a quick wit and a gentle manner. She would get the coin back from him before the night was done, and then some.

"Liss," a voice hissed in her ear. Mona.

"I'm a little busy right now." She held the pirate's gaze and she blinked up at him through lowered lashes, hoping Mona would go away. For once, she was actually looking forward to her night of work.

"We need your help."

"Now? With what?" She snapped, turning to look at Mona. Upon seeing Mona's face, it was immediately clear there was something gravely wrong. Mona had never interfered when Lisbet was working before, and her pale

117

cheeks and wide eyes made Lisbet bolt to her feet in concern. "Mona, what's wrong? Is it the cats? What can I do?"

Mona shook her head, and her voice quivered when she spoke again. "No, it's not the cats…" She trailed off. "Can we go somewhere else?"

"Of course." Lisbet rose to follow her outside. The man she was with protested her departure, but he didn't matter anymore. Her dearest friend was far more important.

"The *Revenge* is no more." Mona burst into tears and Lisbet felt a wave of shock and disbelief break over her. It couldn't be true. *Nimue's Revenge* had seemed as though she had sailed since the dawn of time and would sail til the end of it, immortal. "And the man who sunk her, he's here to kill me and Ellie."

"Here? In Nassau?"

Mona nodded. "In the harbor."

"What can I do?"

"I hate to even ask, but can we stay with you? Only until we work something else out."

"Of course. Mona, you don't even have to ask. You and Elinor mean everything to me, you're the closest thing to family I have anymore." Lisbet gathered Mona into a hug, mind racing as she tried to process what she'd just been told. There had to be a mistake. It was well known that the *Revenge* never lost. But Mona's sobs said it was real. Her heart broke as she held the weeping woman. She needed to be strong for her, and Elinor. Lisbet couldn't fathom their loss, and the fear they must have felt with their own necks on the chopping block.

Kit had been on the *Revenge,* too. The realization hit her like a rogue wave she'd turned her back on and she had to brace her knees to keep them from buckling. A flood of remorse filled her, a wellspring of regret, grief, and despair that threatened to burst through all the dams she had built to contain them. Lisbet had let her pettiness win when she was given a second chance, and there would be no third opportunity to right her wrongs.

"Where's Elinor?" Lisbet asked when Mona's shoulders stopped shaking with her quiet sobs.

"She went to the house to get a few things," Mona said with a shuddery sigh. "She's going to meet us at yours."

"Let's go, then." Lisbet took Mona's arm in hers.

The narrow alleys were a blur as they walked through them, the pungent bodily odors of a drunken Nassau the only thing that cut through Lisbet's numbed senses. She felt like throwing up, but she had to hold herself together. Her friends were counting on her.

Elinor was already waiting at Lisbet's doors when she arrived with Mona. Mona ran to her and the wives embraced, clinging to each other as if they were the only thing keeping the other from drowning. Lisbet supposed it was probably true, and felt the familiar ache of latent jealousy at their unconditional bond. No matter how bad things got, they never had to face it alone.

"Come in," she said, opening the door. "I'll get a kettle for tea going." It felt strange to be the one offering the small comfort.

"Could do with something a bit stronger than tea, if you've got it," Elinor said wryly.

"Of course," Lisbet said, retrieving a bottle of rum from under her bed. "I apologize that there's nowhere to sit. I don't often have guests."

Mona gave her a wan smile as she sat on the bed. "This is more than enough, Liss. We're sorry to intrude like this."

Lisbet turned to Elinor. "And I'm sorry about the *Revenge*."

Elinor shrugged nonchalantly, but Lisbet saw the pain that pinched the corners of her eyes into fine wrinkles before she drank deeply from the bottle of rum. "These things happen. My only concern now is keeping my wife safe."

Mona looked around the small room. "Where's Kit?"

Lisbet's heart, which had been racing from fear and excitement since Mona approached her in the tavern, slammed to a stop. Why was she asking about Kit? Kit was on the *Revenge* with everyone else.

Elinor gave her wife a sharp look. "I've dealt with it."

Dealt with what?

"Elinor," Mona chastised in a tone of voice Lisbet had never heard her take with her wife before. "What did you do?"

"Nothing. I left her for Payne to take care of."

"At the house?"

Elinor nodded. Lisbet looked from Elinor to Mona in confusion. If she was understanding correctly, Kit was on the island of New Providence, just a ten minute walk away.

"Ellie, you can't. This isn't who we are. You know what he'll do to her."

"She betrayed them, Mona. Tristan, Reddy, all of them, dead because of her."

Lisbet's jaw dropped, and she closed it quickly before they could notice her gawking. Kit had betrayed them? She didn't know why she was surprised. It was what Kit did best, was what she had always done.

"We don't know they're dead. She said they might have escaped. She could lead us back to them. But if you leave her to be killed, we'll never know."

Elinor sat on the bed next to Mona, who crossed her arms and scooted away. "Don't hold on to false hopes, my love. It will only hurt more when they're dashed."

"No, you don't give up hope when there's some left." Mona stood. "I'm going to get her."

"You can't." Elinor leapt up to block the door. "What if he's there already? I won't lose you to him, too."

"I'll go," Lisbet offered quickly.

"No," Elinor and Mona said at the same time.

"It's too risky," Elinor said.

"I won't have you dragged into this," Mona said. "It's not your battle."

Lisbet smiled grimly. "I already am in this. And Kit... In a strange way, I feel responsible for her, too. And I may not be a pirate, but I can handle myself well enough around them."

Elinor looked at her, considering the offer. Lisbet wondered why she was waiting for permission to leave her own house. Elinor's air of authority was so strong that it only felt natural, though. She was a leader through and through. Finally, Elinor nodded and stepped aside.

"I can't come look for you if you don't come back," she said. "Payne is a dangerous man."

"I know," Lisbet replied. "I don't want you to. Stay here, stay safe."

She hitched up her skirts and ran towards the beach, praying she wasn't too late. Even though she didn't fully understand what was going on, she knew the consequences would be deadly serious.

The house was dark and quiet, except for Pendragon's meowing as he came around the side of it. Lisbet always wondered how he knew she was coming, no matter what hour she arrived, almost as if he was attuned to her very being. She didn't have time to stop and greet him though, she had to see if Kit was still there.

"Kit!" She yelled, but there was no response. The night was too quiet, and every hair on her body stood up as the wind rustled through the leaves.

Elinor had left the door unlocked and Lisbet entered the house, worried it was already too late. Moonlight filtered in the back window, illuminating Mona's abandoned writings on the table. The inkpot was still uncovered, and Lisbet placed the lid on it out of habit. At first glance, the main room appeared empty, but then she heard the scrape of wood against wood. She peered around the table cautiously, half expecting Payne or one of his men to jump out at her. Instead, she saw Kit, tied to a chair that had overturned and attempting to scoot across the floor. She heard muffled noises and realized Kit's mouth was gagged. When her eyes locked onto Lisbet's, they were wide with relief. It was awful seeing her in such a state, and even worse to think Elinor had been the one to do it. But there was no time to think about that.

Lisbet rushed to her and knelt to undo the restraints, but Elinor was much better at tying them than she was at untying. She was wasting precious minutes and making no progress. The wind gusted outside more strongly than before, rustling the leaves of the palms around the house ominously. It sounded like the attempts of men to move sneakily through the undergrowth, and she jumped to look out the window, fearing Payne's army had arrived ahead of schedule. The dark held no one but for a few pirates further down the beach sitting around their own camp's fire. Lisbet took a deep breath to calm herself. What would a pirate do?

Elinor's cutlass was gone from where it normally hung by the door, so Lisbet rushed to her desk. She felt a brief flash of guilt as she pulled open the drawers, as though she were invading Elinor's privacy, but there was nothing but papers and maps in the desk. If there were any blades in the main room, it was clear Elinor had hidden them or taken them before evacuating her home. Lisbet was beginning to panic. If she couldn't free Kit from the chair, she would have to leave her. Where else would there be blades on the Davies' homestead? She checked the desk drawers again, hoping a knife that had previously escaped her notice would appear, before it struck her. The kitchen outside.

"I'll be right back," she whispered.

Even in the dark, the terror that flashed in Kit's eyes before Lisbet ran out the back door was unmistakable. So were her screams, muffled as they were by the gag. Apparently she didn't believe Lisbet's promise to return. Or maybe she just didn't want to be left alone in the dark again. Lisbet couldn't blame her. She hurried over to a table tucked under the eaves, and pulled a chest from beneath it. Throwing it open, she found the Davies' cooking knives. She settled on the fish scaler- a thin, serrated blade with a wooden handle that was smaller than the others in the crate.

Kit was struggling against her ropes with increased vigor when Lisbet reentered the house, but calmed when her eyes met Lisbet's once more.

"I told you I would be back," Lisbet knelt beside her once again. "Stay still so I don't cut you," she instructed, though it was her hands that shook as she pressed the knife to the rope that bound Kit's ankles to the legs of the chair. She sawed carefully, watching the threads snap and peel away as she cut through the ties. The moment felt oddly intimate even in its terror, and she couldn't help but remember the last time she had knelt between Kit's legs to apply herself to a task. She had been just as nervous then, but for different reasons. Lisbet worked methodically through the knots, pulling the ropes free as she severed them.

As soon as she felt the last fiber give, Kit wriggled free and scrambled to her feet. She reached up and ripped the gag loose from her mouth, gulping in the air before turning to Lisbet with her arms outstretched. Their lips met, and Lisbet kissed her with a hunger she didn't know she had. Tasting Kit again was like the first sip of cool water in the morning or bathing in a warm spring after a long day of work. Lisbet's body was flooded with the warmth of the first gentle rays of sun after a storm, the panic and fear of the night melting away in Kit's arms. She reached up to take Kit's face in her hands and pull her closer, forgetting entirely where they were and why they were there. Their tongues met and danced, and the kiss deepened into something both familiar and new. It was the only thing that mattered; it was everything that Lisbet had yearned for.

"How did you know I was here?" Kit asked, pulling away. Her hand still rested on the small of Lisbet's back.

Lisbet's senses returned in a rush, and she stepped out of Kit's grip. She couldn't believe she had just kissed a traitor. And liked it. " Elinor sent me. We have to go."

"To her? No. She wants to kill me," Kit stated flatly.

"They still need you. And besides, Mona won't allow her to kill you. I won't allow it." Lisbet moved to the door, then hesitated when Kit didn't follow. "Come with me, and make this right."

"Run away with me," Kit pleaded. "We'll go to Bermuda. We can start over. I think you'd like it there, there are—"

"I can't do that, Kit. They're my family."

"So nothing has changed. You should know that family will turn on you as fast as anyone."

"I trust them." Lisbet shifted anxiously. She wanted to get away from the house that could be descended upon by pirates at any moment, but Kit seemed in no rush to leave. "You can, too."

"Only as long as I'm useful."

Lisbet decided she needed to change tactics if she ever wanted to get out of there, so she decided to employ the one she knew best. She walked back over to Kit, and took her by the hand. She held it for a moment, brushing her thumb over Kit's knuckles, then leaned in close to whisper in Kit's ear.

"I don't want to lose you again, Katie." She moved Kit's hand over her heart and held it there, wondering if Kit could feel its pace quicken at the touch. "I need you. Come with me, and make this right, so we can have the chance together we always should have." Her lips brushed the skin where Kit's jaw met her neck, the spot that had always made her melt and give in before. She still remembered Kit's body like it was her own, and she trailed soft kisses down her neck until she felt the skin raise into goosebumps. "Come with me," she repeated.

The words rang surprisingly true for ones that were supposed to be wielded in manipulation and nothing more. Lisbet did desperately, achingly want Kit to redeem herself so she could explore the possibility of something more. Something lasting. Deep down, in spite of everything that had occurred, Lisbet still wanted to believe that Kit was good.

"Promise you won't let her kill me?"

"Do you think I could stop her?"

"Probably not." Kit let out a short bark of laughter. "Though I doubt anyone can. But I'll go."

Chapter 12

"WHERE ARE WE GOING?" Kit asked.

"My house," Lisbet said, picking up her pace as she glanced back over her shoulder.

Kit turned to look, too. The night sky's infinite black was fading to blue in the east, and the stars above were winking out of sight. Dawn was nigh. Ships bobbed peacefully in the harbor, dormant as their pirate crews caroused their coin away on the island. There were no signs of men rowing ashore from the faintly silhouetted *Bonny Lass*, but Kit knew they would come. It was only a matter of time.

Kit's lips hadn't stopped buzzing since the kiss, as though Lisbet's were still locked on hers. She wondered how many others had kissed those lips that evening, then decided she'd rather not know. At least it had been real. Lisbet had kissed her back. And when Lisbet buried her face in her neck, kissing ever so softly, the forgotten longing within Kit awoke more fiercely than she had ever felt it.

"It's just ahead," Lisbet said.

"Wait," Kit said, stopping abruptly. She didn't know when she would have a chance to speak to Lisbet alone again, and she wanted to make sure the moment wasn't wasted. "Did you mean what you said back there? About a second chance for us?"

Lisbet sighed. She looked weary, her eyes devoid of their usual sparkle and her hair an unruly mess of curls that had escaped their pins. She was still so damn alluring. Her mouth opened, then closed again as she considered what to say. Kit wished she could take the question back. She hadn't intended to cause Lisbet pain with the question. That was the last thing Kit wanted.

"You hurt my friends." Lisbet's voice rasped on the words, and she looked up so the tears in her eyes wouldn't fall as she continued, "I don't know if I can move past that."

"You don't understand. If I hadn't told the captain what he wanted to hear, he would have tortured me. If he found me out, he would have raped me then burned me alive with the rest of them. You don't know what it was like. I wasn't ready to die." Was she so wrong for that? Everyone seemed to think so.

"I can't give you an answer right now, Kit. We need to go inside."

There was a long list of people Kit had no desire to be around, and Elinor Davies was near the top of it. Kit could run. There was nothing restraining her, and her clothes were better suited for a sprint than Lisbet's intricate dress with its heavy skirts. She had always been faster. Kit knew the landscape of the island better than most of its pirate inhabitants, and it would be easy enough to slip away into the dense forest where no one would even think to look. But to do so would be to throw away any remaining hope of repairing things with Lisbet. No answer wasn't a no, and Kit wouldn't give up as long as Lisbet said there was still a chance.

Something orange streaked by Kit's feet as Lisbet opened the door, and Kit almost tripped over what she realized was a cat.

"Pendragon, no," Lisbet shouted as she lunged for it, grabbing it by the nape of its neck just before it darted under the bed. She turned to Mona. "I'm sorry, I know Elinor hates cats inside."

"It's your house, Liss," Mona said gently. "He can stay if you want him to."

Elinor was sitting on the far edge of the bed with her head in her hands. She didn't turn around for any of the commotion. Her stillness was unnerving, and Kit shuddered to think what was in store when the intimidating woman turned her attention back to her.

"We were starting to worry you wouldn't make it back," Mona said to Lisbet.

"You needn't have." Lisbet yawned.

"I'm so sorry we're imposing on you like this."

"You aren't, not at all."

"Nonsense, Liss, you're exhausted and we've taken over your whole house."

Elinor stood abruptly. "I have to end this. It's gone too far." She turned her dagger eyes on Kit, and Kit noticed they were rimmed with red and swollen from crying. "They're coming at dawn, you said?"

Kit nodded.

"I'm going to wait for him, then."

"Have you gone mad?" Mona protested.

"I'm not going to spend the rest of our lives running away. We worked too hard."

"You can't face him alone. He'll have his whole crew."

"Not the whole crew," Kit whispered softly. "Twenty men."

"Is that all?" Elinor asked, raising her chin defiantly. "I'm hurt he thinks so little of me." Mona began to protest again but Elinor shushed her quickly. "I just need to kill him, not all of them. The rest will value their own lives too much to avenge him, if they're cowards like Kit." She paced restlessly across the room, and Kit stepped out of her war path.

"I won't let you go, Ellie. You can't do this to me. And what about Tristan? The rest of the crew. They could all be out there, marooned somewhere. They need us."

"How am I supposed to help him now?" Elinor yelled. "I don't have any way to get to him. I don't have a ship, I don't have a crew. I have nothing."

"You have me," Mona said, catching her wife by the arm and kissing her softly on the forehead. "Forever. We'll figure something out."

Kit shifted uncomfortably, wondering if she should say something. She'd had an idea, but she didn't know if Elinor would be open to hearing it from her. It was probably better to remain silent and not risk angering the captain further.

"What?" Elinor wheeled around, as if she could read Kit's mind. Maybe she could. Payne's men had whispered that she was a witch, unfindable and unkillable, in possession of great powers that defied the bounds of human luck.

"Well, uh..." Kit trailed off and glanced nervously around the room, looking for some support, but all three women were glaring at her with their arms crossed. "The *Bonny Lass* will be poorly guarded. They're sending all the strongest men to shore to find you. When he rows in, you could row out and take the ship."

Elinor's frown softened ever so slightly. "How many will they leave on board?"

"Nine," Kit said.

The room was silent while Elinor considered. "Why should I believe this isn't Payne's trap? He sent you here to deliver me right to him, on his ship."

Kit shook her head. "I have no loyalty to him. You and Tristan are some of the few people who have shown me mercy. I want to help. I know they survived. I gave them a knife. There was time for them to cut themselves loose before she went down. We can save them, I know it."

"Even if I take the ship, I have no one to crew it." Elinor seemed unmoved by Kit's plea. "And false hope is a dangerous thing. It can lead people down dark paths."

"I can help you raise a crew," Lisbet said. "How many do you need?"

"To sail a ship the size of the *Lass*? Twelve. To fight? At least twice that many."

"Well, we're four already," Lisbet said.

"Three," Elinor corrected. "And only because I can't leave my wife behind on this island while Payne still lives. But I won't drag you into this any more than I already have."

"I think I can choose well enough on my own if I care to be dragged into this," Lisbet snapped. "And if you're all going, I'm going."

"The only place any of us should be going right now is to sleep," Mona said. "We're all too tired to think clearly anymore. We can discuss everything in the morning."

"I'll need something to tie her back up with," Elinor said, nodding to Kit. "I don't want to give her any opportunity to run back to Payne and forewarn him."

Lisbet rummaged in a wardrobe before pulling out a soft purple sash. "Will this do?"

Kit didn't resist as Elinor yanked her arms behind her and bound her wrists again. Her movements were controlled, but the simmering anger was still evident in how tightly the sash was secured. Kit couldn't blame her. There had been a time when she had felt as strongly for others as Elinor did, a time when betrayals still hurt. But survival had become her only concern, and it seemed as though hers had been granted for another night.

"I'll keep an eye on her. You two sleep first," Elinor instructed.

"I won't try to run," Kit said. "I'd rather be your captive than Payne's."

"You weren't too concerned about that when you sold me out to him and joined his crew."

"Elinor, that's enough," Mona said.

"You're defending her?"

"I went with him once, too. I didn't realize my mistake until it was too late."

"That was different."

"We all make mistakes, Ellie. She's not evil. She's scared." Mona took Kit by the arm and led her to the bed. Lisbet was already climbing under the blanket on the other side. Mona folded back the cover and guided Kit to lay down on the thin mattress that seemed barely wide enough for one. "Sleep."

Kit closed her eyes, knowing sleep would be impossible with Lisbet curled up right beside her. It was almost painful how aware she was of every rise and fall of Lisbet's chest. Oh, how she longed to free herself, just so she could wrap an arm around her and pull her closer. Instead, she listened to the soothing sound of Lisbet's breaths, and slowed her breathing to match them. Kit smiled a little as she realized it was the first time she and Lisbet had shared a bed. She wished it could have been under different circumstances, but it was still comforting to be next to her. Back in the village they'd always had to sneak away to hidden spots in search of even the simplest intimacies, and getting to lie next to her was a small pleasure Kit wouldn't take for granted.

It was a small comfort though, when everything else ached. Her cheek pressed against the mattress, the skin tight and swollen from Elinor's fist. No one had thought to dress her wounds, but why would they? She was just a prisoner to them. Her shoulders were so sore from being wrenched behing her back that they'd gone numb and were sending pins and needles down both her arms. She tried to wiggle her fingers to make the sensation go away, but that hurt, too. But the deepest pain of all was the dull throb in her chest as her broken heart continued to beat out it's lament.

Chapter 13

L ISBET WASN'T THE SLIGHTEST bit refreshed when she awoke. The room was too hot from being overcrowded with four people. Mona and Elinor were both asleep slumped against the wall, and Kit was snoring lightly next to her in the bed. Adding to the claustrophobia was Pendragon, standing on her chest and kneading his paws into her breastbone as he purred loudly. She scratched him between the ears for a moment, then pushed him off her to grab the pitcher on the table. Elinor's eyes jerked open as soon as Lisbet moved, then went to the woman sleeping beside her. She stood and followed Lisbet to the door. Apparently she would have an audience for her morning ablutions.

"I know my wife has already said it, but thank you, Lisbet."

"It's what anyone would have done." Lisbet dropped the bucket down into the well.

"No, it isn't." Elinor reached to help her winch it back up. "I hate to ask anything more, but–"

"I'll do anything I can to help."

"I need your ears in town today. Find out if Payne has come ashore, how many men he brought, where they intend to make camp. And find a man called Avery, if you can. He may have some men he could loan me. He still owes me a favor. If he tries to say no, remind him of that. Agree to any sum he asks for, he knows I always settle my debts." Elinor appeared calm as she rattled off the orders, but Lisbet could tell she was still shaken from the night prior.

Lisbet splashed water on her face. "I'll see to it right away. There's not much food in the house, but you're welcome to any of it you'd like. I'll bring more from town."

Elinor handed her a little leather purse that jingled with heavy coins. "This should be enough for all of it."

Lisbet was about to protest, but Elinor folded her hand around the purse and wouldn't take it back. It must have been unnerving for the woman who seemed like she could do anything to ask someone else for help, and Lisbet realized the purse wasn't because Elinor thought she needed it. Rather, it was the one small way Elinor could still assist when everything else seemed out of her control. Lisbet tucked the purse in a pocket between the folds of her skirt without saying more.

The streets were abuzz as the deviants of Nassau swarmed between the merchant stands. Lisbet was on edge as she walked through them. Did it seem like she was passing more unfamiliar faces than usual? She studied each one suspiciously, wondering if they were Payne, or part of his crew. How would she know? Every buccaneer in Nassau seemed to have become meaner overnight, or maybe Lisbet was just seeing them in a new light for the first time. A man leered at her, beckoning with one hooked finger. She ignored his summons. Even if she didn't have more pressing matters to attend to, she wanted to savor the feeling of Kit's lips against hers for as long as she could, before the memory was washed away again by the crude roughness of her pirate paramours.

She would see about finding Avery first. While she didn't know the captain personally, she knew of him. His crew spoke highly of him and always had plenty of coin to spend. He had a reputation for being reserved, above the debauchery of the pirate haven, and was known among the whores of the island because of his avoidance of them. A tactically-minded former naval officer for the crown, he was one of the older men in Nassau and typically stayed out of the fray.

His camp was the most sensible place to begin her search for him, as Lisbet already knew where it was at the far end of the beach. Metal rang against metal, and she approached to see the captain wielding a cutlass as he parried with a much younger and taller man. Sand flew into the air as the adversary ducked Avery's swing and landed on his knees. He raised his blade to block the next swing, but Avery threw his weapon to the ground and held out a hand instead. The man grasped it and rose, laughing.

Avery noticed Lisbet first. "Whatever it is you're looking for, you're in the wrong place. My men are all away from camp— except for Thomas here— and he's too young for what you're selling."

"I am not," Thomas said, cheeks turning a brilliant shade of red when Lisbet looked at him. Lisbet realized he was no more than a very tall teenager.

"Either way, you still have lessons this morning." Avery looked back to Lisbet, a little surprised she was still there. "Move along."

"I have a message for you," she said. "A request from a mutual friend."

His eyes narrowed as he took her in, then he shooed Thomas away instead. "A friend, you say?"

"Elinor Davies," Lisbet dropped her voice to just more than a whisper, even though it didn't appear anyone else was around to overhear.

He smiled at the name, looking more like a warm father than a feared pirate captain. "Davies is a friend, indeed, and an old one at that. Go ahead, then, I'll hear what you have to say."

"She needs help. She's trying to raise a crew, and wants to know if you can spare her some men." Lisbet tucked her chin coyly and batted her eyelashes, a trick that always turned men to putty in her hands.

"Stop with your simpering, it won't work on me. Why has Davies not come to ask me this herself?"

"She's unable to at the moment," Lisbet said, not wanting to reveal too much.

"I see," Avery stroked his grizzled beard, pondering. "Elinor may be a friend, but if she's set her sights on the seas again, she'll not steal my men to get there."

"She won't be taking them from you. Just... borrowing. For one voyage."

I could ask around to see if three or four of my men are willing. When does she sail? Does she even have a ship anymore?"

"She has a ship," Lisbet said confidently, hoping he wouldn't see through her lie. "She sails as soon as she has a crew assembled. Today if possible."

"What has Davies gotten herself into this time?" Avery chuckled. "No, no, don't answer. I'm sure you won't give a straight one, and I'm not sure I want to know." He winked at Lisbet. "Very well, I'll see what I can do. But only because I like Davies. Be good to see her at a helm again, she's wasting her talents on that shop of hers."

"Thank you," Lisbet said. "I don't suppose you've heard of a Captain Payne?"

"The smuggler?"

Lisbet shrugged. "I don't know him myself, or how he earns his coin."

"I know Payne," Avery said. "He doesn't sail in these waters anymore, sticks to Port Royal and the like. Davies looking for him again?"

"Something like that."

"Tell her not to get my men killed." Avery laughed, but Lisbet could see he was only partly joking. "I expect she'll pay their full wages?"

"Of course," Lisbet replied. Elinor had said any cost.

"Come back in a few hours, then."

Lisbet nodded, grateful to Captain Avery on Elinor's behalf, but it wasn't enough. Elinor had said she'd need a dozen to sail, and even if Avery supplied four, they were still four short. There had to be more she could do, but she didn't know which pirates were trustworthy. If news spread that Elinor was hiring men, it would surely get back to Payne, and that would be disastrous. Even though the pirates of Nassau openly respected Elinor, their reverence was laced with an uneasy tension. Lisbet wondered how many of them would secretly relish the opportunity to rid the island of the notorious woman.

She didn't want to go back to the house until she had better news and more information to share, so she walked up to the tavern to see what rumors might be swirling there. It was only half full with the midday crowd, but Lisbet looked at each man she didn't recognize with suspicion. Maggie was working the floor, carrying full tankards to tables and clearing away the empties as she went. Her dark skin shimmered with sweat as she danced between the long benches with practiced ease. Lisbet took a seat at one and waited for her friend to notice her. Maggie gave her a little wave the disappeared into the kitchen. She reemerged with empty hands and slid onto the bench across from Lisbet.

"Early for you," Maggie said with a smile. "Are you eating?"

"Not today," Lisbet said. "Do you have a moment to talk?"

"Only for you."

Lisbet lowered her voice to a whisper. "Have you heard any chatter about a man named Payne today?"

"Can't say that I have. But I don't pay much attention."

Lisbet rolled her eyes. "I don't believe that, Mags, you're the biggest gossip on the whole island. And everyone tells you everything."

Maggie laughed and tossed her black braids over her shoulder. "Be that as it may, I haven't heard talk of any Payne."

"What about any men looking for work on a ship?"

"You're asking strange questions today. What's going on?" Maggie was too perceptive.

"I'm not sure," Lisbet said truthfully. The others had all seemed so sure Payne would arrive to wreak his horrors that morning, but no one of Nassau had seen hide or hair of the man. It didn't seem like something Kit would have lied about though. "What about you? Were you serious when you said you fancied being a pirate?"

"Me?" Maggie looked surprised. "I'm sure I could never."

"Why not?"

"Well, for one, I've never sailed. The only ship I've been on was the one my father brought me here on."

"I'm sure you could learn. Look around." Lisbet gestured to the men scattered around the tavern. "If these louts can do it, I know you can."

"But the tavern–"

"Ann can manage for a few days without you. This pays more," Lisbet insisted, even though she had no idea how much Elinor intended to pay for the voyage.

"Is everything alright? You're really acting quite odd." Maggie's brown eyes were full of concern.

"Nevermind. I'll find someone else."

"No, I'm interested. Which captain is it desperate enough to take on women then?"

"Elinor Davies."

Maggie looked stunned. "You're having a laugh, aren't you? Everyone knows she swore off the sea for her wife, years ago."

"Well, she's sailing again. And she needs a crew. People who can be discreet and hands that aren't afraid of work. I'm going with her."

"And what makes you think she would have me?"

"She's desperate."

"When does she sail?"

"Tonight, if I can find enough people. I'll come back by later when I know more."

Lisbet had one more stop to make, the last place in Nassau where she knew people would have information they were eager to share. The old house she had lived in with six other women before finally amassing enough coin to build her own. It was early in the afternoon, and she knew most of them would be there. She hoped they would be bold enough to accept the opportunity she offered. A ship where the women outnumbered the men was yet unheard of, but she didn't see why it couldn't be so. And who better to lead the first than the notorious Captain Davies?

***

Elinor was gone when Lisbet returned. Instead she found Kit and Mona chatting inside, Pendragon nestled between them on the bed. Kit's arms were still bound and a flintlock pistol lay on the mattress beside Mona's right hip, but otherwise the scene looked like two old friends catching up.

They turned to look at her, and for the first time, Lisbet noticed the dark bruise that spread across Kit's swollen cheek. She wondered if it had been Payne or Elinor that had meted out the blows.

"Where's Elinor?" Lisbet asked as she took in the strange scene.

Mona's aggravation was clear as she exhaled a drawn out sigh before responding. "At the fort with her spyglass looking out for Payne. You know she can't sit still to save her life. And if she sees him come in, she'll know Kit wasn't lying."

"Is all this really necessary, though?" Lisbet looked at the gun. Thought she saw them every day strapped to the pirate's waists and across their chests, it still made her uneasy to have one so casually in her own home.

"Well, I don't think so and Kit says it isn't, but Elinor disagreed."

Kit was staring at Lisbet hungrily, so much so she almost seemed to be salivating. Lisbet felt her cheeks turn red, wondering how Kit could even think of such things amidst all the tension. She blushed even harder when she realized Kit wasn't staring at her chest, but rather the basket of bread and smoked meat she clutched to it, purchased at the market on her way back.

"Can't we untie her to eat at least?" Lisbet asked. She didn't think Kit was a risk. If she was going to try anything, she would have done it the night before when Lisbet was undefended and her escape would have been easy.

"I don't see why not. Otherwise we'll have to feed her, and I'd rather not."

Kit stood and turned so Lisbet could undo the knots behind her back. The sash was tight, and she fumbled to get the fabric to slide free. When it finally did, Kit let out a whimper of pain as her hands swung around to the front of her body and she doubled over, clutching her shoulders. Lisbet looked to Mona, wondering what she should do, and Mona shrugged. A few moments later, Kit straightened up again, and though she was still wincing, she seemed to have recovered some. Mona tore a chunk from the loaf of bread and handed it to her, before tearing bits for herself and Lisbet and tucking the last heel away for Elinor.

Just as they were finishing their last bites, Elinor burst through the door. She was slightly winded and covered in scratches, looking as though she had run directly through the brush from the fort instead of taking the longer, but more traveled path.

"He's here," she panted. "Coming ashore now. Twenty men, just as Kit said."

"Everything's ready," Lisbet said.

"Avery's lending his men?"

"Including us, you'll have enough to sail." Lisbet wondered if she should tell Elinor exactly who she had recruited, then decided against it. If Payne was coming to shore, his ship was open for the taking, and she didn't want to say anything that would cause hesitation.

"We'll stay here til dusk. I'd rather work under the cover of darkness. And whatever crew remains on his ship won't be expecting us. We should have the upper hand." Elinor spoke with renewed vigor, finally having a plan of action to focus her nerves on. "We'll leave from Avery's beach, it's far enough away from our house that we should escape notice... Who untied Kit?"

"I did," Mona said quickly. "So she could eat. She's not a threat to us."

"She is." Elinor was insistent, but her tone softened as she looked into Mona's eyes. "Once we're on the ship, you can't go against my orders."

"Of course I wouldn't, love. But we aren't on the ship yet and she's no good to us starved to death, now is she?"

"A fair enough point," Elinor said huskily. She wrapped her arms around Mona's waist, seeming to forget that they weren't alone as she slipped into Welsh. "*Dw i'n faelu byw hebddot ti.*"

"*Ti a fi am byth,*" Mona whispered back, as she stared, unblinking, into Elinor's eyes.

Kit looked at Lisbet, who shrugged. Neither spoke the Welsh that the pair so often lapsed into when they were amorously cooing at each other. Finally, Lisbet cleared her throat to remind them of her presence before they could continue further down the path of intimacy they seemed to be on. "What else needs to be done to prepare if we're to sail tonight?"

"We'll need to disguise ourselves to get down to Avery's beach. Payne will have his men searching everywhere for us when he realizes we aren't at the house. And everyone in this town knows me," Elinor said, beginning to pace about the room again. "Payne's men know Mona, and Kit as well. All of us together will stand out."

Lisbet went to her wardrobe and opened it, taking in the assortment of colorful dresses she had acquired over the years. She selected a royal blue one and handed it to Elinor. "Here. This one will look best with your eyes."

"You think I should wear that?"

"We all should," Lisbet said, turning back to pick a garment for Mona. She settled on a dark red, the color of a rich Spanish wine. It would be too short on Mona, who stood almost a full head above Lisbet, but men's eyes didn't tend to make it past the low-cut bodice to inspect if her ankles were showing.

"We'll all be mistaken for whores," Elinor complained. "How are Avery's men to take me seriously as captain if I show up looking like this?"

"What's wrong with being mistaken for a whore?" Lisbet asked, slightly hurt even though she knew it wasn't Elinor's intention.

"Nothing, I didn't mean it like that. I just meant whores attract more attention than anyone in Nassau. Everyone will be looking at us if we four stroll through the market like this."

"They'll all look at us, but none of them will see us," Lisbet explained, "not really. They never do. We're all the same to them, interchangeable, forgettable, there for one purpose. No one will see Elinor or Mona or Kit anymore when you put on the dresses and coiffe your hair. You'll just be another whore of Nassau."

"But–"

"Oh hush, Ellie, and put on the dress," Mona chastised, then looked at Lisbet conspiratorially. "She hates wearing them. I've never seen her in one."

Elinor grimaced. "Then you had better enjoy it, because this will be the only time you see it."

Chapter 14

To anyone passing by, Elinor's grip on Kit's arm would have looked like two close friends walking together. Only Kit could feel the way the captain's fingers dug painfully into her skin. But at least her hands were unbound, and she was allowed to walk somewhat freely. Kit hoped when the shock and anger wore off more, Elinor would be able to see that she genuinely wanted to help.

"Relax, all of you," Lisbet hissed. "You look like you're being marched to the gallows, and it's drawing attention." She let out a forced laugh.

A pirate whistled at the group. "You're going the wrong way," he called as they ignored him.

Kit scanned the crowd growing in the town center as the sun sank down beyond the horizon. Another man reached out to grope Elinor as she passed by, and she dropped Kit's arm to swing at him. Mona quickly pulled her away, and the pirate lunged at Kit instead.

"How dare you?" He asked, not even realizing she wasn't the woman he had just fondled. "Insolent cunt." He spat on her, the glob of saliva landing on her cheek before sliding down her neck. "Ugliest whore I've ever seen too, with hair like a man and flat as a deck timber where it matters."

Elinor, Lisbet, and Mona were gone, swept up into the crowd and happy to let Kit take the blame. If only she was armed. But of course Elinor had refused to give her any weapon, and with good reason. She was a prisoner, a pariah among them. Kit stepped back, wiping her face as she prepared to defend herself from blows, and bumped right into another pirate. Her horror increased as she recognized the second. The quartermaster from Payne's ship.

"Watch your step," he growled.

An arm latched around Kit's waist, dragging her backwards into the crowd and behind one of the canopies over a stand at the edge of the street. She struggled, sure she had been caught. Then she realized the chest she was pressed against was soft and the arm gentle.

"It's me," Lisbet whispered. "Come on. They're waiting up ahead."

"That was one of Payne's men," Kit said, still shaken by the encounter. "Did he recognize you?"

"No, I don't think so," Kit said. Lisbet had been right. Whores were invisible, indistinguishable. She hadn't even seen a flicker of recognition from the man who had given her orders for nearly a week aboard the ship where he was second in command. They rejoined Elinor and Mona where the rough road turned entirely to sand and headed east up the beach together.

"Ah, so you're back with more of your friends," Avery greeted Lisbet first. "When is Davies coming?"

"I'm right here, you old fool. Going blind now are you?" Elinor snapped.

"Could it be?" Avery asked, laughing. "You look like a proper lady in that garb. A far cry from the fearsome Golden Cormorant, the *Bruja del Caribe*. It suits you, though."

"Shut up, Avery," Elinor muttered, her tanned cheeks flushing at his teasing. "Where's my crew?"

"Your crew?" He raised an eyebrow. "My men are just back there. Got six of 'em for you, eager to prove themselves under the most famous pirate to sail these seas."

"You flatter me, Avery. Any extra to row us out?"

"For you, my dear, anything." He bowed, both gallant and mocking at the same time, then whistled to his men. "Anyone sailing with Captain Davies on the *Re–* sorry, what ship are you sailing on?"

"The *Bonny Lass*," Elinor said. "But she'll be getting a new name."

"Anyone sailing with Davies come forth," he hollered.

Kit cringed, hoping none of Payne's men were within earshot of the yelling as they crawled the beach looking for Elinor. A group of men stepped forth from the trees, trailed by four women. Kit recognized one of the women as the barmaid from the tavern, but the other three were unfamiliar to her. They looked like whores, but surely Lisbet hadn't recruited her peers to the ship.

"What is this?" Elinor turned to Lisbet.

"Your crew," Lisbet said.

"I can't sail with this."

"You said you needed twelve, and we're fourteen."

"Twelve seasoned seamen. Not this."

"I didn't know who was friend or foe, so I brought you people I trust." Lisbet stared Elinor down defiantly. Kit admired her tenacity in standing up to the icy captain.

"This is what you have," Mona said. "And you're wasting time. Do you want this ship or not?"

"You," Elinor pointed at the barmaid with long, black braids adorned in cuffs of gold. "Maggie, right? Have you ever been on a ship before?"

"I have. Once," Maggie said, crossing her arms indignantly. "But my father was a bucaneer. It's in my blood."

"And you?" Elinor asked, looking at the woman next to Maggie with a withering glare. "How many times have you trimmed a sail?"

"No times," the woman said. "But Lisbet told us it didn't matter. Said long as we've got a bit o' wits and a bit o' bravery, she swore we was just as fit for the job as any."

Elinor sighed. She looked at the odd group assembled before her for a long moment, then reached for a basked Mona carried. Pulling off the fabric draped over it, she retrieved the flintlock pistol and belt she had tucked in there. It looked out of place as she fastened it around her waist, the black steel and ominous contrast against the soft blue waves of the skirt that rippled beneath it. "Alright," she said, walking the length of her crew and staring each person in the eyes. "Here's the plan."

T HE SECOND BOAT PUSHED out into the ebbing tide, bearing seven of Elinor's newly established crew and four of Avery's that were rowing them out to board the ship. Kit sat quietly at the front next to Elinor, who had given an order of silence. It was well known that sound was carried greater distances when it passed over water, and the captain wanted nothing to give them away.

Anyone looking out from shore would have noticed two boats of whores being rowed out to a waiting ship. Unusual, perhaps, but not anything that would make a man look twice in suspicion. Still, Kit braced herself for the shouts that their ruse had been discovered, alerting the *Bonny Lass* and giving her time to prepare for the impending attack.

Kit swallowed as the schooner loomed closer. Her hands were clammy, and she wiped them on the pink skirt of the dress Lisbet had chosen for her. She'd never fought in a dress before, and worried about how the garment might impede her movement. Her agility was her greatest asset in hand to hand combat, but that was limited by the tight bodice and the too-long skirts she kept tripping over. She hoped Avery's men were skilled enough in combat to make up for it, otherwise the only thing they had in their favor was the element of surprise.

"Remember, I would like nothing more than to kill you. So don't give me another reason to," Elinor whispered so faintly Kit almost couldn't hear her.

She shook her head that she wouldn't, and felt Elinor press the hilt of a short dagger into her hand. A small relief. She wouldn't have to rely on her fists alone to get her through the fight. The knife gave her a chance.

"Hello?" Elinor called, lifting her voice to a flirtatious falsetto. "Gentlemen?"

There were shouts from the deck above, and a small crowd of men gathered at the rail above, holding a lantern over the side to peer into the dark below. Their illuminated faces were shocked to see the two boats full of women, and they paid no attention to the men that had rowed them out there.

"What's this then? How did you get out here?" One called down.

"Your captain sent us," Elinor said seductively. "A gift in celebration of his successes today, to thank you for your part in it."

The men looked at each other, dumbfounded. "Our captain?"

"This is the *Bonny Lass,* is it not?"

"Aye, but Payne's never–" He trailed off as another man pushed him aside.

"Don't ask questions, matey, just get them up here." He grinned lasciviously as the other men shouted their agreement.

They threw a rope ladder over the rail, and Elinor caught it. Kit's stomach turned with nerves. She was meant to follow right behind Elinor, and then the rest of the women would come up. They were bait, meant to distract the men on the ship until Avery's men were aboard. She wiped her hands on the dress again, worried their slick sweatiness would make it hard to get a fast grip on the rope, but somehow she managed the climb. She was so afraid the crew of the *Bonny Lass* would recognize her, she stood petrified on the deck as Lisbet climbed up the ladder behind her.

"Come on, you can do this," she said, pulling Lisbet over to three of the men. "Just be coy, bat your eyelashes a bit, make them feel like they're the only man in the world."

"They're going to know me."

"No, they won't. Not unless you give them reason to. So act like they're complete strangers and you just want to fuck them. It's only a few minutes."

Fucking any of the men on the ship was the last thing Kit wanted to think about with Lisbet so close.

"Oh, boys," Lisbet cooed as she sashayed closer. Three pairs of eyes locked on her. The men were practically salivating at the sight of her, and Kit couldn't blame them. Every inch of her was perfect. She moved to them

152

like a sea siren, enchanting all who looked upon her and binding them under her spell. "Which one of you thinks you can handle me?"

The three crewmen all spoke at once, stumbling over their words as they rushed through them, each trying to be the first to claim the stunning woman throwing herself at them. Even though she knew it was a ruse, jealousy burned like a hot poker in Kit's chest. If only Lisbet would stroke her fingers down Kit's forearm as playfully as she did the stranger before her. Lust burned so convincingly in Lisbet's eyes that Kit wondered if it was truly all an act.

"I don't think any of you can handle me," Lisbet purred. "But I'd wager she can." She pointed to Kit.

"Me?" Kit asked, astounded.

"What do you think?" Lisbet asked the men, stepping to the side and pulling Kit along with her. Slowly the men turned so their backs were to the rope ladder, entranced by the show Lisbet was putting on for them as they nodded their eager approval. "Go on then," she said to Kit, "show them how to really please a woman."

Kit hesitated, but the men were waiting expectantly and she didn't want them to lose interest and realize the trap that was being set. She pulled Lisbet close and kissed her deeply, drawing whoops from the watching men. Lisbet's lips eagerly parted to take her in, and Kit fell into instant bliss without caring if Lisbet's affection was only for show. Lisbet's hand was at the back of her head, holding her in place as their tongues met and swirled around each other. Her other hand was at Kit's neck, her thumb stroking the spot that always drove Kit mad with desire.

Kit could barely hear the men cheering in the background, was only vaguely aware that more were gathering to watch. She saw Lisbet sneak a glance behind the men, and felt Kit's lips move against hers as she counted how many of their own had crept up on deck after the women. Four. They were still waiting for two more. Lisbet's hand was drifting lower, groping down Kit's chest and slipping under the low neckline of the dress. The moan that escaped Kit was real as Lisbet cupped her breast and kneaded firmly. Just like Kit liked it. Her nipples hardened, pressing against the tight fabric that held them uncomfortably in place, and she felt Lisbet smile before switching her attention to the other side.

"I missed you so much," Kit whispered, forgetting where she was as her stomach clenched with desire.

Lisbet pulled away. "How about that? You think you can do better? Who thinks they can make her moan louder?" She asked the gathered men. One stepped forward to grab Kit roughly by the waist, his erection pressing into her. Kit pulled away in disgust, feeling like Lisbet had tricked her as much as them.

"Now," Elinor yelled, ten paces across the deck. "Kill them all!"

Kit's wits had been lost from the moment the kiss began, but she was still able to gather them faster than the stunned man who looked from her to Lisbet to the screaming captain Davies. The slipped into his stomach easily, and she twisted before pulling it out to ram it home again. The sailor was too surprised to even cry out in pain as he sank to his knees. He looked up at her in a mixture of shock, confusion, and betrayal as he tried to staunch the blood draining from his midsection. The same blood was warm on Kit's hand, and she gripped the slick knife tighter as she looked for her next victim. Lisbet shrieked behind her, and Kit turned to see another one of Payne's men pushing her to the ground. Kit sprang onto the man's back, driving the dagger into the base of his neck and up into his skull. Her momentum knocked him down, but there was no need to stab again. The wound was fatal.

The fight was over as quickly as it began. Thick, blue gunsmoke hung in the air, which was odd. Kit hadn't even noticed that shots had been fired. The men of the *Bonny Lass* had been so at ease in the harbor and eager for the entertainment that they'd not even thought to arm themselves, and their bodies lay across the deck, each one soaking the timbers with blood. It ran across the deck, each trickle a sanguine tributary to a larger river that coursed the path of least resistance to spill out of a hatch and into the sea below. The plan had gone off perfectly, and Elinor Davies controlled the ship.

Kit offered a hand to Lisbet, still sitting on the deck, and pulled her up. Lisbet was shaking and her face was pale beneath a splatter of blood. Kit pulled her close and held on tight, the years of soreness between them lost in the intensity of the moment. Lisbet leaned in, letting Kit support her.

"Are you alright?" Kit asked.

"I don't know. I think so." Lisbet sounded dazed.

"But you're not hurt?"

"No. But it seems so unfair. They had no idea what was going to happen."

"At least their final moments were happy ones," Kit said. She squeezed Lisbet a little tighter instead and peered around the deck, counting the heads that were still standing. Fourteen. Everyone had made it.

Elinor stepped through the smoke, looking like a demon raised straight from the fiery pits of hell. Her hair was loose and frizzed in curls around her face, and the arm of the blue dress she wore had ripped along the seam at the shoulder. Blood dripped from her hand and the blade as she raised her cutlass high in the air. Avery's men whooped and Kit joined them, but none of the other women were paying the new captain of the ship any attention.

Elinor scowled, and Kit sensed she was used to a greater response from her crew. "Ahoy," she yelled, and a few more heads turned to listen. Kit felt a shiver of anticipation for what the famous pirate captain would say on her first voyage resuming the role. But Elinor didn't make a speech at all. "Clean the deck and prepare to sail," she said simply, before turning and disappearing into the captain's cabin.

Avery's men sprung into action, while the women Lisbet had recruited stood around looking at one another, still shaken by their brutal introductions to a life of piracy. Kit smiled, feeling oddly nostalgic. She remembered her first fight, the rush of fury that consumed her entire body as she let instincts take over. And she remembered the emptiness that had threatened to swallow her whole when the shock of battle had receded.

"We'd better help," Kit whispered to Lisbet, who hadn't moved since she'd taken her into her arms.

"Help," Lisbet repeated softly. "Help how? What am I supposed to do to help here?"

Kit looked up. Avery's men were in the rigging, working to unfurl the large sail. "We can start by moving the bodies, I suppose."

"Moving the..." Lisbet blinked at her, looking revolted at the thought. "Moving them where?"

"Off the ship." Kit didn't want to let go of Lisbet, but they couldn't keep standing there like statues on the deck while everyone else was working.

"Without a funeral?"

"There's no time for that. We need to leave the harbor before Payne realizes we have his ship."

"Shouldn't we say a prayer? You knew them."

"Not really," Kit said. "And they didn't know me, not who I really am. I was only on this ship for a little while, but I can swear to you, these weren't good men, Liss. None of them are." She knelt by the second man she had slain, who was still facedown on the deck. His pockets contained just two silver pieces, and she slipped them into her own. Then, she hooked her arms under his and started dragging him towards the rail.

Lisbet looked like she was going to throw up, but she joined Kit at the man's shoulders and helped heave his torso over the rail. He dangled for a moment, as if he was suspended between the earthly world and the next, and then gravity took over and his body tumbled into the water below with a splash. Kit peered over the rail and saw one sleek fin slide by next to the ship, then another. The sharks were already circling, drawn in by the blood that had been spilled.

"What are you looking at?" She yelled at the other women, realizing they were all watching. "Help us."

The barmaid stepped forward, her apron stained red. She still gripped a knife in her clenched fist, as though the men might spring back to life at any moment to seek their revenge. Her eyes were wide, but her expression resolute. She looked down at her hands, then tucked the knife into the pocket of her apron and reached to grab a fallen soldier by the legs. Her action was enough to inspire the other women to move, and slowly the deck came alive again.

By the time the creak of the anchor being raised echoed across the deck, all the bodies had been cleared and the unlikely crew was beginning to scrub away the blood that would forever stain it. Elinor reemerged from the captain's quarters, the blood washed away and her hair retamed into a single braid that hung down her back. She had redonned her usual clothing, and looked more at ease as she swaggered across the deck than Kit had ever seen her. She spoke a few words to Avery's men, who adjusted the sails, and the ship began to glide towards the open ocean.

"Everyone, gather 'round!" Elinor called out, and this time everyone obeyed.

"There are rules on board this ship and I expect you to abide them. I'm the captain of this ship, and my orders are to be followed without hesitation. Is that clear?"

"Aye, Captain," the crew said in unison.

"Bagley is the quartermaster for this journey, my second in command. His orders are to be followed as if I gave them. Men will sleep above deck, women below. Not together, or you'll both be punished. You are crewmates, and you need to work together. So whatever you would have normally done on land does not apply here. You're all equals on this ship. You help each other. If you don't know what to do, find someone who does. Is that understood?"

"Aye, Captain."

"Good. And one final thing." Elinor paused, and gestured for Mona to join her. "This ship is no longer the *Bonny Lass*. And you're going to name her."

"Me?"

"You're the best at it, love."

Mona thought for a moment. "*Iseult's Fury*." Everyone looked at her in confusion. "Because the Iseult of yore would have stopped at nothing to get her Tristan back, just as we'll do anything to recover ours," she explained, invoking the old legend of two lovers that had been told and retold across centuries.

Elinor smiled. "It's perfect. Back to it, then." She clapped her hands, shooing the crew away to their tasks before walking over to Kit and Lisbet. "Kit, a word in my cabin?" Her tone was casual, conversational, but Kit saw the pinched corners of her mouth. All was not forgiven yet. Kit sighed, apprehensive of what punishment might still await her.

She followed Elinor into the cabin. Even though the quarters had changed hands, being back there was an eerie feeling, and a shiver ran down Kit's spine as she entered the space where she had been trapped and threatened by Payne. His presence still lingered in the cabin, almost as though he was taunting her. They may have killed a few of his crewmen, but he was safe on Nassau, and would be even more motivated to revenge by the theft of his ship. That was assuming Kit even made it back to Nassau, assuming they found Tristan and the rest of the *Revenge's* crew alive. Otherwise, none of it would be a concern for Kit. She had no doubt Elinor would make good on the promise to kill her.

"You fought well today," Elinor said, circling around her like the sharks that had swarmed the ship.

Kit shrugged, trying not to show how intimidated she really was. Elinor's entire demeanor had changed, and if Kit had ever doubted her ability to lead a ship, those thoughts had long vanished.

"Show me where the *Revenge* went down," Elinor pointed to Payne's desk.

A map was laid out, and navigational instruments cluttered the surface. The devices may as well have been magic as far as Kit was concerned, for she had no earthly idea how little bits of metal could tell a person where they were on the surface of the great, wide earth when there was nothing to be seen but the vast ocean. She stepped forward, looking at the map, then shrugged.

"I can't read this."

"Anyone can read a map," Elinor said derisively. She jabbed one finger at an island. "This is New Providence. Did the *Revenge* sail south? East? What land did you see?"

Kit squinted at the map, trying to remember what she had seen from the deck of the *Revenge*. The sun had risen off their left side, so they must have been sailing south. She traced the route she thought the *Revenge* had taken after it left the harbor of Nassau, hugging the coast of Cuba before turning east to prowl the waters around Hispaniola, and she explained as much to the captain.

"Here," she whispered, her finger finally landing on a spit of land just west of Tortuga. "It must have been here."

"Good," Elinor said, dipping a quill into a pot of ink and marking the spot with an X. She strode back over the the door and flung it open, calling, "Tris– Bagley!"

The newly appointed quartermaster appeared instantly. He was a young man, and rather on the short side, with dark skin and even darker, piercing eyes. He couldn't have been more than twenty, and seemed practically bursting with pride. Kit got the impression that he had never held a rank as high as quartermaster before, and would likely not hold it were he not one of Elinor's very limited options. He seemed eager not to let the formidable captain down.

"Aye, Cap'n?" He said, almost breathlessly.

"Tie her to the main mast for two day's time."

"Captain?" He asked, confused by the order.

"She's a traitor and I intend to make an example of her, so that no one else thinks to turn their loyalties."

"Can't say I'd feel right doing that to a lady," he muttered.

"She's not a lady, she's a pirate, same as you or I," Elinor snapped. "And she'll bear the same consequences as you or I. Did you not see her send two of Payne's men to their maker, and with only a dagger? And you would call her a lady?"

"I'm sorry, Captain, I meant no offense," he said, still looking uncomfortable with the order as he bowed his head in deference to her rank.

Fighting back would accomplish nothing, so Kit accepted her fate quickly and allowed herself to be led out of the cabin. Two days on the mast wasn't bad, provided no squalls sprung up and the weather was mild. She had seen punishments much more severe handed out over much less. And it was two more days of surviving, two more days to prove to Lisbet that she was trying her best do make amends.

Chapter 15

I F LISBET WAS BEING honest with herself, recruiting her fellow whores to work on the ship had been nothing short of a disaster. It was a wonder the ship was making its way through the waves at all, with just under half the crew lacking any experience in sailing at all. She was beginning to see why the pirates preferred to press naval sailors into their crews. There was an amount of discipline and rigidity required aboard a ship that none of the women were used to, Lisbet included, and while the men might have possessed the skills, it seemed they did not have the wills to finish tasks when there were beautiful women everywhere they turned.

Yet somehow, somehow, the newly christened *Iseult's Fury* bumped and jolted her path through the choppy waters and the island of New Providence grew faint in the distance. Kit had disappeared, summoned by Elinor to the cabin, but Lisbet didn't have time to wonder why. She was busy mopping the deck, trying to erase the awful bloodshed that had occurred there before the stains set into the wood forever. The eyes of the man Kit had stabbed still haunted her, the fury as he lunged for her and the stunned blankness as he fell.

He wasn't the first man she had seen killed. Fights happened frequently enough in Nassau. But it was the first killing she had felt a part of, even if it wasn't her hand that had ended the life. Kit had said he was evil, but in the few minutes Lisbet had been around him, she hadn't seen it. She didn't see evil in most of the pirates that prowled the Caribbean, and she had known a fair few. The men weren't thirsty for blood, they sought freedom and gold and often had no other means to attain them. There were some who became drunk with power as they got wealthier, and wielded it in cruel ways, but mostly they were just people doing what they had to to survive.

"Do you think we're wicked people now?" She asked Maggie, scrubbing beside her.

"No," Maggie said thoughtfully. "We're good people who live in wicked times, doing the best we can." She fully looked the part of a pirate, in cut-off breeches and a pistol belted around her waist. Lisbet envied the ease with which she had adapted to life on the ship, as though she had always been destined for it.

Hours of mopping and dozens of buckets later, the remnants of battle were finally erased from the deck. Mona bustled around bearing tankards of hot grog, a spicy, sour mixture of water, rum, and citrus juice. Lisbet laughed a little at how very typically Mona it was to make sure everyone had a mug of something hot after a trying night, even on a ship in the middle of the sea.

Lisbet looked around for someone to drink with, needing a distraction to erase the memory of the dead man's last stare. Everyone else looked busy. Mona was still doling out beverages and Maggie had gone off with one of Avery's crewman, who gestured excitedly as he explained the ropes and rigging to his eager student. Lisbet was sure Elinor was busy with whatever ship captains occupied themselves, which only left Kit. Lisbet hadn't seen her since she'd followed the captain into her quarters hours before.

Lisbet walked the length of the ship, but she didn't see Kit among the crew still working. Finally, on her second pass, Lisbet spotted her. Kit was sitting on the deck and leaning awkwardly against the mast, looking morose. Lisbet's heart jumped at the sight of her, but she wasn't sure she was ready to talk to Kit yet. She couldn't deny how comforting Kit's presence had been right after their ambush, how much Lisbet hadn't wanted her to let go. Even if she was a traitor. Lisbet steadied her nerves and walked over. As she approached, she realized Kit's awkward position and solitude wasn't by choice. Her wrists were bound to the mast.

"Don't think the captain wants you talking to me," Kit said sullenly. "Or anyone, for that matter."

Lisbet shrugged. "I'm not scared of Elinor. It's not as though she'll do anything to me, we're old friends."

"Old friends means nothing when a ship's captain gives an order."

"I'll take my chances," Lisbet smiled. Elinor wasn't the type of captain Kit was accustomed to, so it was normal for her to be wary, but Lisbet really wasn't concerned. After everything she had done for Elinor and Mona, she figured she should be in their good graces for a long time.

"Don't say I didn't warn you."

"I won't." Lisbet sighed. "How did we end up here, Kit?"

"Hell if I know," Kit said with a half smile.

"Why did you turn to this?"

"My uncle was in debt to a merchant in Charles Town. He wanted to use me to pay them, to send me off to work until the debts were cleared. It would have taken me the rest of my life to repay, and he would have never thought twice about me again. So I cut my hair and stole my cousin's clothes and begged my way into being a powder boy on a ship."

"The one that brought you back to Nassau?"

"Aye," Kit winced as she leaned her head back against the pole.

"Is it painful?"

"This? It's not so bad. The memories of that ship are worse."

"I'm sorry," Lisbet said.

"Why did you kiss me?" Kit asked suddenly.

"Which time?"

"Here, on the ship. It wasn't the plan."

"I thought it would be a good distraction to get the rest of the men onto the ship."

"They were plenty distracted already. But you used my affection for you to entertain men, without even asking if I was comfortable with it. And you see nothing wrong with that behavior?"

"Maybe I wanted to kiss you," Lisbet murmured. She still hadn't decided for herself what had compelled her to do it, whether it was for the ruse or her own desire. She'd thought Kit would enjoy it, and was confused why Kit seemed so upset. "I don't know. It's so hard."

"You wanted to or you used me? That doesn't seem hard to me."

"Kit, you betrayed my two closest friends. How am I supposed to feel after that? Even if I do want it, how would I ever look them in the eye again?"

"Then why did you come over here to talk to me?"

"Because I don't know what to do to help the ship and I don't want to be alone."

"This reminds me of the first time we fought. Do you remember it?"

Dread made Lisbet's blood run cold, and her stomach sank. She didn't want to talk about then, about everything that happened before, but she should have known it was inevitable. "Of course I do. You left me at the river to carry back all the washing alone."

"But do you remember why?"

Lisbet shook her head. The argument, the yelling, Lisbet crying by the stream alone, that was still as clear as the finest blown glass. She remembered waiting hours for Kit to come back to apologize for yelling and leaving her there and beg for forgiveness so things could go back to normal between them. But the details of why it had ever happened had long faded from her memory.

"Because I told you I loved you."

The memories flooded back. "And I said I didn't know if I did."

"You've never known, Liss. Anything. You didn't know if you loved me, you don't know why you kissed me... But if you want the truth, I think you're just afraid of it. Because you do feel things for me, and that frightens you, even now."

"I'm not afraid. I just want to be sure. Would you have rathered that I lied?" Except it wouldn't have been a lie. Lisbet had loved Kit then, and somewhere deep down, she still did.

"You asked how we got here, well, isn't that where it all started? The beginning of the end?"

Lisbet shrugged. It was a mistake to have come over to talk to Kit. Instead of the comfort she sought, she was only being made to feel worse. "That was a long time ago," she said weakly.

"But you haven't changed at all. You have no problem using people to get what you want, whether that's attention, coin, or just to entertain your whims. You don't care that you're hurting people." Kit's voice dripped with venom as she glared at Lisbet.

"I care," Lisbet said, blinking back the tears that were welling in her eyes as she wondered if what Kit was saying could be true. It was uncomfortable to consider.

"If you did, you wouldn't have kissed me. You know how I feel, you know what I want. And you did it anyway, knowing it would confuse me." Kit sighed. "But I suppose that's my own fault."

"You're right," Lisbet admitted, letting the tears flow freely as she accepted the realization. "I didn't think about hurting you when I kissed you. And I was afraid to tell you how I really felt then."

"Why?" Kit pressed.

"They would have never accepted us. Loving you meant losing everything, and I couldn't." Lisbet wished she would let it go. She didn't want anyone else on the *Fury* to see her so upset and judge her for it. No one liked an unhappy whore.

"That happened anyway. For both of us."

"I know. And I'm sorry."

"We can't go back. I made mistakes then too, and I'm sorry for those. But what are you afraid of now?"

"Losing it all again. I didn't get to leave the island and start anew where there were no rumors about me, no one shunning me for my sins. Everything I have, I had to earn. Alone." She took a shuddering breath and let the truth of her heart spill forth.

"Liss–"

"No, let me finish. I'm afraid of how much I want to go back to what we had. I didn't think I was ever going to see you again. Twice. And yet here we are again, a third time, and all I want to do is hold you and kiss you and try again, but I'm so scared. You said I haven't changed, and maybe that's true, but you have. I mean, God, Kit, I just watched you kill two men. You sold out your crew, and then turned around and did it again. Of course I'm afraid. I don't even know you anymore."

"So we can get to know each other again. Maybe it's fate that keeps pulling us back together, and we should let it."

"You always said we choose our own fate."

"If that were true, I wouldn't have chosen this one," Kit smiled wryly.

Lisbet wished she could reach for her hand. She ached from the rawness of the conversation and a desperate longing to hold the woman she was beginning to realize she still loved. Kit's eyes widened, and she began to shake her head slightly as Lisbet noticed footsteps approaching behind her. A hand clamped down on her shoulder and spun her around, and Lisbet found herself face to face with Elinor.

"There's to be no talking to prisoners or people being punished, and Kit is both. Go below deck and get some rest, we'll need all hands in the morning." Elinor's coldness shocked Lisbet. The warmth had gone from her eyes, replaced by an icy stare.

"If that's true, then untie hers. She actually knows what she's doing on a ship anyways. Let her help."

"Lisbet," Elinor said slowly, and she could see the captain was fighting to maintain her composure. "I've been patient because you're not accustomed to life on a ship, but that was an order. Kit will receive five lashes now for your insolence."

"That's not fair!" Lisbet protested. "She didn't do anything wrong."

"Then I'll make it ten." Elinor shrugged, and Lisbet found herself dumbfounded at how quickly the friend she knew on land had become so callous at sea.

She opened her mouth to protest again, then thought better of it. She didn't want anything worse to happen to Kit because of her. There was no question it was her fault; Kit had warned her of Elinor's rule, and Lisbet should have taken it seriously. And she couldn't even apologize to Kit because that would be breaking the rules again. Lisbet stormed off, fuming at how unfair it was. There was only one person on the ship who could stop Elinor, and she needed to find her. Mona was collecting tankards that had been left strewn about the deck on crates and barrels as their users had filed off to bed. Lisbet took two from her and walked towards the ship's tiny kitchen with her.

"I didn't know you were still up," Mona said.

"I need your help. Kit's in trouble with Elinor and it's my fault."

"I can't interfere with that." Mona looked away.

"She's going to whip her, and only because I was talking to her. It's not fair."

"It's a pirate ship, Liss, and Elinor's a pirate. It's not meant to be fair."

"I've never seen her so... cruel before. Was she always like this as a captain?"

"She's never hesitated to do what she thought was best for her ship and her crew. And she's angry, and grieving. Best to just do as she asks."

"But it's my fault for talking to Kit. Elinor should be punishing me."

"She is." Mona gave her a sad smile and handed her a cup of tea.

Chapter 16

"I DON'T WANT TO hurt you," Elinor said quietly, glancing around the empty deck. "You've been nothing but cooperative, at great risk to yourself. It hasn't gone unnoticed. But I am going to make an example of you."

"Just don't hurt Lisbet. Please. She didn't know, she's never been on a ship like this. She's never been one to follow orders, either." Kit didn't regret the conversation, it had been worth the price of the lashes. Finally she had some answers, and some hope.

Elinor waved the concern away. "I'm not going to do anything to her except teach her a lesson about listening to her captain that they all need to learn. I don't care if they hate me, or fear me, I intend to bring each one of them home alive." Though Elinor still spoke quietly, her voice was infused with renewed passion. Kit wondered how many crewmen she had lost before. "And I'm not going to do anything more to you. But I'm going to crack this strap and you're going to scream like the devil himself is beating you."

Kit nodded. She understood her role immediately, and the decision renewed her respect for Elinor as a captain. She would have taken the lashes if it meant Lisbet was spared, but she much preferred the alternative Elinor proposed.

"And Kit? Don't tell anyone about this or I really will give you ten. I have a reputation to uphold." Elinor raised the leather strap. "Ready?"

Kit nodded again, then braced her body for the blows she'd been assured wouldn't come. Elinor smacked the strap against a barrel, and before the crack finished echoing through the night, Kit screamed. Four strikes and four screams later, Elinor crossed her arms again, back to her surly self.

"Goodnight, Kit," she said, then added before she turned to leave, "sleep well."

Kit leaned back against the mast, feeling the smooth wood on her back where her shirt had ridden up. She was tired of being restrained, but it seemed Elinor's position on that hadn't softened a bit. It was going to be a long two days, and undoubtedly restless ones. Every part of her ached, and no matter which way she shifted her weight, she couldn't find relief.

She wondered what Lisbet was doing, and craned her neck to look for her, but she wasn't anywhere to be seen. It was going to be a lonely two days, but at least it would give her time to think. Lisbet had all but admitted she'd loved her, and Kit finally believed her. There was something about the haze following a battle that brought hidden emotions out of their dormancy. Especially a person's first one. Spilling blood offered clarity about what was truly important in life, since each fight survived was one closer to the one they wouldn't.

Lisbet had surprised her, though, and Kit began to regret her accusation that she had never changed. The Lisbet she had once known would have always put her own comfort first, even if it meant others were hurt because of it. The lesson in ruthlessness and self-preservation was one Kit had applied to her own life when she took up piracy. Yet, Lisbet had dropped everything else to help her friends in their time of need, abandoning the life she claimed she was afraid to lose in order to be at their side. And she had spoken up for Kit, even if she hadn't understood the risk in doing so. Yes, Lisbet had changed, and it only made Kit want her even more.

Somehow, Kit managed to doze off and on through the rest of the night and into the morning, but by afternoon the sun had shifted and the sails no longer cast their shadow over her. Kit slowly came to understand the real torture of her predicament. It was a hot day, even with a strong breeze filling the sails, and there was no reprieve from the harsh rays. Sweat ran down her body and soaked into the ropes that had rubbed her wrists raw, its salty bite agony against her open wounds. She would have given anything for a drink of water, even just a sip, but everyone moving about the deck continued to ignore her, and she knew begging would only earn her real lashes for the effort.

Night managed to be even worse than day. As soon as the sun disappeared below the horizon, the chill set in and Kit began to shiver uncontrollably. Her legs trembled no matter how she tried to clench the muscles against the twitches. Her sweaty clothes were frigid against her skin, and her teeth chattered so hard she thought they might fall out. She couldn't hold back her cries of pain any longer, and began to think she might have preferred death to the torture she suffered. She forced her head up to look Elinor in the eyes, sure the captain was coming to execute on her promise of harsher retribution. The eyes she met were Lisbet's, anxious and full of pity from across the deck.

Sometime during the darkest hours, Kit began to see things that couldn't have been there. Demons danced across the deck of *Iseult's Fury*, leaving flames as footsteps in their wake as they whirled and spun and set the sails afire. Ash and burning bits of canvas rained down around her as she struggled against her ropes, the faces of the crew of the *Revenge* taunting her from the beyond as they beckoned for her to join them.

"I'm sorry," she tried to say to them, but no sound came out. Her lips cracked at the corners when she opened her mouth to speak, and she licked at the tiny trickle of blood, grateful for anything to wet her mouth that was so dry it hurt to even breathe. The demons cackled. The next thing Kit remembered was the sound of her torso hitting the deck as Elinor cut her down from the mast, then she rolled onto her back, too numb and tired to move further.

"It's over," someone said gently from above. Kit recognized the voice through the haze. Mona.

"Sit her up," Elinor ordered. "Get something in her and get her to a hammock."

Kit felt people pulling her up. She wished they would have let her lie there a little longer. Moving hurt too much.

"Drink this." Mona tried to hand her a tankard, but Kit's hands were shaking too much to take it, so Mona raised it to her lips for her. The liquid was hot and salty, and Kit's vision began to clear as soon as the first trickle passed her cracked lips. "Careful," Mona warned, taking the tankard away, "don't drink too fast, you'll throw it all up again."

Kit reached for it, desperate for its soothing warmth. The sip had barely moistened her tongue, and her throat still burned for something wet. Mona let her drink again, and each mouthful of broth brought Kit further out of the grasps of death and back into the world of the living. When the tankard was empty, Elinor gave a nod and two of Avery's men hoisted Kit to her feet. It hurt to stand, but she refused to lean on them as they led her across the deck to the hatch.

"The women're down there," one said gruffly. "They'll see to it as you have a place to sleep."

Kit was familiar enough with the sleeping quarters of the ship, having sailed on it with Payne, and the promise of horizontal, unbound rest gave her the surge of strength she needed to make it down the ladder. As soon as her feet landed on the planks below, Lisbet was at her side, holding her up and half-carrying her to an empty hammock strung up between two beams.

"Are you okay? Oh, Kit, I'm so sorry. What can I do?" Lisbet cried as Kit sank into the canvas.

"It's not your fault," she said weakly, wondering why Lisbet was crying.

"I should have listened when you said I couldn't speak to you. I never thought she would punish you for it. I'm sorry."

Kit remembered Elinor's deception, and her promise not to reveal it, just before she spoke to reassure Lisbet. She forced a smile. "It wasn't so bad. I've had worse." It was a lie. The beatings she had received before were bad, but she would take them any day over being tied to the mast again. But Lisbet didn't need to know that.

"But I still feel awful. How can I make it up to you?"

"I just want you to hold me," Kit said as she yawned. "Just to be close to you."

Lisbet sat on the hammock and took Kit's hand. "I can do that."

"Lay with me," Kit insisted. She needed Lisbet in that moment as much as she had needed the watery broth up on the deck, or the very air she breathed.

"Are you sure you're alright? I don't want to hurt you anymore."

"You won't." Kit tugged on her hand, and Lisbet gave in, laying next to Kit in the hammock as the boat swayed in the waves.

Kit rolled onto her side to give Lisbet more room, the canvas walls wrapping up around them like a caterpillar encasing itself in a cocoon. Lisbet's arm wrapped around her waist and clung to her, her breath soft and warm on Kit's neck as they rocked gently from side to side. Lisbet was warm, and her touch gentle. Kit sighed as her body finally relaxed, releasing all the suffering she had just been through. None of it mattered with Lisbet beside her. She reached down to run her hand over Lisbet's thigh behind her. She felt Lisbet flinch slightly at the touch, then the arm around her waist tightened even more as Lisbet's thumb began to trace small circles on her stomach.

A snore cut through the silence, and Kit remembered they weren't alone in the shared quarters. There were four other women sleeping off their day of labor in the hammocks around them. But even though Kit was tired to her bones, sleep was the furthest thing from her mind. Lisbet's touch had awakened her, and like a drunken sailor clinging to his empty bottle, she needed more. She took Lisbet's hand with her own and moved it up so it was covering her breast. Lisbet's thumb continued its languid circles, teasing Kit's nipple through the fabric.

"What are you doing?" Lisbet whispered, but continued her stroking. "We can't do this here."

"Don't give in to fear anymore, Liss," Kit said. "We'll be quiet. We won't wake anyone."

"You're in no condition–"

"I can decide that for myself."

Lisbet's touch became firmer in response, and Kit closed her eyes in bliss, all the pain forgotten as her desire grew. The only thing she could focus on was Lisbet's thumb, spiraling around the nipple that had stiffened to a hard peak beneath her shirt. Lisbet pressed her lips to Kit's neck, flooding every inch of her with a warmth that began in her core and spread across her body. Kit held her breath, knowing if she released it too quickly she wouldn't be able to contain her moan of pleasure. She rolled over awkwardly, the hammock pushing her chest tight against Lisbet's. Struggling against its confines, she raised her hands to cradle Lisbet's face.

If Kit could only do one thing for the rest of her life, she would choose kissing Lisbet. Their lips met it and it was as though someone had thrown a fresh log onto a fire from too great a distance. Sparks flew into the air in an explosion of light, whirling and dancing together as they drifted away into the sky and desire set them both aflame. Her lips were so soft against Kit's windchapped ones, and her tongue insistent as she parted them to deepen the kiss.

Both of Lisbet's hands returned to Kit's breasts, teasing them through her shirt. Kit responded by biting down softly on Lisbet's lower lip, twisting it gently in her teeth before returning to taste Lisbet's sweet tongue against hers again. Lisbet was truly driving her mad with her ministrations, and she felt the wetness flood her core as her body readied itself for what was next. Lisbet's knee pushed between hers, prying her legs apart, and Kit eagerly opened them to rub herself against Lisbet's thigh. Intertwined, they pressed into each other, grinding right up to the edge of bliss.

Kit's body was alive with sensations, each one intimate and overwhelming in the best of ways. The need she had been suppressing for too long overflowed as she grasped Lisbet's hand and guided it between her legs. It took a moment– an entire moment too long– to get her skirts hitched up enough for Lisbet's fingers to stroke up her thighs. Kit's breath came in short gasps as Lisbet searched for her opening. She stopped just short, her hand hovering above Kit's mound. Kit nodded in encouragement, their lips still locked together as she silently begged for Lisbet to enter her and sate her deepest need.

Just when she thought Lisbet was going to change her mind and pull away, one finger thrust into her, so suddenly Kit almost squealed with delight. Her muscles clenched desperately around the finger as another joined it in her soft folds. Lisbet stroked her, thrusting her fingers in and out slowly at first, before pushing them deep inside Kit to push back against Kit's throbbing walls.

Kit's breaths were getting louder, and Lisbet clamped her free hand over her mouth to stifle the near moans she was no longer able to control. Her fingers continued their deft succor below, pulling out occasionally to tease Kit's clit before plunging back in to swirl up the desire that threatened to overflow at any moment. Lisbet's touch settled on one spot, and she hooked her finger into it, as if to pull Kit even closer. The pressure was exquisite, and Kit lost all control of herself as her legs began to shake. Her tired muscles spasmed one final time before releasing a flood of warmth that spilled out from between her legs. Kit pulled Lisbet's hand away from her mouth, needing to feel her lips again as she sank into bliss.

"I love you," Kit whispered against Lisbet's mouth. "You don't have to say it back. I won't run away this time. I'll wait until you're ready."

"Shh," Lisbet hushed her. "I love you, too. Now rest. I'll be here when you wake."

Kit nodded and rolled back over. Lisbet's hand settled around her waist again. She was nearly asleep when she realized Lisbet had said the words back. It filled her with a new kind of warmth, one she hadn't known in a long time, and she had to work hard to convince herself it wasn't a lie, or some new manipulation. But it had felt real, and had been said without hesitation. Kit was too exhausted to question it, so she decided to accept it as fact before falling into the deepest sleep of her life.

When she awoke, Lisbet was gone, but judging by the light streaming through the cracks between the timbers of the deck above, it was well past breakfast. Kit bolted out of the hammock, nearly falling as she rushed up the ladder. Everyone was already working, and she was late. All she could do was hope Elinor would look upon the transgression with lenience, because the thought of being lashed to the mast again was unbearable.

"There you are," Mona said, coming from nowhere to stand beside her at the top of the hatch. "Feeling better?"

"Aye, I am," Kit said cautiously.

"Good. There's breakfast and real tea awaiting you in the galley, and then Elinor will see you in her cabin." Mona smiled.

Being summoned by Elinor made Kit apprehensive all over again. She couldn't imagine what the captain could still want from her, or what new transgression she could have committed in the short hours since she had been released from the mast. The breakfast that awaited her was simple– a boiled egg, another mug of the salty broth from the night before, and two stale sea biscuits– but Kit didn't mind. It was better than the nothing she'd been given for two days prior. She dunked the stale biscuit into the soup, softening it to a consistency she was able to bite as she lingered in the kitchen. She couldn't avoid Elinor forever, though.

"Come in," Elinor called as Kit knocked on the captain's door.

She paused to inhale the sea breeze, hoping the captain had no more punishments in store, then pushed the door open. Elinor was hunched over the desk on the far side of the room. She didn't look up from the map she was studying, and Kit stood in the doorway, unsure what she was expected to do.

"There are garments in the chest under the window if you'd prefer to change into something more suitable for work," Elinor said with a wave of her hand. She still didn't turn around.

The chest was open and overflowing with men's trousers and shirts that were left behind by the ship's previous occupants. Kit dug through it, trying to find something that would work on her frame. Near the bottom, she found a pair of black wool breeches that looked like they wouldn't be too long, and a shirt with sleeves that wouldn't drown her hands in their folds. She tucked both under her arm, eager to get out of the bloodstained dress that encumbered her movement and reeked of sweat, and more recently, sex.

"Come over here," Elinor said, and Kit hurried to comply. She handed Kit a gold disc with a glass face that reflected the light that filtered in through the window. Beneath the glass was a tiny needle, painted red, that moved and spun as Kit turned it, always springing back to point the same direction. "Look at the map, and tell me if the ship is going the right way."

Kit felt her cheeks go hot as she looked from the map to the instrument in her hand. "I don't know how. I haven't been sailing long enough." She tried to hand it back to Elinor, but the captain didn't reach out to take it.

"Look here," Elinor pointed to the corner of the map. "Then look at the compass."

Kit squinted at the little symbol, faded on the weathered parchment. "It's the same."

"Exactly. The needle of the compass always points north, and the map tells us which way we need to go. If we need to go south, the needle should point...?"

"Behind us?"

Elinor smiled. "So are we going the right way?"

"Aye, it looks that way," Kit said. "Why are you showing me this?"

Elinor pushed the chair back from the desk and went to a cabinet built into the wall. She pulled out a bottle of rum and two small glasses, filled each, and handed one to Kit. "Because you remind me of me."

It was the last thing Kit had expected to hear. Elinor raised her glass, and Kit mirrored her, drinking the sweet rum in one swig. "What do you mean?"

"You're bold. Reckless, even. I understand why you did what you did, because— were it any ship but the *Revenge*— I would have done the same. And you bore your punishment like a woman. I was proud of you. Whether we find them alive or not, I won't hold it against you any longer." Elinor refilled the glasses. "You have the potential to be a captain, Kit, but not the experience. So I'd like to teach you."

Kit had never pictured herself as a captain. It seemed impossible. Elinor had only been able to do it because she'd spent almost her entire life aboard a ship, but Kit had been sailing for less than a year.

"You don't look convinced," Elinor said. "Of course, I can't force you to learn. You can go back to swabbing the deck and running powder, if that's what you prefer."

"No, I want to, it's just a lot to take in." She'd gone to Elinor's cabin fearing the worst, and was taken aback by the grace the captain was giving her.

"Change your clothes and let's walk. I'll wait outside."

Kit finished her last sip of rum and set the glass down on the desk before finally stripping free of the tattered dress. She stepped gratefully into the breeches, and found they fit her almost perfectly. The sleeves of the shirt were too long, but she could roll them up. They weren't clean by any means, but they were far cleaner than what she had been wearing, and smelled vaguely of sea water, as though someone had attempted to wash them at some point. Feeling like a new woman, she stepped out of the cabin to join Elinor.

Kit was amazed to see the difference in the crew from their first bumbling night on the *Fury*. Everyone had settled into their roles and to an outsider, it might have seemed if they had been sailing for years together. She looked to Elinor. "How did you do it?"

"You have to find the balance between fear, respect, and inspiration. They have to want to do it, and want to do it for you because they believe you'll lead them to their riches. I'll admit I had my doubts about them, but they're strong, and eager to learn. They all came for a reason." Elinor handed Kit the compass again. "Which direction is the land from here?"

Kit looked off the side of the ship at the mass of land that seemed to stretch forever along the horizon, and then down at the needle. "South and west from us."

Elinor nodded her approval. "You learn quickly. That's a good quality for a captain."

Kit tailed Elinor the rest of the afternoon as Elinor explained the intricacies of sailing that Kit hadn't yet been exposed to. She saw Lisbet only once throughout the day when their eyes locked across the deck and Lisbet blushed a flattering shade of pink. Kit felt a stirring between her legs, recalling the night before, and imagined how she would give Lisbet the same exquisite pleasure as soon as the sun set and they descended to their hammocks.

It was for the best that that was the only time Kit saw Lisbet, otherwise she wouldn't have been able to focus on the things Elinor was teaching her. When she was finally dismissed from the captain's tutelage for the day, she rushed to find Lisbet. Most of the crew had gathered at the stern to watch a shooting demonstration by Mona, and Kit found her among them, watching with rapt attention. Kit would never have guessed the soft-spoken, warm woman was such a sharp shot, but she handled the flintlock pistol with ease as she fired off round after round, reloading faster than Kit had ever seen.

"Pretty good, isn't she?" Kit said, sidling up to Lisbet.

"Good?" Lisbet's eyes lit up when she noticed Kit. "She's the best. Haven't you heard? She saved Elinor's life with an impossible shot."

"Do you think we could ever be like them one day?"

"Mona and Elinor?"

"Their life seems so perfect."

Lisbet flinched as another shot tore through the air and Mona's ball hammered home, shattering the empty bottle she'd set atop a barrel. "I'm sure they have problems too, everyone does."

Kit reached down to intertwine her fingers with Lisbet's. "Can I ask you something?" She lowered her voice to a whisper, but no one around them was listening anyways. They were all lining up for their turn to try to outshoot Mona.

"Anything," Lisbet said, squeezing her hand.

"Reddy said... I don't know if it's true...Liss, is there anything between you and them? Anything intimate?"

Lisbet stifled a laugh. "Between me... and Mona and Elinor? No, never. It's never even come up. But I won't lie to you, I have known Elinor that way in the past. She paid for my services a time or two, years ago."

Kit already knew that, but she appreciated the honesty from Lisbet. It made it easier to believe everything else she was saying. "They're all going to be distracted with this shooting competition for a while. Come on, I know somewhere we can go."

Chapter 17

L ISBET FELT LIKE A teenager again, sneaking off with Kit while everyone else's backs were turned to do forbidden things away from watchful eyes. A shiver ran down her spine at the exhilaration, and she stifled a giggle as they clambered down the hatch.

"This way," Kit said, her eyes gleaming mischievously in the red light of the setting sun that slipped through the deck and the portholes.

"Should we really be doing this?" Lisbet asked. Elinor had made the rules of the ship clear, and she didn't want to run afoul of them again. But at the same time, her desire burned so hotly she couldn't deny it. Every moment not wrapped in Kit's arms seemed like a moment wasted, and Lisbet wasn't willing to forgo another opportunity.

"I know somewhere they'll never find us," Kit said breathlessly. "But they won't come looking."

Lisbet opened her mouth to remind Kit that Elinor and Mona knew the ship as well as anyone, but Kit stopped her with a kiss, pushing her against the curved wall of the ship's hull. Kit's fingers curled into Lisbet's hair and

and she urged her mouth open with a hunger that bordered on desperation. Lisbet's whole body was hot, emanating her desire as she submitted to lust.

"In here," Kit said, pulling away and opening a door. The hinges squealed, but the sound was drowned out by a shot on the deck above. They entered the ship's storeroom and Kit pushed the door shut with one hand as she pulled Lisbet close again with the other. "God, you don't know how much I need you."

Lisbet's body was humming, and every stroke of Kit's hand only served to set her further aflame. Across her waist, around to the small of her back, and then lower to grip her ass. She gave in to all of it, thrusting her chest forward as if to beg for Kit's touch on her nipples. Her knees felt weak, like they might collapse if not for Kit's hand holding her up. Her breasts throbbed, desperate to be soothed by Kit's warm kiss, but Kit's mouth was still pressing down on hers, unyielding. Finally, just when Lisbet thought she couldn't bear the agony of denial any longer, Kit's hands drifted to the hem of her shirt. Lisbet gasped as the rough garment passed over her sensitive peaks. Kit's mouth clamped down with the same rough affection she had doted on Lisbet's lips, and Lisbet sank onto one of the crates in the vast storeroom, unable to stand any longer. Kit knelt in front of her, sucking one breast as she massaged the other until soft whimpers escaped Lisbet's lips.

"Shh," Kit quieted her. "We don't want to be found out."

The risk of being discovered only added to the exhiliration of the moment.

Kit's other hand moved to the crotch of Lisbet's pants, lazily stroking the seam between her legs. Lisbet could just barely feel her touch through the supple leather, teasing and tantalizing, and she thrust her hips forward in hopes that Kit's caresses would become firmer. Kit chuckled as Lisbet's body betrayed her need, then moved to the waistband and tugged the trousers down to Lisbet's ankles. Lisbet leaned back, supporting her weight on her hands as she opened herself to Kit. She felt like a goddess, wanton and pagan, one of the false idols that parents warned their children against. Men may have laid their coins at her altar, but Kit knelt reverently and offered her soul.

"I wanted to do this last night," Kit said huskily, and plunged her face between Lisbet's legs.

Lisbet yelped in surprise at how sensitive she already was. Kit's tongue flicked lightly out, lapping circles around Lisbet's clit until her hips were grinding against the crate and she was engorged with arousal. The sensations jolting through Lisbet's body were almost too overwhelming, but she missed them as soon as Kit moved lower to thrust her tongue into her.

"Don't stop." Lisbet held Kit's head in place, entwining her fingers in the short hair that suited her so much, and pulled her face back up. The vibrations of Kit's throaty chuckled made her quiver in anticipation, and Kit resumed licking her nub with renewed vigor. The pressure inside Lisbet was building, building, building until it consumed her entirely. Kit slipped a finger inside her, then a second, thrusting them slowly until Lisbet's thighs were quivering. She was closer to the edge than she had been in a long time. Her legs shook uncontrollably as the warmth spilled out, seizing her inner muscles and drenching Kit's face as she lapped up the liquid with delight.

Lisbet felt like she had just been dropped into a hot bath, all her worries melted away into a puddle of warmth and wet beneath her. The warmth filled her with something she had never felt before. Completion. Not just in the physical sense, though her body still quivered with ecstasy, but also emotionally. The words she had whispered to Kit in the dark the night before were true. She was fully, madly, profoundly in love with the rakish pirate, for better or for worse.

"Liss, what's wrong? Was it something I did?" It was only Kit's concerned voice that snapped Lisbet out of her reverie, and she realized she was crying.

"Nothing is wrong," Lisbet panted, still out of breath. "And it was everything you did."

"I don't understand. Tell me how to fix it." Kit reached up to wipe the tears flowing freely down Lisbet's face.

"No one but you has ever done that to me," Lisbet said. "They all take their pleasure from me, but none have offered it in return. I'd forgotten how good it could be."

Kit's smile was barely visible in the dark storeroom, but she looked pleased with herself. "I'll remind you anytime you like." Another shot rang out from the deck. The competition was still ongoing. "We should get back before they notice we're gone. I'll go up first, so no one sees us together." She kissed Lisbet on the lips, then bent to Lisbet's still-exposed breast and kissed it as well, sending new jolts of longing into Lisbet's core. She moaned, and Kit pulled away. "Anytime you like," she said with a smile.

"Kit, wait," Lisbet called as she scrambled to pull her shirt back down and her trousers back up.

Kit paused by the door. "Yes?"

"I love you," Lisbet said. "I want to be us again. Together. I don't want to have to live my next five years without you in my life."

"I want that, too." Kit smiled. "More than anything. But we don't have to figure it out tonight."

As soon as Kit shut the door behind her, Lisbet's tears began to fall again. She knew Kit wasn't walking away from her because she wanted to, but it didn't change the fact that Lisbet was alone. All she wanted was to be held for a spell, have her hair stroked and soft words whispered in her ear. She wanted to be allowed to feel in love, not hide it. But she shuddered to think what Elinor would do to Kit, or her, if she ever found out. She understood why Kit had to walk away. She didn't understand why she hadn't said 'I love you' back.

She shouldn't have mentioned the men she'd been with. Kit was without comparison, and the topic always made her jealous. It had been a terrible idea to bring it up in her moments of purest bliss, but the words had slipped out before she thought of how they might hurt Kit. She had a habit of doing that. She would have to find a way to make it better, to let Kit know she was all Lisbet desired.

Lisbet waited until her cheeks had cooled and the sound of pistols firing ceased before making her way back up to the deck. Mona spotted her as she climbed out of the hatch and waved her over to the stack of crates she and Elinor were perched on, eating their supper. The rest of the crew had found their own spots to tuck into steaming plates of beans and salt pork.

"Go get your bowl and sit with us," Mona said. "I feel like I've barely seen you since we set sail."

That was by design. Lisbet was still disappointed with her friend for refusing to intervene on Kit's behalf, and had been avoiding her as much as possible on the small ship. Kit put on a strong face, and she refused to let Lisbet even see the wounds she had caused, insisting she was well on the mend. In spite of Lisbet's irritation with her friend, the request still felt like an order with Elinor sitting beside her, and Lisbet begrudgingly complied.

"So, how are you finding the voyage so far?" Elinor asked.

"I think the land is more to my liking," Lisbet said diplomatically. She didn't want to complain, and she didn't regret helping her friends, but the work on the ship was more than she cared to do. She found herself missing her simpler days in Nassau, where the food was plentiful and good and the work wasn't so endless. The only thing *Iseult's Fury* had that Nassau didn't was Kit.

Lisbet scanned the deck, finding her immediately. She was resplendent, practically glowing in the lantern light that bathed her in warmth and made her eyes sparkle as she laughed with Avery's men and Maggie. She fit in so well among them, only making Lisbet feel more inadequate in comparison. She knew she should stop staring before it became obvious to Mona and Elinor that the flame had rekindled between them, but it was so hard to tear her eyes away. Everything about Kit was perfect, and Lisbet ached to go to her, to fall back into the embrace that stopped time itself.

"Liss?" Mona asked, noticing where Lisbet was looking and giving her a knowing smile. "I asked what you think the cats are doing without us?"

"Having to make their way actually hunting the rats they were put on the island for," Lisbet said with a laugh. She missed Pendragon, but she wasn't worried about the surly creature. He would surely fend well enough for himself until she returned. She was more concerned about finding the crew of the *Revenge* and clearing Kit's name.

"Do you suppose they'll be angry at us for leaving?"

"They're cats, Mona, I would expect nothing less," Lisbet said dryly. She wondered how many days away they were from where the *Revenge* was lost.

Elinor laughed, and Lisbet saw shades of her old friend hidden beneath her tough captain's exterior. It was so hard to forgive her for hurting Kit so cruelly, even though Kit herself seemed to have moved past it, having spent the whole day with Elinor. Yet another reason Lisbet couldn't envision a life aboard a pirate ship. Their code of morals and ethics— of fairness— made no sense to her.

The realization stabbed like a knife through her heart. Their world was too foreign to her, and hers too incomprehensible to them for anything between Kit and Lisbet to ever work. Perhaps that was another reason why Kit hadn't returned the declaration of love. She had already come to understand they were too incompatible for one another. Their lives were too different. And one thing was certain for Lisbet– she didn't want to return to a life of secrecy and sneaking away, living in constant fear of being caught and what the repercussions would be. If she was going to love Kit, she wanted to do it honestly, openly, not constrained by the rules set by someone else.

And that was all she wanted to do, for the rest of her days. If there was one thing Kit's return had taught her, it was that second or third chances were never to be taken for granted. Something had reawoken in Lisbet, and she began the happiness she had constructed for herself was nothing more than an illusion. She needed someone who would worship her with the love she deserved. A friend, a partner, a lover. Someone to complete her in every way. And she had never met anyone who fit her so perfectly as Kit.

Chapter 18

"IT WAS HERE," KIT said as she peered through the captain's spyglass. "Just on the other side of that spit of land."

"Are you certain?" Elinor snatched the tool from Kit and raised it to her eye. Kit pretended not to notice her slightly shaking hands.

"I'm certain," Kit said. "I remember that cluster of logs on the beach, under those trees growing from that rock. It was here." More than two weeks had passed since the *Revenge* had been set ablaze, and any traces of the black smoke that had billowed from it were gone from the serene beach in the distance, but the rest of the landscape was exactly as she remembered it.

"They weren't far from land."

"Almost close enough to swim," Kit confirmed.

Within an hour they were gliding past the spit that formed the mouth of a small bay. Goosebumps rose on Kit's arms. For as much as it looked like paradise, she feared they were sailing across a cemetary where she had dug all the graves. Mona had joined her and Elinor at the rail, squinting at the beach as though Tristan and the crew would appear if she just looked for them hard enough. Her white-knuckled hands gripped the rail as *Iseult's Fury* rocked in the choppy waves.

"Drop the anchor, lower the skiff!" Elinor yelled out orders from the helm of the ship. She looked as tense as Kit felt, and Kit knew they were both thinking the same thing. The chances of ever finding any of the men of the *Revenge* wear slim. But not impossible. "Kit and I are going ashore, everyone else is to stay here and ready the ship for battle."

"You're not leaving me behind," Mona said when Elinor walked over to join her and Kit at the rail.

"Captain's orders," Elinor said, pulling her wife close and kissing her. "You're needed on the ship, gunmaster."

Mona laughed at the title. "And what battle are you preparing for?"

"Whichever one may find you while I'm gone. This could be an ambush, or another ship may decide we look like a merchant whose load they're looking to lighten. One can never be too careful."

"But I don't want to be apart from you," Mona pouted playfully.

"It's too unsafe for you to come. We don't know what we'll find there." Elinor laid a finger softly on Mona's lips before she could protest again. "It's only a little while, my love. I'll be back before you know it."

Kit turned away, pretending she couldn't hear as Mona and Elinor's conversation descended into saccharine nothings. She caught Lisbet's eyes and rolled her own, evoking a smile. Sensing that Elinor and Mona wouldn't be done fawning over each other any time soon, she walked over Lisbet to say her own farewells.

"I wish she hadn't picked you," Lisbet said, reaching for Kit's hand, then pulling away suddenly.

"What?" Kit asked. She pulled Lisbet's hand back and raised it to her lips before intertwining their fingers together.

"We're in plain sight of everyone."

"So are they," said Kit, nodding to Mona and Elinor.

"The rules don't appear to apply to them. Elinor does as she pleases, but affords no one else that luxury." Lisbet frowned slightly. "Be careful, Kit."

Kit longed to lean up and smooth the two wrinkles of worry that appeared between Lisbet's dark eyebrows with a kiss, but she held back. "I will," she promised. "I have a reason to be now."

"Good," Lisbet said, smiling once more. "And when you get back…" She leaned in to whisper in Kit's ear.

Kit felt her cheeks burn hot at what Lisbet suggested. It took every ounce of willpower she had in her body not to grab Lisbet right there and then, drag her to the storeroom, and demand she demonstrate what she'd promised to do on Kit's return. "You're wicked," she said, shaking her head as she felt herself getting wet. "You've got me all bothered when you know I have to leave."

"I'm just making sure you miss me while you're gone."

"I've missed you since you left my hammock in the wee hours this morning," Kit murmured. Lisbet was entirely bewitching, and since she had cast her spell on Kit, she had been able to think of nothing else.

"Come on, Kit!" Elinor called.

Lisbet gave her one last sultry smile, then turned and sauntered away. Kit watched her go appreciatively before joining Elinor.

"After you," Elinor gestured to the rope.

Kit slid down and landed in the skiff with a thud. Elinor was right behind her, and they each took up an oar. The sea was calm, and the water clear as crystal when Kit looked into the depths below. There was a dark shadow on the sea floor, just barely visible against the dark blue of the deep water, but the longer Kit stared, the more recognizable it became. It was the tall mast of a massive ship, broken off to rest atop the sprawling reef of coral. Kit supposed the fire must have eaten it away before the ship sank. Kit looked further beyond, and saw what remained of *Nimue's Revenge.* She looked at Elinor in horror. The captain had tears in her eyes, and she knelt on the floor of the dinghy, staring at the seafloor as though she was in a trance. Elinor trailed her fingertips across the surface of the water.

"It's her," Elinor said. "My ship."

"I'm sorry," Kit said.

"You've apologized enough. She would be there if you were on her or not. I just didn't think we'd be able to see her, that she went down in such shallow waters. She's got a good resting place here, at least, in waters she's known since even before my time." Elinor let out a shuddering sigh. "Did Tristan at least give them a good fight?"

Kit nodded, and Elinor picked up her oar again.

They rowed towards the shore in silence, sliding easily onto the sandy beach. After pulling the skiff well out of the water, they both scanned the beach. There was no other boat intact on the sand, no other skiff that had been rowed to shore. The only sign of human life were the dozens of burned planks scattered about— pieces of the *Revenge* that had broken off and been washed ashore. Elinor bent to pick up a piece of charred timber the length of her forearm and nearly as wide and tossed it into their skiff.

Kit walked further up the beach, looking for any sign someone had come ashore. There were no footprints she could see in the sand, but that didn't mean there hadn't been. Two weeks was plenty of time for the wind to have worn them all away, if they were ever there to begin with. Elinor was still picking up pieces of scorched wood and loading them into the skiff, moving with the desperation of a woman trying to cling to an ethereal past. She had said she no longer blamed Kit, but the guilt still weighed heavily on Kit's heart and her hopes of finding the crew alive were fading.

Kit followed the curve of the bay as it stretched towards a narrow spit of land that jutted into the sea nearest to where the *Revenge* went down. If the crew had made it to shore, they wouldn't have stayed at the beach. They would have headed inland, in search of water and food, well out of sight if Payne decided to return. Kit squinted at the elbow where the spit joined the larger island. Something looked strange about the brush, but it was hard to tell from a distance. She jogged closer.

"Elinor," she yelled in excitement when she realized what it was. A path. Cut through the thick vegetation, the smooth breaks and fallen boughs could only have been caused by a human forcing their way through. "You need to see this."

Elinor dropped the boards she was holding and ran over to Kit. "This is recent," she said, her eyes lighting up with excitement as she inspected the hewn undergrowth. "Be careful, we don't know who made it."

Kit nodded and let Elinor take the lead as they entered the dense brush. The path meandered to and fro, as though whomever had carved it had no sense of where they were going. The forest was thick and lush, and seemed mostly uninhabited by humans, but for the ones whose trail they were clearly following. Elinor stopped and held up a hand, listening. Above the chirping of birds and buzzing of insects, Kit heard the faint sound of running water. The path curved towards it. Her heart began to race with anticipation. A few minutes later, Kit smelled a whiff of wood smoke on the breeze, faint but unmistakable. Elinor broke into a jog, and Kit knew she hadn't imagined the scent. Elinor had smelled it, too.

All the hope she had tried to abandon rushed back as they ran down the path. The dense foliage around them broke just over the next hill, and the sound of water grew from a trickle to a roar. Kit began to hear voices, distinct even above the noises of the dense forest and their own pounding footsteps. A laugh she recognized. She felt her face split into a smile. Reddy. They crested the hill, and descended into a ramshackle encampment filled with pirates.

"Ellie," Tristan cried in disbelief as she ran straight into his arms.

"Captain Davies," she corrected, grinning from ear to ear as tears streamed down her face. "I thought you were dead."

"Captain?" He raised an eyebrow. "I never thought I'd see the day when you took up a helm again."

"Nor did I," she laughed, "but my idiot friend lost his ship and needed a hand."

"How did you find us?"

"Kit led us to you. "

All eyes turned to Kit, who had hung back at the edge of the camp. She was sure they were none too pleased with her. Tristan beckoned her forward, and reluctantly she walked over to meet him.

He stared at her for a long moment, then reached for his waist and unsheathed a knife. Her knife. "You forgot this." He spun it around to grasp the blade, and offered her the hilt with a wink. "We'd be at the bottom of the ocean if not for you."

Kit took it, breathing a sigh of relief as she did. "Thank you," she said softly, not just for the knife but the apparent forgiveness of her sins.

"What do you say, gentlemen? Ready to sail home?" Elinor asked.

The crew of the *Revenge* cheered loudly and rushed at her, drowning her in their embraces. Kit marveled at the sight. She'd known Elinor was beloved as a captain, but she hadn't realized how deep the men's loyalty ran. Elinor emerged, laughing, from their pile of affection.

Reddy walked up to Kit, Diego right behind him. "Thanks for coming back for us," he said, opening his arms to offer her a hug.

"Of course I did," Kit said, forgetting to disguise her voice from them. It wasn't as though her secret would be maintained much longer, anyways; as soon as they returned to *Iseult's Fury,* the subterfuge would be spoiled. "I... have something I should tell you both."

"We already know," Diego said. "Tristan told us everything. Made a lot of sense after he said it. I just can't believe I didn't see it sooner."

Reddy still looked bothered. "You could have told us, though. We wouldn't have thought any less of you for being a woman."

"I'm sorry," Kit said. "For everything."

"Did you bring rum? That might help make up for it," Diego said.

Kit laughed. "There's plenty back on the ship."

If the men needed any more motivation to break their camp and hurry back to the beach, that was it. They had few belongings that they had salvaged from the *Revenge* before she went under, and within a few minutes the whole group was underway, following Captain Davies back through the jungle.

"Whose ship did you have to borrow to come rescue us, and how much do I owe them?" Tristan asked Elinor. Kit hadn't seen him stop smiling since they'd arrived in camp.

"I didn't borrow a ship," Elinor replied, raising her chin. "I took Payne's. Had to beg a few men off Avery that'll be expecting a purse after this, though."

"The *Bonny Lass?*"

"*Iseult's Fury,*" Elinor corrected. "We had to rechristen her."

Tristan grinned. "Mona?"

"Of course."

"Is she here?"

"I couldn't very well leave her in Nassau with Payne, could I?"

"So he's there?"

"I assume so, seeing as I took his ship."

"We'll have to deal with that, then."

"I already have a plan," Elinor smiled.

Chapter 19

MONA RAISED THE SPYGLASS to her eye again, looking towards the dark hole where Kit and Elinor had disappeared. Sighing, she collapsed the instrument and tucked it back into her pocket to resume her pacing. Lisbet walked the length of the deck beside her, just as anxious.

"They'll find them," she said to reassure herself as much as Mona.

"I'm they will," Mona agreed. "But I still hate to have her out of my sight."

"I know what you mean."

"I'm sure you do." Mona gave her a devilish smile.

"What do you mean by that?" Lisbet asked, playing innocent.

"As if it isn't quite obvious how you and Kit have been entertaining yourselves these past few days." Mona chuckled. "Don't worry, Elinor's not going to do anything as long as no one else figures it out."

Lisbet blushed furiously. "How did you know?"

"The way you look at her and have a conversation with your eyes, and then disappear for a spell together, then reappear separately with both of you practically walking on air. Anyone with two eyes and half a bit of sense could see what you've been doing."

Through her embarrassment, part of Lisbet was relieved that her dearest friend knew. She had been so desperate to talk about it, to share her joy with someone else, and having to keep the secret from Mona had been weighing on her.

"How is it?" Mona asked slyly.

"Like I was swimming underwater for too long, and finally came back up for air," Lisbet sighed. "I didn't know I could be this happy. It's perfect. She's perfect."

"I'm glad for you," Mona said. "Just don't get too caught up too quickly. I don't want you to get hurt."

"I won't."

"She's still a pirate. What will you do when you return to Nassau?"

"I don't know," Lisbet said. She hadn't thought about it, not seriously. It didn't matter. She and Kit would figure it out together.

"Just be careful," Mona cautioned, then her head whipped around. She pulled out the telescope again just as the movement on the beach caught Lisbet's eye.

"Is it them?" Lisbet asked. The distance was too great for her to identify the figures making their way across the beach.

"It's them," Mona said breathlessly. "They found them."

"Kit did it," Lisbet said. The impossible had happened. "It's a miracle."

"It feels that way." Mona was crying as she strode off towards the kitchen. "I can't believe it. We have to prepare them something to eat, and a hot grog. They'll all need it after this ordeal."

Lisbet followed her, eager to have something to do with her hands to expel all the nervous energy that had been pent up while she waited. Maggie joined them, helping to hammer the hard seatack into chunks to be soaked in broth that would make a filling, if unappetizing, gruel. Lisbet sliced limes and squeezed their juice into a vat that already held two full bottles of rum and a large scoop of coarse, brown sugar, keeping one eye out the door and on the little skiff that bobbed slowly through the waves. Even though Kit had only been gone a few hours, Lisbet had missed her more than she cared to admit. She stirred the grog, feeling the weight lift from her shoulders. Kit had kept her promise and exonerated herself, and Lisbet was free to love her.

All of a sudden, the deck burst into a flurry of activity as the skiff bumped up against the hull and the beleaguered men of *Nimue's Revenge* began to climb up the ropes. They looked better than Lisbet had expected them to after nearly three weeks of being marooned, but many of the men were gaunt shadows of their former selves, their cheeks sunken in and bones protruding where they shouldn't have. She rushed to bring them bowls of the hot gruel, which they took appreciatively as they sank down on crates to finally rest from their ordeal. Only after they had taken their first few bites did they begin to look around the deck, their eyes widening in awe. Lisbet knew exactly what they were thinking.

It seemed Elinor did too, because she quickly stepped to the front of the group and addressed the men. "Many of you sailed with me on the *Revenge*, and I'll have you know my expectations for conduct on *Iseult's Fury* are the same, even if her crew may look a little different than what you're accustomed to. No fighting, no gambling, and any man who lays a hand on a woman of this ship will lose it in payment, whether she wills it or not. Am I understood?"

The newcomers grumbled their assent, while still leering at the handful of whores among them. Lisbet couldn't help but smile at the loophole

Elinor left, and wondered if it was intentional. It had to be, otherwise Elinor and Mona would be afoul of the edict, too. She looked around for Kit and spotted her sitting between Reddy and Diego across the deck, listening intently to Elinor's words. She wouldn't meet Lisbet's eyes but she flushed red under her stare, and Lisbet felt the pang of hurt that came from being ignored. She tamped it down. Kit was allowed to have bonds with others, too, and Lisbet knew she wanted to make amends with the men who had welcomed her aboard the *Revenge* as one of their own. Still, she'd thought Kit might have missed her as much as she'd missed Kit.

"The men will move to the hammocks on the lower deck, and the women will share the cabins. Otherwise, this crew is like any other. Bagley will remain quartermaster, his command is to be followed as mine." Elinor smiled at Tristan, and then her wife. "Mona, you're being demoted. Tristan will take over as master gunner until we get home."

Tristan raised one dark eyebrow in question, but didn't ask anything as he folded his arms across his chest. Lisbet could tell he was less than pleased with the arrangement, but doubted he would say anything to contradict Elinor publicly.

"Well, what are you waiting for?" Elinor asked, clapping her hands. "Hoist the anchors, we're going home."

Lisbet didn't have a chance to speak to Kit again until a few hours later, as dusk began to fall and the ship picked up speed in the night wind. She stood at the stern, gazing back towards the island they were powering away from, her mind dwelling on Mona's earlier words. It was easy to love Kit on a ship, when they were near each other with no other entertainment and the real world of New Providence seemed so far away. But perhaps Kit had already grown bored with Lisbet. She certainly had seemed disinterested as she stopped to talk to everyone on deck except Lisbet.

It was quieter near the ship's stern, away from the men who crowded around the galley and the women who fawned over them. Lisbet wandered in that direction to stare off into the creeping fog that settled over the sea, making it appear as though *Iseult's Fury* was floating through clouds instead of waves. The night was calm and the ship rocked gently, a pleasant reprieve from the choppy waters that had turned her stomach earlier. She would be glad to return to land, but she worried Kit would want to stay at sea.

"You're deep in thought," Kit remarked, strolling up and startling her. "Care to share them?"

Lisbet turned away. "Wouldn't you rather be talking to your friends?"

"Are you really upset about that?"

"You didn't even greet me when you reboarded the ship."

"Liss." Kit glanced around the deck before wrapping her arm around Lisbet's waist. "I just don't want anyone to catch on to us. I was waiting for the right moment, when no one would notice."

"They already know. Mona told me they figured it out right away."

"And Elinor is going to allow it?"

Lisbet shrugged. "I suppose so, as long as we remain discreet. She did say if any *man* touches a woman, and we certainly aren't that."

"You know we're sharing a cabin now, right?" Kit slid closer, sliding her hand up Lisbet's wait to caress her breast. "And you promised me something. I've come to collect."

Lisbet squeaked at the sudden spark of arousal that flared when Kit touched her there. She wriggled out of Kit's grasp before she melted into it, across the point of no return. She had made Kit a promise, and she intended to deliver on it as soon as their cabin door was barred for the night. But that was later. She crossed her arms as Kit reached for another feel, the question still heavy on her mind.

"And then what happens to us? When we get back to Nassau, I mean."

"We keep going as we have been. Hopefully forever." Kit pulled at Lisbet's arms, trying to uncross them so her roaming hands could continue their work.

"Do you mean that?"

"Of course I do. I love you."

"But what about my work? You'll be jealous."

"You still want to go back to those men after me?" Kit asked, and Lisbet could see the hurt on her face.

"It has nothing to do with that," Lisbet insisted. "It's how I earn my coin. What we share can never be compared to that. It's you I love, but it's them that keep me fed."

"Because you still want to be with men."

"I want to be with you. See, you're already jealous. A pirate should understand that a coin is a coin, and we all come by them however we can."

"I don't want to share you."

"And are you going to give up pirating?" Lisbet asked, her temper flaring. "Or are you going to leave me behind to only love you a few weeks out of every year?"

"We could go together."

"I wouldn't be happy. I thought this life seemed exciting, but it's not for me. I can't obey senseless orders or live my life according to someone else's mandates. And I miss the land."

"We don't have to figure this out now," Kit said. "I'm tired and I just want to be with you."

"If this is just a passing amusement for you, then tell me now before I give my whole heart to you."

"Liss, I love you. I always have. And I want this more than anything. So we'll figure it out together, one day at a time." Kit tugged at her hand, and her heartstrings. "Let's go see our new cabin."

LISBET WAS IN A freefall, tumbling faster and faster with no way to stop herself and no desire to. Love was an even more powerful emotion than she'd expected, once she had set aside her fear and allowed herself to leap into it. Waking beside Kit each morning brought a sense of stability Lisbet had been longing for, a deep and fulfilling feeling that she finally wasn't alone. *Iseult's Fury* was more than amply crewed, and Lisbet began to enjoy the journey once the expectation of labor was lightened to what she considered a more reasonable load.

Nassau came sooner than she wanted it to, the island of New Providence appearing through early morning sea mist just eight short days after they reunited with the crew of the *Revenge*. It was a stark reminder that they had resolved nothing, come to no agreement. Sailing was Kit's calling, that was plain enough for Lisbet to see. She spent all her days shadowing Elinor, returning to Lisbet in the evenings overflowing with excitement about learning a new navigational skill or tying a particularly difficult knot.

Nassau was where decisions would have to be made. But before they could even contemplate that, there was still the matter of Payne. Elinor didn't think he would have been able to find a ship to chase them, so he must have remained on the island, waiting for her return to enact his revenge. She had devised a plan, as simple as it was brutal. And it was time for the crew to enact it, and neutralize the threat Payne posed once and for all.

"You should stay on the *Fury*," Kit implored as the harbor came into view. "It will be safer for you here."

"I want you to stay then, too. What if something happens?"

"Then I'll be in the company of the fiercest band of pirates to sail the seas," Kit said. "I have to do this."

"Why?"

"Because Payne is evil, and I want to personally assure he never has an opportunity to lay another hand on a woman or child again. And because Elinor ordered it."

"Then I'm going with you."

"Absolutely not. We're well armed and these are good fighters. You'd only be in the way."

Lisbet was hurt, even though Kit was right. She would be more hindrance in any battle than help. She couldn't stand the thought of waiting on the ship, though, ignorant of what would be happening on the shore until it was over. And if they lost, if Payne came to reclaim his ship... Lisbet's stomach turned at the thought.

Kit must have seen the look on her face. "Don't worry. Avery's men are staying here, and so are Mona and some of the other women. You'll be safe. They'll defend you if anything goes wrong."

"I just got you back. I don't want to lose you again."

"Trust in fate to bring us together, as it always has before."

There Kit went talking about fate again, as if their lives were all woven into some grander design, with no control over where their threads lay. Lisbet nodded anyway and squeezed her hand tighter. There was nothing more she could do.

Chapter 20

"I F THEY'RE EVEN HALF good at what they do, they'll be waiting for us," Elinor warned the crew gathered around her. "Payne will recognize his own ship in the harbor and realize we've returned for blood."

Indeed, bloodlust was in the air on *Iseult's Fury* that night. The thrill of anticipation sent a shiver across Kit's body. Maggie caught her eye and grinned. They were the only two women who had been selected to go ashore for the hunt, except for the captain. Kit couldn't help but feel it was a test, and all the men would be judging them for whatever happened. She hoped she would be the one to land the killing blow to Payne, though she knew she wasn't the only one with such aspirations.

She wasn't worried about the fight. They had the advantage in numbers, and the burn of revenge was a powerful motivator. She just wanted it to be over so she could turn her attention completely to Lisbet and to building what they deserved together. In the face of all life's uncertainties, there was one thing Kit knew was sure. She was meant to be with Lisbet. Why else would they have been born in the same village on the same island, thrown

209

apart and pulled back together? Their paths were as entwined as their limbs had been the night before.

"And if they surrender?" Reddy asked.

Elinor looked at Tristan, who shook his head. She nodded slightly. "No prisoners. No survivors. Their sins are so egregious as to be irredeemable."

The decree would receive no challenge from Kit, though she silently wondered if all the men of the *Bonny Lass* deserved the angry end that was spilling over rails of their former ship into the waiting vessel below. Payne was undeniably evil, but were all his men responsible for the misdeeds ordered upon them by their captain? Kit was glad not to be Elinor then, faced with the decision of who lived or died.

She swung her leg over the rail, taking one last look at Lisbet as she did. Staring back was a face with anguish written so clearly upon it that Kit almost abandoned the shore party to run to her. But she had to go, if only to see with her own two eyes that Payne would never cause problems again.

"Ready?" Diego asked from beside her in the skiff.

"I think so," Kit said, nervously fingering her knife.

"With Captain Davies, we can't lose. She's lucky, you know."

Kit wished she had his confidence. And his pistol. She was grateful the task of rowing because it gave her somewhere to direct her nerves, but each stroke brought them closer to the shore where she could already see men gathering, their weapons glinting menacingly in the moonlight. She looked around at the men in the boat wondering which of them were going to die, for surely they wouldn't all make it out alive. For the first time, Kit wondered if it would be her.

"It's him," Elinor confirmed from the front of the skiff, spyglass to her eye. "Payne awaits us."

His men formed a line on the beach, drawing their pistols and muskets as one and aiming at the little boat approaching the shore. Kit saw the flashes of gunpowder an instant before she heard the volley of shots, and then the balls began to hit the water around them, sending up a sizzle of spray that was too close for comfort. The men in the boat were readying their own guns to return the gesture as soon as their captain gave the command. Kit had never felt more useless in her life, or more vulnerable. There was still too much distance between the boat and the beach, and Payne's men would have ample time to reload and fire at least once more before they reached it. They were an easy target in the water, all clustered together. And she had no gun to loose on the waiting pirates.

"Fire!" Elinor ordered.

Her men let their shots fly into the night, and Kit saw one of Payne's men stagger and fall to the ground in the surf.

"Hold," Kit heard Payne's voice drift across the water, raising goosebumps on her arms. "Give up Davies and the rest of you will live!"

Elinor didn't even deign to respond, but Kit noticed her glance worriedly over her shoulder at the crew. None of them moved from their positions in the boat. None of them would betray her.

Tristan clapped a hand on her shoulder. "We're with you til the end."

Kit felt the unmistakable scrape of the skiff cutting through the soft sand below the waves as it ran aground in shallow water. Elinor pulled her cutlass from her waist and held it high in the air, screaming like a demon from Hell as she leapt off the prow of the skiff and charged through the surf. The men roared to life behind her as another volley of shots ripped through the night.

Kit's ears rang as she splashed into the waves, nearly losing her footing when the water was deeper than she expected. She kept her grip on the knife and ran towards the closest of Payne's men she could make out through the salt burning her vision, echoing Elinor's haunting scream of rage with a shriek of her own. The man paused as the briefest flicker of recognition flickered across his face, followed by confusion at her banshee's wail. Kit used the moment to her advantage, swiping forward with her knife as the man scrambled to free his cutlass from its scabbard. The extra second was all she needed, and she felt her blade hit flesh and tear through.

The wound was only enough to spark his rage, but not hinder him, and he pulled his weapon as blood streamed down from the recently opened gash in his arm. Kit darted to the side just in time to avoid the blade that sliced through the air a hairs-width away from her neck. She heard yelling around her as blades connected with their targets and men screamed in pain, but she couldn't see any of it. Her vision was closing in, leaving only a narrow tunnel locked on her man as he spun and slashed at her in a deadly dance.

Kit was tiring quickly, but so was he, and each swing of his sword had a little less strength behind it. Still, she was unable to push through his parries to sink her own blade home. He stabbed towards her and she jumped backwards, falling to the sand. It was a dreadful fighting surface, loose and shifting beneath her feet, and the misstep cost her an opportunity to strike. Luck was on Kit's side though, and her opponent stumbled as well, falling to his knees in the sand beside her. She lunged toward him, straddling him as he fell onto his back. The knife, already slick with his blood, shone in the sliver of moonlight that broke through the clouds.

"Please," he begged, eyes round with terror. "I surrender. Please."

No survivors. Elinor's words rang in Kit's head as she plunged the knife into his throat. Scrambling back to her feet, she became aware of the fight still raging around her. Elinor and Tristan were both in combat with Payne, pushing him further back from the shoreline as their blades sang through the night in perfect harmony. Someone grunted behind her, and she turned to see where she could help. Reddy was fending off an attacker with his fists, protecting Diego as he reloaded his pistol, spilling powder into the sand in his rush. Kit ran towards them.

Blood trickled from a gash on Reddy's temple, but he was still fighting furiously. Kit jumped into the fray, helping to repel the man swinging the butt of his pistol wildly in the hopes of catching Reddy in the head again.

"Move," Diego yelled behind them.

Kit and Reddy fell back to flank him as he raised the pistol and fired. Gunsmoke burned Kit's nostrils, and she heard the man's scream before the smoke cleared to reveal him motionless in the sand. The beach in their near vicinity was momentarily calm, and all the fighting had pressed toward the main road into Nassau. Kit bent over panting as Diego reloaded his weapon, taking the brief second to catch her breath before bounding over to rejoin the fight.

Half a dozen bodies lay still on the beach. Not enough. Reddy and Diego overtook her with their longer strides as they sprinted up the beach. A musket ball intended for someone else slammed into the sand at Kit's feet and she shrieked in surprise before dashing over to the treeline. It would be easier to sneak up on someone when she was creeping through the shadows. Her hands were shaking and her legs trembled with exhaustion. It was the longest fight she had ever been party to, and it seemed as though it was just beginning.

Kit didn't even hear the man come up behind her, thinking the faint rustle was her own movement through the overgrown vegetation. At first, it felt like someone had given her a hard shove right on the shoulder, and she stumbled forward. The pain hit her as she spun around to face him, a burning that spread from her shoulder down into her arm. Her fingers went slack, not of her own accord, and her blade tumbled to the ground.

It was the most pain she had ever felt, white-hot and blinding. She heard screaming in the distance, then realized they were coming from her. Blood ran down her back, trickling along her spine in a warm rush. The man who had just stabbed her was staring at her in horror.

"I didn't know," he stammered. "I thought you was one of them. I didn't know you was a woman. I didn't know." He backed into the shadows, but Kit knew he was still there, watching her. Waiting for her to die.

She reached for her shoulder, stunned by what had happened. Her fingers came away wet. The island of New Providence began to lurch beneath her feet, spinning like the waters trapped in an eddy and pulling her down. The pain came in waves, crashing down upon her and then receding only to pummel her again with renewed force. Kit knew with perfect clarity that she was dying. There was no one coming to help her. Only the soft sand beneath her. She closed her eyes, thinking of Lisbet. Kit had been so sure Lisbet was her destiny. She had been so wrong. All she wanted in her final moments was comfort that no one was there to give.

Kit had come to know death as a violent thing, doled out by the unmerciful on their quests for greatness. It surprised her how peaceful it was. The blood soaked night disappeared with all her pain as she was transported back to the field below the little village up the hill, verdant after the long winter rains. The sun shone brightly overhead, making Lisbet's hair gleam ahead of her. Lisbet turned back to smile at Kit, and Kit reached for her, pulling her close.

"Aren't you worried someone will see us?" Lisbet asked breathlessly.

"Not anymore," Kit said, kissing her deeply, as though it would be her last chance to do so.

Chapter 21

NO MATTER HOW MUCH Lisbet squinted and strained, all she could see on the beach was silhouettes grappling against one another as the sound of gunfire filled the air and shattered the peace of the cloudy evening. She couldn't tell who was who, or if they were winning. Mona stood beside her, wearing the same worried expression Lisbet could feel clouding her own face.

"I think that's Ellie," Mona whispered, pointing at a shadow moving up the beach. "Ugh, I can't tell from here."

"I thought it would be over by now," Lisbet said. The skirmish on the ship had been over in minutes, but the one happening on land seemed as if it had been raging for an hour.

"They know what they're doing," Mona replied, but she didn't look convinced.

Soft rain began to fall, splattering on the deck. Lisbet couldn't help but be reminded of the blood that had been spilled there, that was still stained into the wood in patches that would never disappear. A final shot rang out, and then there was silence from the shore.

"Were they victorious?"

"I don't know."

Waiting was torturous. Time seemed to have stopped entirely as shadowy figures clambered across the beach, stopping to kneel by those wounded or dead. Lisbet looked for Kit's tiny frame and graceful stride, but she didn't appear to be among those trawling the beach to rob the fallen.

"Look," Mona said excitedly.

Lisbet fixed her gaze on the spot Mona pointed out, but didn't see anything at first. Then, a wave swelled and the skiff crested it, rowing its way back to *Iseult's Fury.*

"That's Ellie, I'm certain."

The skiff held four occupants and Lisbet realized Mona was right. The captain was returning to her ship, triumphant. The other three in the boat were clearly men, even if Lisbet couldn't make out precisely who, and disappointment collided with fear in her gut, almost causing her to double over.

"Where are the rest of them?" She gasped, trying to quell her panic. "Are they the only ones who–"

"Stop that thinking right now," Mona hushed her. "Everyone else is on shore, tending to the wounded and making camp. You'll see her soon."

That was easy for Mona to say, with the woman she loved fast approaching. It was harder for Lisbet to feel reassured. She wouldn't stop worrying until Kit was safely in her arms again, holding her and stroking her hair and telling her everything was alright. That they would be alright. The skiff bumped against *Iseult's Fury,* and moments later Elinor's blonde head popped over the rail. Mona ran to her first, embracing her as though they had been apart a year, not an hour. Lisbet was right behind her.

"Where is Kit? Is she alright?" Lisbet asked before they even pulled apart.

"She's with Tristan and Maggie," Elinor said, her eyes telling Lisbet everything she needed to know.

"She's hurt," Lisbet said, feeling as though Elinor had just hit her in the stomach.

Elinor nodded.

"How bad?"

Elinor shrugged, and her brow pinched together in concern. "She was still breathing when we found her."

"How bad?" Lisbet asked, her voice rising in terror. It couldn't be good. Elinor was usually direct, but she was avoiding answering the question. Lisbet's heart hammered against the walls of her chest, and her stomach felt like someone had clamped it in a vice and was wrenching it as tightly as they could.

"She lost a lot of blood before we found her," Elinor said. "Her wound is deep. But they're looking after her. They'll do everything they can."

Lisbet sank to her knees, her anguish escaping her body as deep sobs. It couldn't be. Not Kit. Not when they had just found each other again, just begun to open themselves up to the potential of a life together, a future together. Mona and Elinor were beside her, each taking her by an arm and lifting her back to standing. Lisbet was too numb to feel any of it. She felt as though she was the one injured in the battle, her chest blown open and gaping as every daydream she'd had of true love trickled out to mingle on the deck with the falling raindrops.

"Liss, I know you're scared but you have to calm yourself," Mona whispered. "We'll go to her, but you have to calm down. You need your wits and your strength about you to climb down the ladder."

Lisbet would have dived into the ocean and swam to shore if that was what it took, she wasn't worried about a simple rope ladder. Yet when she threw her leg over the rail and tried to grasp the rung, her hand wouldn't close around it. She had lost all control of her body, consumed by grief and fear.

Mona covered Lisbet's hand with her own, molding the fingers in place around the rope. "One step at a time," she said gently.

The next thing Lisbet remembered was the skiff bumping up against the shore. The remaining crew must have followed her into the boat, because Avery's men were around her, pulling the skiff onto land. The other women were staring at Lisbet with concern.

"Thank you," Elinor was saying as she shook the hands of Avery's men and dismissed them. "I'll bring the coin owed to your camp in the morning."

Lisbet hovered near the boat, waiting for Elinor to finish. "Where is she?" She asked as soon as Avery's men cleared out.

"The tavern," Elinor said.

Lisbet ran as fast as she could, fearing the worst, fearing she would be too late. She needed to be at Kit's side, holding her hand and telling her all the things she'd held back. All of Nassau seemed to be in the street, drawn forth by the excitement of battle right at their doorsteps, and Lisbet wove through the crowd, elbowing people aside in her haste. She almost ran right into Tristan, who was striding down the road towards the beach, his face grim. The tightness around his eyes relaxed a little bit when he saw her.

"Good, you're here," he said, grabbing her by the arm and hauling her to the back of the tavern.

The table in the kitchen had been cleared of its normal stack of deep pots and dirtied tankards. A figure lay atop it, completely still and sickly ashen. Kit. Lisbet was afraid to look, but she forced herself to anyway, and breathed a deep sigh of relief when she did. She wasn't too late. Kit lay face down on the table, but her back rose and fell as she breathed. She was still alive, if barely.

"What happened?" Lisbet choked out, new tears blurring her vision as she gazed upon Kit's nearly lifeless body.

"She was stabbed," a man Lisbet hadn't even noticed said. He stepped forward, wiping bloody hands on a borrowed kitchen apron before offering it to Lisbet to shake. "Got her sewed up best I could, rest is in God's hands now."

Lisbet bristled at the mention of God and the reminder of the deeply faithful community that had rejected her and Kit. Perhaps if the village had accepted them instead of casting them out as sinners, none of it would have come to pass. Kit wouldn't be dying before her, with her helpless to stop it. God had done nothing for her, why would she trust him then?

"Who are you?" She asked angrily, wheeling on the man. Who was he to say there was nothing left to do?

"Murray was a surgeon on one of the crown's own naval ships," Tristan said, laying a calming hand on Lisbet's shoulder. "The best in Nassau."

"Is she in pain?"

"Not while she's sleeping," Murray said.

"I want to be alone with her."

Boisterous singing came from the main room of the tavern, but Lisbet barely noticed it as she crouched near Kit's head and took one clammy hand between hers. Her skin was so cool to the touch, but moist with clammy sweat. Kit moaned faintly at the disturbance, but didn't awaken. Lisbet swallowed hard, determined not to cry. If there was nothing else she could do to help, at least she could be strong for Kit.

"This is all my fault," she began, her voice cracking on the words. "We wouldn't be here if it wasn't for me. I should have listened to you all those years ago. I shouldn't have been so afraid." She stopped to regain her composure. "In truth, I would have gone my entire life without ever knowing real love if not for you. I need you. I can't lose you now." Lisbet squeezed Kit's hand, hoping against hope she would feel the gesture returned. Nothing.

Lisbet didn't know how long she crouched there, looking up every so often to make sure Kit was still breathing. Eventually she heard rustling behind her, then soft footsteps moving across the wood floor.

"We need to move her," Maggie said gently. "She'll rest better in a proper bed."

"Bring her to my house," Lisbet said. She had the distinct feeling that if she let Kit out of her sight again, the worst would happen. "I'll look after her."

"We thought you would," Elinor said, stepping into the room with Tristan close behind her. She had washed up and was much cleaner than the last time Lisbet had seen her, the blood on her face replaced with a thin, white bandage that wrapped around her head.

"The surgeon said you're to clean the wound often, with the strongest spirits you can find. Keep it from festering." Tristan stepped up to the table. "Help me roll her over."

Lisbet stood, her knees screaming in protest after having been locked in a crouch for so long. She barely noticed it. Was it just her imagination, or did Kit's fingers twitch ever so slightly when Lisbet's palm left hers? Even touching Kit was frightening; Lisbet didn't want to hurt her further. Gingerly, she helped turn Kit onto her back, supporting the injured shoulder with an arm around her ribs so it wouldn't hit the table. Tristan scooped Kit into his massive arms, making her look even smaller than usual. She groaned, and then her eyes fluttered open and she began to writhe in Tristan's grasp.

"Shh," he said gently. "It's just me. We've got you now, the fight is over."

"Put me down, I can stand." Her voice was shaky, but Lisbet heard the underlying strength. Kit was still fighting.

"How about you try sitting first?" Tristan lowered her back to the table, keeping a steady arm at Kit's back.

"Liss. What are you doing here?" Kit asked, noticing her for the first time since waking.

"I wouldn't be anywhere else. Oh Kit, I was so worried."

Kit smiled crookedly, wincing as she did. "I told you fate would bring us back together again."

"You're in pain."

"Of course I am, I just got stabbed."

"This will help," Maggie said, offering a glass that was nearly overflowing with the amber liquid. Rum.

Kit took it with her uninjured arm, which still trembled as she tried to raise it to her lips. Lisbet reached to help steady it, and Kit smiled again at her touch.

Kit was slurring her words by the time the crowd had cleared out of the kitchen, though she insisted on walking back to Lisbet's hut. Tristan accompanied them, and halfway through the short walk, Kit began to lean heavily on him as the fatigue of her ordeal set in. She staggered into the house and lay face first on the bed, moaning slightly as she jostled her shoulder. Lisbet rushed to her.

"Be careful," she chastised, "You don't want to make the injury worse."

"I can think of something that would make it better." Kit was slurring her words as she turned her head to look at Lisbet. "Come here."

"Kit!" Lisbet blushed furiously. Tristan was still hovering by the door.

He chuckled and gave Lisbet a knowing smile before bowing out and closing the door behind him. Kit giggled on the bed. The color had returned to her cheeks, and though her eyes were bleary with drunkenness, they sparkled as she looked at Lisbet.

"Take that off and come join me," Kit demanded.

"Really? I'm sure that's not a good idea. You need to be resting."

"I don't care. I need you." Her eyelids began to droop.

"I'm right here," Lisbet said, climbing into the bed beside her. "And I'll be here tomorrow, and the day after, and then when you've healed a bit we can do whatever you want."

"Whatever I want?" Kit yawned.

"Mhmm," Lisbet hummed, then wrapped her arm around Kit's hips, taking care she was well away from disturbing the freshly stitched wound on her upper back. Kit sighed happily and her breathing settled into the rhythmic pattern of a person enjoying a deep slumber.

"DAMN IT ALL," KIT swore as the knife slipped through her fingers to stab into the ground again.

"Try again," Lisbet encouraged. Three weeks had passed since the fight, and while Kit's wound hadn't festered and she was well on the mend, the struggle of relearning how to use her arm was a growing source of frustration for Kit.

"So I can fail again? I'm not ready."

"Well, are you ready for this afternoon?"

"I suppose so," Kit said, sitting down on a stump in the yard and wiping her brow with the back of her hand. "What do you think Elinor is going to announce?"

"Probably that she's giving the *Fury* over to Tristan." What would become of Elinor's newly acquired ship had been the source of rampant speculation in Nassau, with some rumors saying the famed captain would take the helm again and rejoin the growing band of pirates in their reign of terror across the Caribbean. Lisbet thought that was unlikely. She and Mona had had an ideal life before the *Revenge* was lost, and if she knew them as well as she thought she did, they would both be eager for a return to normalcy.

"Do we really need to be there for that?"

"Of course, it's a celebration. Don't you want to be with your crewmates when it happens?"

"They're not my crewmates. I'm done pirating. Look at me. I couldn't if I wanted to."

"You'll be strong again someday. I think the real reason is you're hiding from them." Many members of the *Revenge's* crew had come by to see Kit in her recovery, but she had refused every one of them.

"Why would they have me back? I betrayed them, then failed them in battle."

"You didn't fail them. You were wounded fighting with them. And all of them have transgressed in their lives. You may have betrayed them, but you saved them, too. And Tristan has already been by to ask when you'll be fit to sail."

"And what about you?" Kit asked.

"The sea is your calling, I won't hold you back from it."

"You'll get lonely while I'm gone."

"Absence will make your returns all the sweeter. Besides, I have Mona and Elinor and the cats to keep me company."

"And all the men of Nassau," Kit muttered.

"What was that?" Lisbet felt her temper flare up. They hadn't talked about her profession at all during the weeks since their return to Nassau. She had been too focused on Kit's recovery and their bliss at being together at last to even consider it. "Don't you trust that I love you? After all this?"

"I do, but even if what you do with them isn't love, it still makes me sick to imagine. They don't see you, they don't understand that you're meant to be worshiped, not used for their pleasure. They don't deserve you. And I'm frightened you'll meet one you like and forget about me."

"You don't have to worry," Lisbet said. "I don't intend to go back to that. I wouldn't be able to, not now that I've found you again. Your love is worth more than any gold."

"Then my love you shall have." Kit's eyes darkened with lust as she stepped towards the house. "I can think of a way we can work on strengthening my shoulder before the announcement."

"Oh?" Lisbet asked innocently, as if she didn't know what Kit had in mind. Her insides clenched with anticipation.

"Let me show you." Kit planted a firm kiss on Lisbet's lips beneath the frame of the doorway. Wrapping her weak arm around Lisbet's waist, she pulled her to the bed.

Chapter 22

"WE REALLY HAVE TO go now, we're going to miss the whole announcement," Lisbet murmured as her fingers moved lazily inside Kit.

"I don't want to. Let's just stay here instead." Kit gasped, feeling Lisbet's thumb slide across her clit. It was almost too sensitive to bear, already tender from the attention Lisbet had lavished upon it.

"I promised Mona." Lisbet pulled her hand away and wiped Kit's juices from her fingers before turning to run a comb through her disheveled hair.

Kit thought she was the most beautiful she had ever been in that tender moment of disarray following a long bout of lovemaking. Her tousled waves framed her face seductively, cascading over naked shoulders and a back that glistened with sweat. Her breasts hung heavy, nipples in the halfway state between pert arousal and softened relaxation, and Kit longed to reach out and pinch one to see it rise into a stiff peak again. She nearly groaned with desire as she imagined the excited squeak Lisbet would emit if she did. But alas, Lisbet was right. They needed to go.

Kit stretched, her shoulder twinging as she moved it around. Every day brought a little less pain, but she was frustrated with how long it was taking and was beginning to wonder if it would ever feel the same again. She could live with a bit of pain, though. The ship was waiting, and since she finally knew Lisbet supported her return to seafaring, she was eager to know who would be captaining the crew she hoped to remain a part of. Especially since she no longer had to worry about Lisbet straying from her in her absence. A flicker of doubt nagged at her as she rose to get dressed. It was easy for Lisbet to say she would be faithful while Kit was standing right there, but she could always change her mind as soon as Kit was away. But Lisbet had seemed sincere, and Kit decided she needed to trust her.

After all, it was Lisbet who had been by her side through her convalescence, changing the dressings on Kit's wound and lavishing her with attention. It was Lisbet who cried at her pain and held her until it melted away. Living with her was comfortable, and Kit savored every moment of learning each other's routines. It was easier than ever to imagine spending an eternity next to her. Kit was just waiting for the right time to ask Lisbet to become her wife, waiting for the moment when she was sure the answer would be yes.

Kit clung to Lisbet's hand as they meandered through the streets of Nassau. The outward display of affection was such a little thing, but Kit's heart swelled with pride to so clearly signal that Lisbet was hers. A man whistled at Lisbet, but to Kit's delight, she didn't even turn to look at him. By the time they arrived at the beach, small crowd had already gathered in the yard at Elinor's supply shop, waiting to hear what the two captains had to say. Elinor and Tristan stood on the porch, both dressed in what looked to be their finest garb, striking figures of fearsome wealth and power.

"I've decided to keep *Iseult's Fury*," Elinor began to speak just as Kit and Lisbet arrived. "For now. As a ship to train sailors who wouldn't otherwise have the opportunity." She looked at Kit and smiled.

The crewmen murmured to each other in shock and confusion. They quieted when Tristan stepped forward.

"I'll be finding another ship soon," Tristan said, "and I'll need a good crew with me. But I understand if none of you care to wait. I appreciate everything you did for the *Revenge* and for me."

"You were wrong," Kit whispered to Lisbet playfully. In truth, she was just as shocked as everyone else standing in the yard.

"I'm glad to be," Lisbet said. She looked excited. "There's no one better to teach women to sail than Elinor."

"You think that's what she meant?"

"I *know* that's what she meant." Lisbet gestured to the crowd, and Kit realized Maggie was there, along with two other of the women who had sailed on the rescue mission. "Why shouldn't we be sailors? Well, not me, of course, I hate it. But there are plenty of women who don't."

"Tristan looks none too pleased about it." Kit noticed. He was standing on the porch with his arms crossed, scowling uncharacteristically as his men shouted questions at him.

"I suppose he'll have to get over it," Elinor's voice behind them startled Kit. She had snuck up on them. "I gave him one ship already and we can all see how that worked out. He'll have to find his own this time." She laughed, looking pleased with herself. "But enough about that, Kit, I trust you're recovering well?"

"Well enough," Kit said, flexing and rolling her shoulder. Pain shot down her arm, but she stifled her grimace.

"Good. I thought we might sail in the morning."

"So soon?" Lisbet asked.

"Just a short one, around the island. We're not on the hunt for gold, just learning the ropes. A day at sea, maybe two, so I can see how you manage without seasoned crewmen about."

Kit balked at the suggestion. As much as she tried to pretend the fight hadn't affected her, the memories of dying in the sand still lingered. And she still couldn't swing a knife without dropping it. But she knew the longer she waited to get back to sea, to get back to being a buccaneer of the Caribbean, the harder it would be. And if she waited too long, she might never return to what she loved.

"Tomorrow will be fine for me," she said. Lisbet squeezed her hand in encouragement, picking up on the hidden waver in her voice.

"Good." Elinor smiled. "If there's truly to be a republic of pirates as they're saying, we need to be ready to claim our seat at the table. Where we deserve to be. We can't leave all the gold to the men."

Kit nodded, and Elinor walked away to speak to someone else in the crowd. She wasn't sure she deserved to be at any table with how poorly she's done in the battle. All she'd wanted was to give the final killing blow to the man who had caused her and so many others such anguish, but she hadn't even been conscious to see it happen. Seeing his head driven into a stake in front of Elinor's house– a clear warning to other pirates that Captain Elinor Davies was not one to be trifled with– felt like a hollow victory.

"Come, let's stop at the tavern for supper," Lisbet said, linking her arm through Kit's and giving her a peck on the cheek.

The weather was even more perfect than usual that evening, with only the faintest of breezes rustling the palm leaves overhead as they walked. Kit leaned in to lay her head on Lisbet's shoulder, soaking in their island of calm amidst the street's debauchery.

"Lisbet, Kit, wait!" Maggie called behind them, jogging to catch up. "What did you make of Elinor's announcement?"

"It was surprising," Lisbet said, "but I'm happy for it. And I assume you'll be joining?"

"Elinor just asked if I wanted to." Maggie beamed with joy. "Of course I said yes."

"But who will run the tavern?"

"I might sell it, I haven't decided yet. I just feel like the ship is where I'm meant to be. Like my father, before he met my mother."

"He would be proud of you," Lisbet said.

"I hope so." Maggie gestured for them to enter the tavern before her. "Sit, I'll bring food right over."

The room was already crowded with pirates who all seemed to be gossiping about the same thing: Captain Davies's decision. Kit and Lisbet sat across from each other at the end of a table near the back. Three men sat at the other end, and turned to stare at Kit and Lisbet. His face broke into a slow smile, devious but not unfriendly.

"You're on Davies' new ship, are you not?" He asked.

"I am," Kit said, sitting up taller on the bench as she swelled with pride. It was such a change from the first time she had been in the tavern, desperate to hide who she truly was and trying to escape attention. She smiled at the memory that seemed so distant, glad that she was finally free to be her true self.

"Well, I would wish you calm seas and gentle winds, but alas." The pirate shrugged. "I already wagered a hundred silver pieces you'd be lost at sea."

The other men laughed. Kit felt her smile falter and her determination harden. They didn't think she could do what they did, but she and the rest of Elinor's crew would prove them wrong.

"Only a fool would place a bet against Captain Davies," Lisbet said lightly, but Kit could see the annoyance in her eyes.

"It's not Davies I'm doubting, it's the rest of them. Whores and housewives have no place on these seas."

Kit rolled her eyes and turned back to face Lisbet, ignoring the mens continued jeers. She wouldn't let them get to her.

"Are you nervous about tomorrow?" Lisbet asked softly, taking both her hands across the table.

"Of course I am," Kit said, "what if I can't do it anymore?"

"Elinor wouldn't have asked you if she didn't think you could."

"I'm just glad I have you. I wouldn't even be here without you. I wouldn't have any of this." Kit smiled. So much had changed, not just with Lisbet, but with everyone. Lisbet and Mona and Tristan and the rest of the crew had visited her regularly, checking in to make sure she was recovering well. Tristan had even offered her the same pay he gave Avery's men and the other women who had sailed to save the crew of the *Revenge*, insisting she take it no matter how much Kit tried to refuse. But most importantly, they accepted her exactly as she was. She had never been happier in her life. "I understand it now, why you call them your family."

"Much better than ours ever were," Lisbet agreed, squeezing Kit's hands. "We finally found our place."

Maggie dropped off steaming plates of rice, beans, and warmly spiced seafood, but Kit was too lost in Lisbet's gaze to notice. Her face glowed with excitement for Kit's new adventures, and her smile was brighter than the lanterns lighting the tavern. Kit couldn't believe how lucky she was to have all her dreams come true all at once. They held hands across the table, and, even though they were surrounded by people, Kit again had the sense that she was alone in the world with Lisbet.

Lisbet giggled. "The food is going cold."

"I don't mind," Kit said. She never wanted to let go of Lisbet, even if the smells rising with the steam of the hot food were most appetizing.

Lisbet gave in first and pulled away. "I could hold on to you forever, but I fear I'd starve to death."

Kit followed her lead, realizing how ravenous she was when the first spoonful hit her lips. A few tankards of ale did wonders to loosen the stiff muscles of her shoulder, and by when a ragtag band of buccaneers struck up a jaunty tune, she and Lisbet rose to dance. Their feet moved quickly, matching the pace of the lively jig as Kit held tightly to Lisbet's waist and spun her around the floor. It was everything she had ever dreamed of, and no one could stop them.

She saw the hand before she saw the man, reaching out to clasp Lisbet on the shoulder mid-whirl. It wasn't unusual for men to approach Lisbet when they were out, and Lisbet always chased them off quickly, telling them she was no longer for hire. But Kit's heart sank when she looked up and realized who the hand belonged to. Andrew, the village boy who had stolen Lisbet's heart so many years before. Kit blinked. It couldn't be him. But looked exactly like him, just older. He same thick jaw and bushy brow, the same contemptuous stare. It was him. And in the space between three heartbeats, her world came crashing down.

"I've been looking for you for days," he said, still gripping Lisbet's shoulder.

"Go away, Andrew, I'm not interested."

"I think you will be," he said, then turned to Kit. "Run along boy, she has no use for you now." He hadn't recognized her.

Kit looked at Lisbet, desperately hoping that Lisbet would tell her what she was seeing wasn't real. It was as though all her nightmares had come to life before her, the moment she feared was upon her. "Lisbet?" She choked out, her heart pounding with dread. There had to be an explanation. There had to be a mistake. It couldn't be happening. Not again.

Lisbet didn't say anything, though her cheeks flushed a deep crimson that gave Kit all the answers she needed. She looked terrified as her eyes darted from Kit to Andrew, each with a hand on her as if to lay their claim.

"Wait a moment," Andrew said thoughtfully, "I know you, don't I?"

"Leave her alone," Kit said, feeling for the knife at her waist.

"Little Katie Murphy, isn't it?" He smiled, though the gesture looked more threatening than friendly. He had never liked her, even before Lisbet had involved herself with him. "Didn't know you'd come back to Nassau. I must say, I liked to better when you hadn't. So, run along."

"Run along?" Kit spit out, rage rising. Who was he to speak to her like that, and what was Lisbet still hiding? "Why is he here?" She asked, certain she didn't want the answer but needing to know it all the same.

"Kit, you should go," Lisbet said.

"Go? Why?"

"Because she wants me more." Andrew's words stabbed her more painfully than the knife she had taken to the shoulder. He sneered. "Just like she always has." He wrapped his other arm around Lisbet's waist, then reached up to grope her chest.

"That's not true," Lisbet insisted, but she didn't push him away. "Andrew, what's this about?"

"Your sisters," he said without elaborating further. "Come with me and I'll tell you everything that's happened."

"No, you can tell me here."

"That's not our arrangement."

Kit's head was spinning, and it wasn't just the ale. Lisbet had never mentioned she was still in contact with Andrew, or that they had any arrangement. And knowing Lisbet, knowing her past, there was only one thing the arrangement could be. Kit's heart felt like it was shattering, and she looked down in a daze, expecting to see her own blood spilling across the floor. Surely there was some mistake. Lisbet would explain, and then everything would be fine.

"Lisbet, what is he talking about?" Her voice trembled with rage when she was able to speak again.

"Kit, I'm so sorry."

That wasn't what she wanted to hear. She didn't want an apology that all but confirmed her suspicions, she wanted denials. She wanted to hear that it wasn't true. Why wasn't Lisbet telling Andrew to go away? Kit should have known better than to be fooled twice, in the same manner by the same person.

"It's getting late," Andrew said, stepping backwards and pulling Lisbet away with him. "We need to go."

Lisbet reached for Kit's hand, but she pulled away. "Listen. I need you to listen. This is nothing. I'll explain everything later. Just go home and wait for me."

"Don't go with him," Kit said, her voice breaking.

"I have to. Please, Kit, believe me." Lisbet's face crumpled and she looked on the verge of tears.

"No. Don't go. If you do, all of this is done and you'll never see me again. I can't do this again."

"I'm sorry." Lisbet's face said she truly meant it, but that her mind was set and there was nothing Kit could say to change it.

Getting stabbed was less painful than watching Lisbet turn away from her to Andrew. Kit wished they would have let her die there in the sand. At least she would have died knowing love, instead of being fated to relive the same heartbreak all over again. Maybe it was God punishing her, as her parents had sworn he would do when they discovered her desire to be with women all those years ago. Or maybe it was Kit's own fault for believing the wrongs of the past could be righted, for believing that people could change.

If Kit still had any question about what Andrew was there for, it was answered when Lisbet linked her arm through his, leaning in and batting her eyelashes as the anguish disappeared from her face she transformed back into another one of Nassau's whores. Kit should have known better, but she had always been one to trust blindly, even when her instincts were screaming at her otherwise. She needed to learn to listen to them more.

Men and whores whirled around her as the band struck up another merry reel. Kit stumbled off the dance floor, torn between wanting to drink every bottle of rum in the tavern until she could think no more and a need to escape from the tavern, the island, and any memory of Lisbet. Drinking was the easier option, so she flagged down Maggie and asked for a bottle of rum to be brought over to the table. Then she stared at the empty spot where Lisbet had been sitting only moments before and waited for her relief to arrive.

"Is everything alright?" Maggie asked with a concerned look as she set the bottle down. "You look terrible. Where's Lisbet?"

"She chose a man over me. Twice." Kit's voice cracked on the last word, and she quickly washed the rising tears away with a long pull from the bottle. Fortified, the words spilled out and she told Maggie everything in a cascade of grief and disbelief. How Lisbet had abandoned her for Andrew after Kit gave her everything, their reunion, and their attempt to rekindle a fire when they should have just let the embers burn out.

When she was done, Maggie closed her hand around the bottle and took it back. "I know it hurts, but you can't numb it with this. We have an early morning tomorrow on the *Fury*."

"I'm not going," Kit slurred. "What's the point? Who am I doing it for, if I don't have her?"

"For yourself," Maggie said. "You love it, don't you? Sailing, fighting, living as they do?" She nodded to the pirates around them.

Kit nodded miserably. What did it matter if she loved it? Everything she had loved before had hurt her.

Maggie looked her up and down, then let out a sigh full of pity. "Come on, then. I'll make you a place to sleep in the house. I'll not let you miss this opportunity because of all this, or you'll come to regret it."

Kit didn't argue as Maggie led her through the back of the tavern and across the yard to the small house that stood behind it. Maggie steered her onto a stool and she sat with her head in her hands wondering where it had all gone wrong, why her love hadn't been enough to make Lisbet stay. Such a useless emotion, love. It never ended well. Maggie went into one of the rooms and emerged with an armful of blankets. She folded one carefully and laid it out on the floor beside the stool.

"I'm sorry I can't offer something more comfortable," Maggie said, holding out a second blanket for Kit to take. "But I suspect you're drunk enough you won't mind."

"I just wish I could have been enough for her." Kit tried to stand, but the room was spinning and her knees wouldn't hold her up. Maggie caught her by the waist and pulled her close, helping her stand. She was warm and smelled of spices and freshly baked bread, a testament to the hours she toiled in the tavern.

"There are other women out there who want the same things you do," Maggie whispered, her full lips inches from Kit's. "Women who would never consider leaving someone as remarkable as you for a man."

The intensity of her gaze was enough to confuse Kit. Was Maggie saying what she thought she was saying? She was beautiful, Kit couldn't deny that. Her dark skin glowed warmly in the flickering candlelight, and her deep, brown eyes almost seemed to be staring into Kit's soul as she waited for a response. She was alluring, and Kit was tempted to give into the flash of desire that sparked in her. But Kit soon realized her desire wasn't born of lust, but of a need for revenge. A need to prove that, despite the rejection, she was still worthy of affection. Maggie's hand at her waist tightened, pulling her closer as her mouth lowered towards Kit's, waiting for her to close the distance.

"I can't," Kit said, turning away before her drunkenness led her to decisions she would regret. "It's too soon. I still love her."

"I know," Maggie said, letting her go. "But one day it will hurt less, and when that day comes..." She trailed off as she helped Kit lie down on the makeshift bed on the floor. "You're stronger than this, Kit, you'll be alright."

The floor was hard and the blanket a poor substitute for a mattress, but what Kit missed most of all as she fell asleep was Lisbet's arms around her. A feeling she would never know again. Finally, the tears broke free and she sobbed, mourning the loss of the dreams she had clung to for far too long.

Chapter 23

"I DIDN'T KNOW KATIE was back on New Providence," Andrew said. His arm was still wrapped possessively around her waist, and his tone was triumphant.

"She goes by Kit now," Lisbet said defensively. And she didn't want to think about her. She knew she might have just ruined everything, but she just needed a chance to talk to Kit. She would understand once she knew everything. She had to, because Lisbet couldn't lose her again over someone as detestable as Andrew. "Is something wrong with my sisters?"

He shrugged, ever playing his game. "You give me what I want first, then I'll tell you. That's always how we've done this."

"I hate you," she said as he pawed greedily at her decolletage.

"So you say. Don't you remember what you said last time we met?"

"No," Lisbet said honestly. So much had happened since then, and when she had made her promises to Kit she had been so caught up in the whirlwind of love that she hadn't even considered that she would have to stop seeing Andrew to honor them. When Kit was near, Lisbet forgot everything else.

"You said you would do anything I wanted for more time with your sisters. Did you mean it?"

"What are you offering?"

"More time. Yes or no?" He didn't offer any more specifics. He never did.

"Yes." Lisbet glanced around. There was no one in sight; they were well away from the main part of town and no one was likely to happen across them there. She bent forward, bracing her palms against the trunk of a tree.

"No," he said, "turn back around." Lisbet heard him undoing his belt. "I want to look at you while you beg."

LISBET'S EYES WATERED WITH pain and shame. Andrew hadn't held back on her promise to do anything he pleased, until— just as he had predicted— she'd begged him to stop. Across the hundreds of men she had known, none had made her feel so degraded or humiliated as Andrew had that night. She swallowed, trying to rid herself of his thick, salty taste that still coated her mouth. She still had a performance to put on for him, still had to tell him what he wanted to hear so he would uphold his end of their agreement.

"When can I see them?"

He sneered. "I don't think you've earned it yet."

"What else do I have to do?" She asked warily. He'd already taken every part of her and left her so sore she didn't even know how she would manage the walk back to her house. What more could she give? And at what point was it no longer worth it?

"Anything I want, wasn't that the arrangement?"

"And I just upheld my side of it."

"That paid for their food the past week, since your mother died."

Lisbet stared at him in stunned silence. Her mother, dead? It was the last thing she had expected to hear.

"Oh, you didn't know?" He mocked. Of course she didn't know. There was no one to tell her but him. "Your sisters are living with me now. My wife was reluctant to take on the extra mouths to feed, but I convinced her it would be the most pious thing to do. Charity to orphans, you know?"

"How did she die?" Lisbet asked. She didn't even care, but the question would buy her more time to process everything else he had just revealed to her. Her sisters were living with Andrew. It wasn't right. They were her family.

"The girls said she was out of sorts one evening, complaining of a wicked headache, and the next morning they couldn't wake her. God must have determined it was her time."

Lisbet wished he would stop talking about God as if he was an example of piety after he had just violated her body and spirit to fulfill his carnal whims. "I'll take the girls. I wouldn't want to burden your family any further."

"You'd have them if you'd married me. They'll be better with us in the village, where they can learn and grow to be proper women. Your den of debauchery is no place for two young girls. And I'll let you see them whenever you'd like."

Of course he would, as long as she paid for it with her body. She realized that was the only reason he'd willingly taken them in. It made her easier to manipulate. All he had to do was threaten them, and she would do anything to appease him. She couldn't say no, or they would have no one left to protect them. They were all alone in the world now, and they needed her, however she could be there for them. Even if it meant she lost everything. "Tomorrow?"

"Tomorrow you can earn their next week's food, and then maybe we can discuss a visit."

"Earn their food?" She echoed, dazed.

"Unless you don't want them to eat. Two more mouths are expensive in this time of want."

He was the vilest person Lisbet had ever met. "I'll see you tomorrow then."

"Sunset, at the storehouse," he clarified. "Oh, and Lisbet?"

"What?"

"Do tell Kate it was lovely to see her again."

She watched him leave, checking the shadows to make sure he wasn't lingering in wait to follow her home. It was the one sanctuary she still had from him. She spat on the ground, wishing his taste would leave her. It had all been too good to be true, and she knew Kit would never accept her bending over for Andrew's every whim. But she had no other choice. Her sisters were relying on her, even if they never knew it, and she couldn't abandon them.

Each step was misery. And he expected to do it to her again tomorrow. She didn't know if she could bear it, but then she realized she wasn't expected to. He was going to break her, thoroughly and completely, take everything she had to give, and maybe even kill her. He didn't still care about her after so many years, though he might have believed he did. Deep down, Lisbet knew there was still a part of him that hated her for the embarrassment she had brought to him and his family. Her humiliation was his goal, his revenge.

Kit wasn't at the house when Lisbet arrived, and she didn't return at all that night. She might normally have been glad to not have Kit see her in such a state of emotional disarray, but Kit's threat to never return weighed heavily and Lisbet only longed to be folded in her arms once more. The later the hour got, the more it seemed Lisbet was to be cut adrift again, marooned alone on an island of discontent with no hope of closure. She was starting to believe in Kit's idea of fate, though instead of being fated to be together, she thought it was more likely the opposite.

She woke before the sun and considered going down to the harbor to see if she could catch Kit before *Iseult's Fury* left on its first journey around the island with Elinor's hand-selected crew. But it was better to give Kit a few days to cool off and calm down before Lisbet tried to offer an apology. Even if their love wasn't going to win out, she wanted Kit to know her reasons. She wanted Kit to know she loved her. And more than anything, she wanted Kit to succeed on the voyage and win Elinor's approval. She deserved it all, and Lisbet would only be a distraction. Yes, it was better for any conversation to wait.

Lisbet went outside and checked the plate of pork she'd left on the stoop before she and Kit had left for Elinor's announcement the day before. Their moments of joy already seemed so distant. Irretrievable. The plate was empty. There was no way of telling if Pendragon had eaten the scraps, it could have easily been any of the other cats on the island. He seemed to have been avoiding her, as cats were sometimes wont to do, but she knew he was around because she'd seen an orange streak disappearing into the garden when she opened the door some mornings. It seemed even he was mad at her.

When she was certain *Iseult's Fury* had left the harbor, she made her way down to Mona's house. Her mind was set. It was time to end Andrew's reign of terror over her once and for all. Her sisters deserved better than to be used as tools for his manipulation. She deserved better, too, she realized. The happiness she had felt the past few weeks with Kit was worth fighting for one last time.

"Heavens, Lisbet, what happened to you?" Mona asked as Lisbet rounded the house and entered the cat yard.

"Does it look that terrible?"

"Aye, it does," Mona said. "Your neck's all brown and blue. Who did this to you? Not Kit? I noticed you didn't come to see her off this morning."

"Not Kit," Lisbet said quickly. "Someone else from my past." She took a deep breath, anxious over what she was about to share. Mona was one of her closest friends, but Lisbet still worried she would be judged for it. Oh well. She couldn't hold the secret in any longer. Exhaling, she told Mona everything from how she had first taken a silly, teenage liking to Andrew and how he had become her occasional client, trading information for having his lust sated between her legs. Lisbet's voice cracked as she spoke about his demands of her body, and she cried anew telling Mona the control he had over her sisters. "And he wants to see me again tonight."

"No," Mona said adamantly, pulling Lisbet into a secure embrace. "You're not going to him, tonight or ever. Never again will he hurt you like this."

"But he could still hurt my sisters. I need to get them away from him, away from the village."

"And there's an entire pirate crew camped just across the yard that thinks fondly of you and is looking for work," Mona said, nodding towards the

Revenge's camp in the trees. "Come, let's find Tristan. He'll know what to do."

L ISBET GRIPPED HER SKIRT nervously as she walked up the hill. The sun had begun its descent lower toward the horizon, though dusk was still a few hours off. She had to be there early, to give no chance for him to arrive before her. Her stomach turned as she remembered Andrew's hands gripping her throat and robbing her of breath as he'd pushed into her and she broke into a cold sweat imagining it happening again.

"Are you alright, Miss Lisbet?" Diego asked politely from a few paces ahead, stopping to wait for her to catch up.

"Yes, of course," she said distantly. His presence was doing little to calm her nerves. There were still too many things that could go wrong, both at the storehouse and further up the hill in the village. Tristan had seemed confident in the plan, and his men were eager participants once they saw the state Lisbet was in. Still, she wondered if she was putting her sisters at too much risk by agreeing to it. But he'd sworn it would be simple, mundane for crew, and nothing would go wrong. She hoped he was right; she couldn't take another loss.

"I'll be near the whole time. He won't lay a hand on you, or I'll kill him." Diego withdrew his cutlass partway from its scabbard, showing off the gleaming metal with its freshly honed edge.

"I'd rather you didn't," Lisbet said. "He has a wife, and children, and I'd prefer he focus his attention on them instead of me. But I don't want him dead."

Diego shrugged and raised an eyebrow, a mannerism the young pirate had almost certainly picked up from his captain. "I have my orders." He pointed up the hill and across the field. "Is that the storehouse?"

Lisbet nodded. The ruined building stood just a few hundred paces away.

"Then this is where we separate. But don't be frightened, I'll be watching. He won't hurt you."

Diego crept off to hide among the overgrown vegetation around the storehouse, disappearing from sight within minutes. Lisbet hoped Tristan had chosen well when he'd selected Diego to accompany her. He had grown into a strapping young man, tall and well-muscled from labor, but he was still just a teenager. But it was better than being alone, and his hidden presence was a comfort, no matter how modest.

Lisbet paced nervously in front of the burned shell of a building as she waited for the sun to set. Just as it turned from orange to crimson, Andrew arrived. He seemed cheerful, completely unaware of the trap that had been laid for him. Completely unaware that she was his bait, and she was about to put on the best performance of her life.

She stepped towards him, lowering her eyelids and looking up seductively as she ran a finger down his chest. "I missed you."

"Did you?" He looked surprised.

"Of course I did," she lied. "I always have. You were right. It should have been us married." She felt the bulge in his trousers stiffen and twitch against her thigh, and she pulled away as bile rose in her throat. Her job was to keep him talking, keep him distracted and away from the little village as long as possible.

"I knew your contempt for me was just an act. But I would never marry a whore."

Lisbet's face burned at the word, an insult when hurled from his lips, but she wouldn't let his smug smile bother her. She glanced towards the trees where the village lay hidden, wondering if Tristan and his handful of pirates had begun their foray to retrieve her sisters yet. The plan was simple. She had described the village to them as well as she could remember, and they would sneak in under the cover of darkness while she distracted Andrew and Diego protected her. The sky had already darkened to an indigo befitting of the rich and royal, and the first stars were beginning to twinkle to life overhead. The party in the woods would be descending on their prey soon

"Look," she said, pointing up the heavens.

"What?" He followed her gaze skyward.

"It's beautiful, isn't it?"

"I suppose. I didn't come here to look at stars with you, though." He stepped towards her, reaching to fondle her breasts as she pulled away again. Anger flashed across his face, and his tone turned threatening. "Stop wasting my time, woman. You owe me a service, don't make me take it from you."

Diego leapt from the vegetation, nearly silent as he landed on his feet between them. "No, it is you who will stop," he ordered Andrew, jabbing forward with his cutlass. "On your knees."

"What's the meaning of all this?" Andrew demanded, looking at Lisbet as he complied. "Do you know him? Another jealous lover, perhaps?"

"A loyal friend," Diego corrected before Lisbet could reply. "And you will not harm her again if you wish to live."

"Tell him to remove his blade or you will never see your sisters again," Andrew threatened. "I'll have them sent away to earn their keep on their own in the Colonies."

"Hold your tongue if you'd like to keep it," Diego said, and Lisbet got the impression he was rather enjoying the opportunity to dole out orders. He pulled a strip of cloth from his pocket and began to bind Andrew's feet. "Go to meet your sisters, Lisbet. I'll keep him here until Reddy comes for me."

Lisbet nodded, and her hands began to shake as she realized it was over. As soon as she was reunited with her sisters, Andrew would hold no power over her. There would be nothing he could use to manipulate her any longer. She inhaled, the night air refreshing and cool as it filled her lungs. She was free.

A shot rang out from the forest, but she didn't have time to wonder who had fired it as she raced back down the hill to Mona's house. That was the rendez-vous point where she would be reunited with her sisters. Another shot echoed in the distance. It sounded like the village was giving more resistance to the invading pirates than anticipated. Lisbet hoped no one was seriously injured. As much as she resented the villagers, it was never her desire to see them hurt. Or worse. She couldn't fault them for not understanding her and Kit. There were few who did.

Mona welcomed her in, pressing a warm cup of tea into Lisbet's hands as she ushered her to a seat. Lisbet took a sip and nearly choked on the liberal nip of rum Mona had added to the drink.

"I was hoping they'd have arrived already," Lisbet said, glancing anxiously at the door. "It's well past dark."

"They'll come," Mona said as if she knew it to be certain.

"They don't even know who I am." The reality of her situation was setting in. The last time she had seen her sisters, neither had recognized her. "They'll be terrified. They'll think they've been kidnapped by pirates."

"But surely once you explain–"

"How am I supposed to explain who I am? They'll never believe me. Oh, God, Mona, how am I supposed to look after them? I've no idea how to be a parent." Lisbet was beginning to panic. She was no person to take on the care of children.

"We'll help you." Mona slipped another splash of rum into Lisbet's drink. "You won't have to do this alone."

"Nassau is no place for children," Lisbet countered. It wasn't safe, her life wasn't stable enough. And she didn't want them exposed to the seedy doings of pirates, or see that the only place for women in Nassau was to sell themselves for men's pleasure. "I don't want them to follow the path I did."

"They won't," Mona said. "Elinor can take them on the ship sometimes, and I'll teach them to read and write and do calculations. You aren't alone, Liss."

"I don't want them to be pirates, either. I want them to be children, free of worry and despair." Lisbet sighed, knowing her sisters had already had too much of that in their short lives. "I want them to be happy."

"And that's why you're suited to look after them. Because you love them, and you want the best for them. No decisions have to be made today about the future. There will be time aplenty for that in the tomorrows. And we'll always stand by you, as you've done for us."

Footsteps pounded across the porch, and Mona rushed back across the room to open the door. Tristan stepped in, sweaty and ragged-looking, holding Adeline. More of his men were right behind, shepherding in Charlotte, who looked around the room with wide eyes. Lisbet rushed over to take Adeline into her arms, laughing and crying as she brushed the hair back from her little sister's face.

Charlotte glared at her. "Leave my sister alone, you rotten buccaneers." She stamped her foot, a tiny vision of ire surrounded by dangerous men thrice her size.

The men in the room laughed at the childish insult, but Lisbet's heart went out to her sister. "We're not going to hurt you," she said softly, so as not to spook the suspicious child. "We're going to make sure you're well cared for."

"I can care for Addie just fine," Charlotte said, raising her chin defiantly. "I'm the elder sister. It's my responsibility."

"Oh, Lottie," Lisbet said. The girl looked startled by her use of the casual nickname. "You may not remember me, but I'm the elder sister. You are my responsibility, and I finally have you back."

"Our oldest sister died," Charlotte crossed her arms. "Five years ago."

"No, I didn't." Lisbet winced, knowing the truth she was about to share would hurt both girls. But they needed to know. "Our parents lied to you. They didn't want you to know about me because they were disappointed in some of my actions then. But I'm here now. And I'll never leave you again."

Chapter 24

"NOT LIKE THAT," ELINOR said impatiently, taking the rope from Kit's hands. "I've shown you this twice already, and this is one of the simpler knots. You make me wonder if you even want to be here. I thought you heard the call of the seas."

"I do," insisted Kit, embarrassed that she had left her mind wander again during the demonstration.

"Then what's gotten into you? You've been distracted ever since we left Nassau, and I need you present. We can't sail with this small of a crew and not have everyone fully committed. You're putting us all at risk."

"I am committed," Kit said, yawning. And she was. But she felt like she hadn't slept in days. Every time she closed her eyes, she pictured Lisbet turning to Andrew and her heart broke all over again.

Elinor set the ropes down and leaned on the railing. "But you aren't the Kit I saw the promise of a captain in. Are you sure everything is alright? Have you changed your mind about a life of piracy?"

"No," Kit admitted when it was clear the captain wasn't going to let the issue go. "It's Lisbet."

"No need to worry about her while we're away. Better to have her safe in Nassau than fighting at your side," Elinor said with a grim smile. "Believe me."

"It's not that. She chose someone else over me."

Elinor immediately looked like she regretted prying. "That's unexpected news. You seemed so happy at supper last week."

"We were. But then he turned up at the tavern, and she went with him without even hesitating."

"A man?"

"Not just any man, the one she left me for before. She told me she could explain, but I don't even know if I should give her the chance to do so. What explanation could there even be?"

"What does your heart want?" Elinor asked.

"Her." Kit's answer was swift, without thinking. "Always her. But not like this."

"Then listen to her when we return to Nassau. I've known Lisbet for a few years, and I know her to be a good person. Hear her explanation and then decide if your heart is truly broken. But for now, I have something else to distract your thoughts." Elinor waved Maggie over to join them and retrieved two wooden cutlasses from a crate on the deck.

Kit groaned. Her body already ached from Elinor's grueling notions of training, and her wounded shoulder was sore from a morning spent climbing rigging and trimming sails. But Elinor was right, the mock combat would be a good distraction, and Maggie was a worthy opponent. The other women gathered around to watch and wait for their turns.

The fake wooden blade was too light and too bulky to properly mimic a real cutlass, but it did have the advantage of being far safer to train with. Kit shifted her weight onto her back foot as Maggie mirrored her stance. Elinor raised her arm, signaling the start of the contest. The movement distracted Maggie and she glanced off to the side, giving Kit an opening to strike. Driving off her back foot, she lunged, thrusting the blade towards Maggie's torso. Maggie responded just in time, parrying the blow away and spinning to the side. Kit was thrown off balance and stumbled forward into the space where Maggie had been. She had expected her strike to land, and didn't know which way to turn next. Maggie's blow glanced across her lower back before she could recover, and the contest was over as quickly as it had begun.

"Quickness is nothing without a plan. Kit, you had none. Go again," Elinor commanded.

Kit flushed at the rebuke. She hated training on the cutlass. It was an elegant weapon, but she was an inelegant woman only further hobbled by her mending injury. She missed her knife, the short blade that was so comfortable in her hand that it almost felt like an extension of her. But Elinor insisted she learn. Sighing, she sank back onto her hind foot again and raised the weapon before her.

The second time Elinor gave the signal, Maggie didn't flinch. The two women circled each other slowly, each waiting for the other to pounce first. Maggie's eyes darted to Kit's left hip a tiny motion that betrayed Maggie's intention a heartbeat before the wooden blade arced through the air. Kit blocked the strike without looking, the swords clattering together as she pushed Maggie back and away. The effort made her shoulder throb, but she ignored the pain. She wasn't going to lose a second time. Maggie struck again, and Kit repelled her, spinning with the momentum of her blade and striking before Maggie could recover. Kit began to press, knowing she needed to end the bout quickly before her shoulder gave out. Putting a little more force behind each strike, she knocked the blade from Maggie's hands and thrust the wooden tip of her own into Maggie's stomach.

"Better," Elinor said, nodding her approval, then motioning for the next two women to step into the circle.

Kit handed off the wooden sword, grateful Elinor hadn't insisted on a third round. The underworked muscles of her shoulder seized, and she rubbed it as she stepped back to observe the next fight. Two by two, the other women on the ship took their turns practicing combat, with Elinor breaking in to demonstrate techniques and offer praise or criticism. None of them were as skilled as Kit or Maggie, and Kit felt a small rush of pride. Maybe she had redeemed herself a bit with the stern captain. It surprised Kit how much she wanted to please Elinor, and show she hadn't made a mistake in showing Kit leniency before.

After everyone had taken a turn at wielding the cutlasses, Elinor called Kit into her cabin for another lesson in navigation, followed by supper, more practice at tying knots, and then, finally, bed. Lisbet didn't cross Kit's mind again until there was nothing else to think about when she lay in her hammock below deck, confronted by the silence of night. Kit ached with questions unanswered, and she knew Elinor was right. She needed to hear Lisbet out, even if it was just to gain closure from it all. If closure was even possible after she'd been played for a fool twice before. One question burned stronger than the others, fueling a flicker of hope. What had Andrew meant about Lisbet's sisters?

The next morning, *Iseult's Fury* blew off course, a mistake Kit suspected was intentional when she saw Elinor's broad grin as she instructed the women in righting their direction. It was the crew's most difficult challenge at sea yet, and it took everyone working together to wrangle the sails to catch the wind that would send them back into Nassau's harbor. Little by little, they brought the ship back around, and by afternoon Elinor was giving the order to drop the anchors and lower the skiff. The impossible had come true, and a crew composed only of women had made a successful voyage around the island.

A crowd gathered on the beach to greet the skiff as news of their return spread, and Kit wondered how many men had gambled away too much of their gold betting on the *Fury's* demise. They would be sorely disappointed, and those who had wagered on the women would need new belts to hold up their pocketfuls of coin.

Kit scanned the faces as the skiff ran ashore, but didn't see the one she was looking for. That was for the better, she wanted to talk to Lisbet alone and avoid a confrontation in front of everyone. Tristan greeted Elinor with a bottle of rum, calling for a toast to the newest pirate crew of Nassau, and a second for Captain Davies. Kit drank when she was passed the bottle, thanking Reddy and Diego half-heartedly as they congratulated her on the voyage.

"Where's my wife?" Elinor asked Tristan with a worried look on her face, and Kit realized Mona was also absent from the beach celebration. "I thought she would be here."

Kit stepped closer to listen to Tristan's response. As close as Lisbet and Mona were, it wouldn't surprise her if they were together.

"A lot has happened since you left," he said vaguely.

"We weren't even gone three full days. What could have possibly happened?"

"Not here," Tristan pulled Elinor away from the crowd, then noticed Kit eavesdropping. He motioned for her to follow. "You may as well come, too."

They didn't have to walk very far up the beach before Kit realized what Tristan was referring to. Lisbet and Mona were in the cat yard filling dishes of water while two young girls ran around, chasing cats and laughing as the startled felines darted away.

"Tristan? What have you all gotten into?" Elinor asked warily. "Whose children are those?"

"Lisbet's sisters," Kit said softly, recognizing them immediately. Even though Kit hadn't seen them in years, they still looked just like Lisbet. She couldn't believe how big they'd gotten. The flicker of hope grew brighter. Maybe Andrew's sudden appearance was less of a betrayal than she'd thought. He'd said he needed to see Lisbet for some matter regarding her sisters, and Kit found herself hoping she had too hastily jumped to conclusions. Elinor was right, she needed to at least give Lisbet a chance to explain herself.

Mona waved happily as the trio approached. Elinor jogged over to her wife, lifting her off her feet in embrace and spinning her around. Kit wanted to run to Lisbet and do the same, but Lisbet still hadn't even looked at her.

"I made tea when I saw you rowing in," Mona said. "Come inside and we'll tell you everything that happened here."

Elinor and Tristan followed Mona inside, but Lisbet made no move to go with them. Kit stayed in the yard with her and the girls, not knowing what to say but not wanting to hear explanation from anyone but her. Lisbet sat heavily on a stump, and an orange cat climbed into her lap, purring loudly as she stroked his head. She closed her eyes for a moment and turned her face to the sun, almost looking to be in prayer. Kit noticed dark bruises creeping up her neck from beneath her collar as she stretched to the sky. The girls shrieked, and Lisbet's eyes fluttered open again. They were running happily after a small black cat, blissfully unaware of the awkward anguish that hung between Kit and Lisbet just across the yard. The black cat darted under the fence and out of reach. The girls turned their attention to a pretty calico lazing in the sun.

"Girls!" Lisbet called, and they both turned to look at her, noticing Kit for the first time. Charlotte stepped in front of Adeline and crossed her arms. "You're supposed to be helping, not terrorizing the poor beasts. Go draw up some water to finish cleaning the cages," Lisbet chastised.

"I assume they're Charlotte and Adeline?" Kit asked, gesturing to the girls.

Lisbet nodded. "They're in my care now."

"For how long?"

"Forever."

Kit listened closely as Lisbet told of her mother's death, the daring plan to save her sisters, and the longstanding arrangement she'd had with Andrew. She sat in silence long after Lisbet had stopped speaking.

"He did this to you?" Kit asked, her skin crawling at the thought of his hands on Lisbet. Her temper flared with Lisbet's nod of confirmation.

"I'm sorry," Lisbet whispered, interpreting Kit's anger as being towards her. "I didn't want to go with him. I never would have if he didn't have my sisters to use against me. And I never will again."

"I'll kill him," Kit vowed.

"No. It's over. Diego assures me he'll never be a problem again."

"Diego should have killed him." Kit reached out to cradle Lisbet's chin, tilting it up so she could see the marks Andrew had left there. It filled her with fury. Lisbet deserved so much better, and Kit felt guilty that she hadn't been there to stop him. She had formed her conclusions too quickly and believed the worst of Lisbet even after she had shown she'd changed.

"I asked him not to." Lisbet noticed Kit's scowl. "Not because I care for him in any way. I just don't want his blood on my hands. He has a wife and children of his own that rely on him."

"Let her come to Nassau and earn her own keep."

"She shouldn't pay for her husband's sins. She would never survive here."

"What are you going to do with them, then?" Kit looked at the girls again. "What good prospects do young girls have in this den of thieves?"

"Better prospects than they had in a dying village. They've no wealth nor title. Marriage was their only future. Now Mona will teach them to read and write, Elinor will teach them how to sail. They can have whatever future they choose."

"And what of our future?"

"I thought you didn't want that anymore."

"I never stopped wanting it." Kit sighed. She needed to be completely honest. "But I don't see how anymore. I understand why you did, but watching you go with him was the worst pain I've ever known."

"I never wanted to hurt you."

"Then why didn't you tell me all this about Andrew before? All the hours we spent in bed, talking about the village, talking about our lives since then, yet never once did it occur to you to mention that? That's what hurts Lisbet, just as much as what you did with him. But at least that I understand."

"I should have. But what we had was so perfect, and I didn't want to spoil it with talk of him. I knew it would only upset you, and I couldn't have that. Not while your were still recovering from the fight. I was going to tell you someday."

"If we're going to spend our lives together, I need to know these things. How many other arrangements do you have?" Kit dreaded Lisbet's answer, but she needed to know. The time for secrets was over.

"None." Lisbet grabbed both of Kit's hands and looked her earnestly in the eyes. Through all of her account of the ordeal with Andrew and rescuing her sisters, Lisbet had only stared vacantly out to sea. But as she stared at Kit, Kit saw the tears threatening to spill over. "You've given me more chances than I deserve, but I'm begging you for one more. I love you, only you, more than I've ever loved before. And yes, it frightens me, but I would rather face that fear with you at my side."

"I just have to know you're committed to me. No more hidden arrangements, no more men. Only us. And if that isn't enough for you, I understand and we can fully end this. I won't hate you for it."

"Never," Lisbet . "You're all I want, Kit. I swear. I'm in love with you."

Staring into her tear-moistened eyes, Kit finally believed her. She had no doubt it would be difficult, and there would be days when her jealousy burned so hotly it would be hard to control. There would be times when the past would rear up to haunt her with doubt that she would have to battle. But Lisbet was worth it, and Kit knew that time would heal the pain that still lingered in her heart.

"I love you, Liss. Forever." Kit sighed. There was still one thing they hadn't discussed, perhaps the biggest obstacle of all. "But I don't see how it will work with the girls. Are the four of us all to live in one room together?" And am I supposed to become a parent? She left the second question unasked. Motherhood was something she had never bothered to consider, certain it was out of her grasp. But she didn't think herself incapable. She had spent plenty of time minding the village children when she was growing up, and she didn't hate the idea. It was just sudden.

"I've already hired Tristan's crew to begin expanding the house. They'll begin as soon as they acquire the materials. It will be tight at first, until they finish, but we can sleep in a hammock outside together, just like on the ship."

"And what about us? Won't they be confused by two women in love? I don't want to have to hide anymore. I can't got back to pretending to be your friend until we can sneak away."

"What's confusing about love? Besides, children accept whatever you tell them. They already know that Mona has a wife and it hasn't bothered them at all. And that's what I hope to make you someday— my wife."

"I don't know if I'm ready. When I pictured us, I never pictured—"

"Raising my sisters? I'm not ready either, but all we can do is our best, one day at a time. The girls are old enough to look after themselves most of the time, and we'll have help from Mona and Elinor and the rest of the crew. There are other children for them to play with it town. We'll find a way to manage." Lisbet gripped Kit's hands as though she never intended to let go. "Don't you believe in fate? Don't you believe this is meant to be?"

Kit did, more than she believed anything. She leaned over to kiss Lisbet, wiping away her tears as she held on like her life depended on it. She was overwhelmed by emotions— seething rage at Andrew, fear for the future, confusion— but most powerful of all was the surge of love and longing that washed over her when their lips met. It felt like coming home. The rest they would figure it out together. As long as they had each other, Kit didn't care about anything else.

Epilogue

OCTOBER 1710

"A RE YOU APPREHENSIVE AT all?" Mona asked, running a coarse boar bristle brush through Lisbet's loose curls.

"I wasn't until you asked," Lisbet replied, fiddling with the sash tied around her waist. Committing her life to someone else wasn't an act she took lightly, but she was ready. Every day she had spent with Kit had brought more happiness than the one before it. "I wish we could have a real wedding, though."

"What do you mean, real wedding?"

"In the eyes of the church and the law," Kit said. As open as their community in Nassau was to the unconventional matches, it would never be recognized beyond New Providence. Neither the church nor the crown would see past their womanhood to witness the deep, abiding love they had cultivated.

"And what authority do they have over our lives?" Mona asked, setting down the brush to pick up strands of Lisbet's hair. Her fingers moved quickly as she pinned and tucked wisps into place. "I was meant to marry a man, a marriage that would benefit our fathers more than us. That marriage would have been less real than the one I have with my wife. If your days are filled with love and you want to grow old beside her, your wedding will be more real than most."

Pendragon meowed at the door, and Charlotte pushed past Adeline to scoop him up and bring him in. He gave Lisbet a doleful look as he was paraded past her, hind legs dangling in the air. His orange expression was annoyed and his ears folded back, yet he still purred loudly, contradicting himself. Charlotte dumped the cat unceremoniously in her sister's lap. He kneaded his paws a few times, then lay down and shut his eyes, rumbling in contentment all the while.

"Girls," Mona scolded lightly. "Put him back outside. You're going to get cat hair all over your pretty dresses."

"He needs ribbons, too," Addie whined.

Lisbet and Mona burst out laughing. The precocious children were hard to say no to, especially on a day that was meant to be festive. "Just a few," Lisbet agreed. "Then you need to run along down to the beach house to see if Elinor needs help with the preparations."

The girls sifted through a basket of ribbon scraps, searching for a suitable one. Charlotte selected a pale blue one that was nearly as wide as her wrist and held it up triumphantly. "This one is perfect for him." She handed it to Adeline. "Make the bow Kit taught you."

Lisbet smiled. Charlotte was already showing Elinor's influence in the way she ordered her sister about, still gently guiding her to learn all the while. Both girls had taken to the captain immediately, following her around when she wasn't training her crew at sea. And when *Iseult's Fury* was away, Charlotte took over, strutting about and handing out commands to anyone who would heed them. They were adapting well to Nassau.

She had taken them back to the village once, because they had begged, and because morbid curiosity had drawn her back. The villagers were all gone, finally driven off the cursed island by the pirate raid and kidnapping that returned Charlotte and Adeline to her. After years of destruction, droughts, and withering crops, they had decided that enough was enough. The pirates threatened their way of life and left them stranded from the rest of the world and the crown they still pretended to serve, so they hired a ship to take them to the nearby island of Eleuthera. Lisbet hadn't heard if they made it, or if the pirates they'd hired had seen them to other, more nefarious ends. She didn't care.

She and Kit had walked between the buildings hand in hand while the girls collected flowers to lay on their parents' graves. The village had already fallen into shambles as the buccaneers swept in to scavenge whatever materials they could find for the growing town of Nassau. They both knew they would never return. There would be nothing to return to. In one final act of defiance, they had kissed in front of what still stood of the church. There was no one to stop them. They were victorious.

"All done," Mona said, stirring Lisbet from her thoughts. "You look beautiful."

Lisbet stood and twirled for her sisters. "Do you approve?" The deep green dress swirled around her. It was modestly cut compared to most that she wore, but it was finely embellished with gold buttons on the sleeves and intricately embroidered flowers along the hems. She was certain it was the finest dress in all of Nassau, and she was impatient for Kit to see her in it.

"Almost as pretty as Pendragon," Charlotte said slyly. She was picking up Diego and Reddy's biting humor as well, and applying it in her own childlike fashion.

Adeline's brow furrowed as she looked from Lisbet to the cat, considering her options . "I think Lisbet is prettier," she concluded.

Mona stifled her chuckle. "Get down to the beach now, both of you. Your Aunt Elinor is waiting."

The girls ran out the door, with Pendragon trotting behind them. Any affection for Lisbet from him was forgotten as soon as her sisters moved in.

"Do you think Kit will like it?" Lisbet asked, peering in a small mirror at her distorted reflection.

"She'll love it," Mona assured her, pulling her close for a hug. "I'm so happy for you both. I always knew this was meant to be."

Lisbet poured a cup of rum to settle her stomach as the sunset hour drew nearer. She wondered if Kit was doing the same, then decided she almost certainly was. Tristan, Reddy, and Diego had shown up early that morning to whisk her away so she and Lisbet could ready themselves apart. Lisbet couldn't wait to see her again. Another swig of rum later, and Mona beckoned her to the door.

"It's time."

Lisbet and Mona walked arm in arm through streets that were coming alive with the pirates' debaucherous revelry. Nassau was awash in the tropical colors of the setting sun, vibrant and airy on the warm evening. Lisbet marveled at it all. She had thought she had everything, but she had been so blind to the beauty all around her until Kit came back into her life to open her eyes. The fleeting joy she had known before felt so wan and simple in comparison to the wonder that was every day with Kit.

The yard was filled with people she loved, people who had become her family through shared hardship and adventure, people she knew without any doubt she could rely on as kin. Her heart swelled as she realized they were all there for her and Kit. Elinor and Mona had turned the yard into the most beautiful sanctuary of glowing candles, with flowers overflowing on tables and their friends spilling off the benches. The girls were across the yard, wriggling in their seats beside Maggie. Their faces lit up when they noticed Lisbet had arrived, no doubt dreaming of their own weddings one day in the distant future. Tristan smiled and nodded as Lisbet walked past him, the playful glint ever-present in his eyes. He was surrounded by members of the *Revenge's* crew, and they waved cheerfully at Lisbet. She barely saw them. There was only one person she was there for, her reason for being.

Her heart pounded when she didn't see Kit at any of the tables. Maybe Kit had changed her mind at the final hour, had decided that it was all too much and she was better without her. A hush fell over the murmuring crowd, and finally, she spotted her. Kit stepped out of the house and onto the wide porch that wrapped around it's sides. The sunlight hit her face as she emerged from the shadows, and Lisbet stared at her in awe. Kit's hair was freshly cut, and she pushed a few rakish strands out of her eyes as she scanned the crowd, looking for Lisbet. She glowed in the setting sun, the gold buttons and woven threads of her brocade coat making her seem as regal as the King George himself, or as wealthy as one the of richest captains. Lisbet's heart swelled with pride. She couldn't believe how lucky she was, that she would be the one to call Kit her wife.

Lisbet ran to Kit with tears in her eyes. She didn't care if she was supposed to wait for Elinor to speak some special words before taking Kit into her arms as they had planned, she needed her then and every day thereafter. Kit met her halfway, and they fell into an embrace that made their friends around them whoop and cheer. Kissing Kit then may not have been appropriate in full sight of everything, but there was nothing that could have stopped her.

"I love you," Kit whispered against her lips.

"Forever," Lisbet replied. As it was fated to be.

Author's Note

This book is a blend of history and my imagination. Where it was possible, I tried to keep dates and places historically accurate, but *Nimue's Revenge, Iseult's Fury,* and their crews are all figments of my imagination. While we know women pirates like Anne Bonny and Mary Read were active during the Golden Age of Piracy in the Caribbean, there are otherwise very few records of women aboard these ships. It is hypothesized that many more women worked aboard these ships disguised as men, so the real number of women pirates is lost to history. Kit was inspired by these brave women, who did what society told them they couldn't.

Pirate society was somewhat more egalitarian than elsewhere at the time. Pirate ships and havens were diverse, and crews comprised of different races and nationalities worked together, and interracial marriages and same-gender partnerships, known as matelotages, were not unheard of. The opportunities for women, however, were still scant. Through Lisbet, I wanted to tell a story of a woman in that time who wasn't particularly inclined to piracy, and what options she had available to her.

The places mentioned are all real. Nassau was home to what would be known as the Pirate's Republic, and Hispaniola— where the *Revenge* sailed on her final voyage— is now known as Haiti. This story takes place a few years before Nassau developed fully into a pirate haven. Prior to the 1710s, the island of New Providence was colonized by the British and destroyed in multiple raids by opposing fleets. Many British privateers seized the opportunity to base their operations there, as it was an island largely ungoverned and with few inhabitants. The few remaining settlers fled to other islands in the Bahamas, such as Eleuthera, or even further to the colonized territories that would one day become the United States.

In *The Pirate's Pursuit*, I tried to bring this time period back to life while imagining what it would have been like if women had played a greater and more open role on these ships and what unique challenges they might have faced. I hope you enjoyed my creative interpretations of life at sea and exploring the islands of the Bahamas while falling in love.

About Author

WREN TAYLOR is a sapphic romance novelist. A passion for history and stories of empowered women serve as her primary inspiration when writing. She lives in the Pacific Northwest with her two dogs. When she's not dreaming up her next book, Wren enjoys cooking, painting, gardening, and enjoying the natural beauty of the world.

The Thief's Treasure

COMING SPRING 2023

The Sapphic Seas series continues in an all new adventure with characters you already love, and some you haven't met yet!

Wales, 1711

Sara Jones has never traveled beyond Ogmore-by-Sea, let alone outside of Wales. One day, a letter arrives from her employer's long lost daughter, and Sara is compelled into a journey across the sea to retrieve her. When their ship is caught in a violent storm along the way, their only hope may be a band of notorious female pirates. Aboard their ship, Sara soon finds herself caught in a dangerous web of lust, love, and lies.

Made in United States
Troutdale, OR
08/19/2023

12200540R00170